She was just a girl really . . .

A girl full of modest blushes and curiosity. A girl whose heart had beaten with untested passion as he'd purposefully held her near. The way to win her over was no mystery. He was halfway there already.

He lay in her bed. There was no mistaking the herbal scent that clung to the pillows. The same fresh fragrance was in her hair. Soft hair, soft lips, soft shape easily molded to his own.

From the other room the music she played started up again, sweet remembered tones played too poignantly. A peaceful sleep stole over him, his first for a very long time.

And in the gentle dreams that followed, a beautiful angel beckoned to him with a heart of gold. Calling to a soul he no longer believed he possessed . . .

THE MEN OF PRIDE COUNTY

THE PRETENDER

ROSALYN WEST

AVON BOOKS ◆ NEW YORK

AVON BOOKS, INC.
1350 Avenue of the Americas
New York, New York 10019

Copyright © 1999 by Nancy Gideon
Inside cover author photo by McLain Images
Published by arrangement with the author
Library of Congress Catalog Card Number: 98-94817
ISBN: 0-380-80302-X
www.avonbooks.com/romance

First Avon Books Printing: June 1999

AVON TRADEMARK REG. U.S. PAT. OFF. AND IN OTHER COUNTRIES, MARCA REGISTRADA, HECHO EN U.S.A.

Printed in the U.S.A.

WCD   10 9 8 7 6 5 4 3 2 1

Prologue

Pride County, Kentucky
1866

Better it burn than belong to another.

Deacon Sinclair stared into the flames, that thought consuming him the way greedy tongues of fire devoured the well-aged wood. Smoke enveloped him, its acrid scent parching eyes already raw from lack of sleep, but he didn't draw away. He continued to watch the blaze, seeing his hopes, his dreams fall away in ashes.

Everything he loved, everything he'd sacrificed for, would soon be gone.

Today the fertile acres and the majestic house standing proudly upon them would pass from his grasp into a stranger's hands. Tonight a stranger would make the decisions he'd been bred to. Tonight a stranger would sleep in the bed where he'd been conceived. And he would sleep under someone else's roof, accepting charity where he could find it.

Except he'd never learned how to do that. Humility, like apology, were things he'd never

1

been schooled in under his father's harsh tutelage. He knew how to command his future and that of those around him. He knew how to survive by any means at hand. But he didn't know how to bend to a bitter fate and graciously admit to failure.

Failure was a luxury he'd never been allowed.

But what else could he do that hadn't already been done? Tyler Fairfax had sold off the mortgage and the new owner was on his way to claim what Avery Sinclair had died to preserve. A way of life, an inheritance of pride, all gone. And for the first time, Deacon was glad his father had died in battle so as not to witness the shame of his trust betrayed.

Avery Sinclair would never have bent. Nor would he have allowed his home to pass out of his hands. He would have destroyed it first.

He would want Deacon to do the same.

But Deacon couldn't force himself to take a piece of kindling from the fire burning in the grate before him to turn his family home into a pyre of defiance. It was the last monument to all he held dear, to all he'd aspired to. In destroying it, he would lose himself as well.

There had to be another way.

Anger flickered then flared white hot in defiance of his despair. After all he'd done, after all he'd let escape him—happiness, love, even the basics of his humanity—he was not going to quietly sit by and lose it all anyway. The unfairness of it fanned his fury. This house, these lands, were his inheritance, not just given but earned: every board foot, every acre through brutal work and endless self-deprivation. Lost in a moment of weakness. Gone upon a schemer's whim. And though he wished he could cast the blame elsewhere, it settled hot and chokingly within him, a victim of his pride. He'd failed to protect one of the two things he'd vowed never to compromise—his family lands and his family name. What good was one without the other?

He would find a way, perhaps not today or tomorrow, perhaps not for weeks, months, or years, but he would have back what was his. In making that promise, he leaned back from the blaze.

There is no such thing as honorable surrender. There is no substitute for success.

The war hadn't taught him that. His father had.

"I'm ready."

The sound of his mother's soft tones squeezed about Deacon's heart. It was a moment before he could stand and turn to face her with an impassive front. That, too, was expected of him. Her brave, accepting smile was bereft of accusation. And that small forgiving gesture nearly broke him. He had to look away or lose the last of his control. Words failed briefly. What could he say to her that would reduce the pain of leaving her memories and security behind? He took a breath, then another to ease the constriction in his throat.

"Patrice and Reeve should be here soon to see you to the Glade."

"You aren't coming with us?"

"No. I need—I need to take care of things here. I'll come by later to make sure you're settled in."

"We'll wait with you."

Her concern shot a spear of anguish to his core but his reply was carefully void of emotion. "No. I'd rather see to it alone." Alone, the way he'd handled everything in his life. Alone was preferable. No witnesses to his fall from grace.

"What ever you want, dear."

He squeezed his eyes shut. What he wanted? He wanted to give her back her home. He wanted to return dignity to his family name. He wanted the vision of the future his father instilled with relentless and unswerving zeal. He wanted to stand tall just once in his life, knowing he'd met every expectation. But this wasn't about what he wanted. It was about what had to be.

"Mama?"

Because he rarely addressed her so informally or with such raspy feeling, Hannah Sinclair drew close, all at once consoling, yet not sure how to comfort. "What is it, Deacon?"

"I'm sorry."

She placed her hand on his coat sleeve, inviting him to turn into her embrace, well knowing that he wouldn't. Her husband had quite effectively and quite ruthlessly weaned him from the need for compassion—hers or anyone else's. That was the only cause she'd ever had to curse the man she'd adored. Because she knew he would accept honesty more readily than sympathy, she made her reply one of quiet earnest.

"Don't be. You did everything you could do."

His head bowed.

Sensing his uncommon vulnerability, Hannah was about to say more when the sound of an approaching company interrupted. Immediately, Deacon stiffened, self-contained and unapproachable once again.

"That'll be them. Are you sure you have everything you need, Mother?"

"All I need is my family."

He looked at her then, his features expressionless, emotions swallowed up and sealed away by years of training. If his heart was breaking, he gave no evidence of it. "I'll bring down the rest of your bags."

But her hand remained upon his arm, staying him as if there were more she meant to say. Because he couldn't bear to hear those sentiments, Deacon gently carried her graceful fingers to his lips, pressing a respectful kiss upon them. Asking for and receiving her silent obedience with a remote gentility that was so like his father's, it brought tears to her eyes. Hannah blinked them away, not wanting him to mistake their cause. She withdrew her hand and softly said, "I'll let them in."

Deacon watched her move toward the foyer,

all fragile grace and Southern charm, while he choked on the fact that this was the last time she'd play hostess in her own home. One more sin to weigh upon his soul. He was about to start for the stairs when a familiar voice grated against the last of his reserve.

Tyler Fairfax, come to gloat in smug victory.

Damn him!

Bringing with him the new masters of Sinclair Manor.

Deacon didn't know much about them. He didn't need to know more than the fact that these people were laying claim to generations of sweat and sacrifice by virtue of having the one thing he lacked . . . money. Not having much character to begin with, Fairfax displayed a greed which overcame all promises he'd made to allow Deacon the time to buy back his inheritance. The town banker told him that the new owners had paid an unprecedented sum to snatch up the Manor's mortgage in a time when much more could be had much more cheaply. In the aftermath of war, plantation property was easier to come by than credit. But it was more than money where Fairfax was concerned; it always had been. Something had prompted the little weasel to sell, something more than the amount. The Fairfaxes had more money than God. No, this was about pride, about wanting to rub Deacon's face in his misfortune just for the malicious enjoyment of it. There was something about this offer, about these buyers, that had

Fairfax smirking with pleasure. Gritting his teeth and gathering his dignity, Deacon went to discover what it was.

The truth nearly killed him.

Fairfax might have hoped it, but never could he have dreamed the full effect the owner's identity would have.

Deacon stood in the doorway, rigid with shock, while Tyler, smiling a Cheshire grin, introduced the well-dressed couple standing in the hall.

"Might I present Mister Montgomery Prior and his lovely wife?"

"A pleasure, Mister Sinclair."

The man who spoke with a clipped British accent extended his hand in an affable manner, but Deacon never saw the gesture or truly noticed the man. His disbelieving stare was fixed upon the stunning woman whose new name and glamorous look couldn't distract from the way Deacon's heart seemed suddenly to still in his chest as she smiled and purred, "I believe the pleasure is all ours, Monty. Hello, Deacon. I'll bet I'm the last person you ever expected to see again."

The understatement left him speechless.

Because here was one unresolved slice of his past that he'd never dreamed would come calling—even as he dreamed about her every night without fail.

His onetime hope for happiness had become his living hell.

Chapter 1

Cumberland Gap, Kentucky, five years earlier
1861

From his place on the ridge, Deacon had the perfect view of the modest farm below. It was like many others nestled into the steep embrace of the Cumberland. A house, a barn, a well, and an old wagon. A neat garden plot covered by a dusting of snow. A scattering of hens. A horse for the wagon and a cow for milk. An existence without luxury but with a peaceful sort of comfort. He watched, although he knew the routine by heart. He'd been observing the farm for almost a week and the pattern was as familiar as it was predictable.

Just after dawn, the door to the house opened and a single figure, bundled in a heavy overcoat with hat tipped against the chill, hurried toward the barn to tend the needs of its meager inhabitants. A puppy that was all mammoth head, whip tail, and plate-sized feet bounded after. Deacon waited until the door closed, until the undisturbed serenity settled back over the inti-

8

mate scene. Then he drew his pistol to calmly check its chambers.

He drew a slow breath and steeled himself for the unpleasant business ahead.

Echoes of the shot rolled down into the quiet valley creating an avalanche of sound. Though gunfire wasn't uncommon, its proximity startled the dog into frantic barking. The lone figure emerged from the barn to scan the surrounding hills fretfully, but reverberations off the wooded slopes confused the origins of the shot. Just as he'd planned.

What he hadn't planned for was the intensity of the pain.

The image of the valley below faded as blood begin to seep between the press of his fingers. He'd nicked nothing vital, but that knowledge didn't stop his swells of nausea. He tried to holster his still smoking gun, missing the first time, managing the second in an uncoordinated effort. That was when the first shock of fear hit him. His meticulous plan would fall to ruin if he fell off his horse and bled to death, unnoticed, right here in full sight of his goal.

Fighting back the swamping dizziness, Deacon gathered his reins in a bloodied hand and nudged the animal forward. Movement sent fresh waves of hurt pounding up from his side to beat in blackening pulses behind his eyes. What seemed so simple and logical in the planning stage was now close to insurmountable as he swayed in the saddle. Breathing in short, quick snatches to keep the darkness at bay, he lay along the horse's neck, his eyes closing against the blur of passing shapes. Not much farther. Not much farther.

Hang on. Hang on. How are you going to accomplish the rest if you can't manage this simple thing?

Awareness ebbing, he lost all direction, all focus. And then he was falling. For such a long time—or at least that was how it seemed. Pine needles and powdery snow cushioned his impact with the ground, but the blow was jarring. If he fainted, he would fail. He clung to that like a lifeline, struggling to hold to it even as he felt himself slipping away.

And just as consciousness left him, he had one last impression, that of an angel bending near. Only angels weren't supposed to be shaped to tempt sinful thought, were they?

Perhaps this was hell, and damned inviting it was.

He blinked once, twice, trying to retain the alluring vision as it came closer. He desperately wanted to hear the words those ripe cherry-sweet lips were forming, but concentration faltered and he sank into oblivion.

Garnet Davis believed in answer to prayer, but never had she expected such a quick response . . . and one so singularly attractive.

Only moments before, as she knelt beside their cantankerous cow trying to coax a steady stream of milk, she'd been brooding over a frequent wish, a wish that she wasn't so alone she felt like screaming. A wish that when she spoke, a human voice would reply.

She meant no offense to Boone. The affectionate hound was a most attentive listener, but not so good when it came to giving advice. He'd cock his huge head as she poured out her woes, giving quick comfort with a long swipe of his tongue, but as far as an opinion, his was always a tail thumping, "Whatever you like is fine with me." On some topics, that just wasn't good enough. She wanted another's point of view or even an argument—something to challenge the sameness of her days and the loneliness of her nights.

Of course, she'd been hoping for her father's early return, or perhaps a simple visit from one of their neighbors, but she knew the distance and the danger prevented both things. She wasn't afraid to be by herself, even though it gave her father no end of worries. She'd been hunting turkeys and small game since she'd been big enough to hoist her papa's scattergun. It would take more than the threat of enemy armies to scare her from her daily duties. An empty homestead was an invitation to the riffraff combing the countryside. The sight of her steady double barrels was usually all it took to discourage the shiftless wanderers. Knowing the solitary drifters weren't the main cause for her father's concern, she'd promised him she'd escape to the woods should true danger arise.

She knew every hollow, every cave, and could live off the charity of the land until the freebooters moved on, or could make her way to the closest Union camp if necessary.

But that would be a last resort. It would take John Hunt Morgan and a battalion of gray coats breathing fire to chase her off her property. But she'd promised, to give her father's mind ease. No man liked the notion of a daughter all alone in times this troubled, especially when he had no guarantee of when he could return.

Garnet didn't ask for guarantees. She was a patriot, proud to know her father was doing his best to hold their country together. She wrote of that pride, of her willingness to sacrifice his company for the sake of the nation, in nightly entries in a big tattered book filled nearly front to back with her innermost thoughts and dreams. But writing about them in private narrative and speaking them to another were two very different things as the lonesome winds wailed through their valley, echoing the melancholy in her soul.

But it was an echo of a very different nature that drew her out of the barn, one hand twisted in Boone's rope collar and the other toting the heavy rifle. As Boone strained and barked, Garnet stood fast, listening. A single shot. Maybe a hunter. Maybe a signal. Then it was more than the morning chill chasing shivers through her.

She saw the lone horseman heading down out of the treeline. She waited to greet him with the purposeful end of the long barrels. Recognizing the Federal blue of his uniform, she relaxed somewhat, but not completely. She'd learned from her father's warnings that danger didn't ride with one side over another. Bad men came in both blue and gray.

So she waited, at the ready, as the single rider approached, not opposed to giving him a hot breakfast and some feed for his horse, but determined to share no more than that. The weary pair entered her yard.

"That's close enough, mister." She pitched her voice purposefully low and gruff, keeping her hat tipped low to conceal her features as well as her gender. "State your business. Be quiet, Boone." She gave his collar a jerk, but the dog continued its frenzied barking. "I said that's close enough!" She raised the barrels to punctuate that claim.

Instead of reining in, the rider decided to dismount in a sloppy spill, hitting the ground in a soundless heap. Garnet hesitated, wary as well as concerned.

"Mister, you all right?"

That's when she noticed the bright blotching on the snow.

"Oh, Lord have mercy!"

Forgetting the danger, she raced toward the fallen figure, shoving a growling Boone aside so she could kneel down by the nearly insensible man. Now she knew the destination of that single shot. The entire side of his uniform jacket was soaked with blood. The middle of her front yard, in full view of whomever had done the firing, was no place to check the extent of the damage.

Boone sniffed around the soldier's feet, rumbling fiercely. If another source of threat was near, he'd be distracted. Still, it wasn't safe to linger outside any longer than she had to.

"Mister, I've got to get you inside. You hear?"

His eyes blinked open and fixed with a brief understanding upon her. His gaze was the color of the slated sky, stormy and intense, mesmerizing her into a long moment of inaction. But then his focus faded, releasing her from that compelling stare to do what needed to be done.

Wedging the rifle beneath one arm, she gripped him by the shoulders of his jacket and began to drag him toward the house. He offered no resistence or complaint, but no help either. By the time she'd pulled him as far as the front porch, she was winded and perspiring despite the cold. For all the long-limbed leanness of his build, he was no lightweight. She paused for a bit to catch her breath, forcing it by habit to come as slow and easy as possible, then she tugged him up the stairs. Not the most gentle of rides but the best she could manage under the circumstances.

The heat from the fire hit like a physical push as she dragged the wounded man inside. Boone bounded in after them, still growling with enough menace to bristle his thick neck. When his awkward legs tangled with Garnet's, she gave him a swat. With a startled yelp, the pup scuttled away to regard her and their guest glumly from underneath the table.

The floorboards probably weren't the best place to examine a gunshot wound, but Garnet needed to see what she was dealing with. First, she unbuckled his gun belt and drew it out from under him. Until she knew who'd shot him and why, she couldn't afford to treat him with anything but caution. She tossed the armaments out of reach. The soldier offered no protest when she unbuttoned his jacket and carefully peeled it away from the site of injury. Powder burns and blood discolored woolen long underwear. Whoever had pulled the trigger had done so at close range. Swallowing grimly, she ripped the saturated fabric to lay bare the wound.

She'd picked shot out of countless fowl and four-legged game without blinking an eye, but this was her first dealing with a human sporting a bullet. She tried to pretend there was no difference—tried, but was not as successful as she'd hoped to be. There was no mistaking the hard contour of abdomen and the warmth of skin as anything but man. Her fingertips were resting on the crisp hair beneath his navel. She yanked them back, blushing in horror even though there was no one to observe her unplanned familiarity with the stranger's body.

It was an awkward second before she could focus anywhere other than that naked stretch of masculine furring. She'd never seen so much as an inch of an unclothed man before—not even her father. Her insides were all jumpy with the forbidden shock and sudden wonder of it. But this man was going to bleed to death if she couldn't pull herself together. She drew a deep breath and forced herself to concentrate upon his injury.

The piece of lead had torn a nasty furrow along his ribs before chewing a chunk out of his side and exiting cleanly. It wasn't terribly deep, which she hoped meant it wasn't fatal, but it bled something fierce. That she would have to take care of, and quickly.

Gripping the edge of the linen tablecloth, she jerked it toward her, sending her breakfast plate and cup tumbling to shatter on the floor. Boone scrambled out of sight behind the quilt curtaining off her bedroom.

"Coward," she muttered, hastily ripping the cloth. She wouldn't think of the mess or the loss of her last piece of good linen. She concentrated instead upon the man's life's blood leaking out onto her pegged flooring. She daren't move him again until she was certain he wouldn't lose any more of it.

After pressing a wadding against the wound, she rolled him as gently as possible from side to side, working the linen beneath him so she could bind it tightly about his middle.

"There. Let's hope that holds you."

She rocked back on her heels to consider her

handiwork. Not an expert dressing, but one that would suffice. Still, the soldier was deathly pale and scarcely breathing. Her worries were far from over.

She couldn't lift him, so Garnet dragged him over to the fire. There she bundled him in a shaggy bearskin to combat the effects of shock and cold. He never made a sound.

Though she hated to desert him now, she couldn't leave his horse unattended—or in the open, should someone less friendly be following. She went back out into the swirl of snow.

The animal still stood where it had been abandoned. It went gratefully with Garnet into the shelter of the barn and was soon muzzle deep in grain. She removed its standard military issue tack and rubbed it down. Then, lashing the door shut behind her against the tug of the wind, she took a moment to study her yard. Would someone be able to tell he'd come here? That she'd taken him in? Convinced that fresh blowing snow had already covered all signs of his passing, she hurried back to the house.

Was she crazy to take in this wounded stranger? He could be a deserter. He could be anything, and she'd brought him inside her house, inside her circle of safety. Unwise, perhaps even crazy, but she couldn't have left him out there to bleed to death. She took a firmer grip on the gun. Besides, she could always add another hole to his hide if he proved to be less than gentlemanly.

She slipped out of her bulky outerwear, then quickly, nervously, cleaned up the broken crockery, which was all that remained of her breakfast. Garnet settled cross-legged near the fireplace and waited for her company to regain consciousness. Either he would die or he would recover. She prayed for the latter as she watched his faint breaths stir the coarse nap of the robe. At the very least she wanted to know his name so she could notify his family and his unit.

And she wanted to hear his voice.

She gave a slight start as Boone burrowed his cold nose under her hand. He whined until she lifted her arm, letting him crawl halfway across her lap. He was content to lie there, keeping a distrustful watch on the figure beneath the robe.

Who was he, this injured stranger? Was he a scout, a messenger? Surely there was no other reason for him to be alone. Which of the Union companies combing the hills did he belong to? She wished she knew so she could contact them to come and get him. Then she could go back to the sameness of her days without the intrigue and interruption.

But where was the thrill in that?

This was the first exciting thing to happen in her valley since duty had called her father from home. And she admitted to herself, ashamed of her own selfishness, that she was in no rush to send the soldier on his way.

Little news wound its way into the lonesome valley. Perhaps he would know the direction the

war was taking, offering some idea as to when
her life could return to normal. She'd never been
outside the valley to visit the world beyond
except through books. He could provide that
link to what she didn't know but still could long
for. Where was he from? She leaned forward,
studying the asymmetrical lines of his face as if
they could reveal some truth. A city, perhaps.
Did he have a family, a wife, or a fiancée waiting? Suddenly, Garnet hungered to know everything about him for the simple joy of connecting
with another.

An answer to prayer.

She smiled.

Her father had always told her to be careful
what she wished for. But while she was usually
cautious, she was rarely careful. Careful
allowed one to grow old safely, but it didn't
permit the freedom of realized dreams. Garnet
had a lot of dreams, most attached to what lay
beyond her valley. While she would never
think to abandon the farm while her father was
at war, her dreams remained unfulfilled,
though never forgotten. Perhaps she could
taste some of them through this man Provi-
dence had provided. If only he'd survive.

As if in answer, he muttered softly. Those
storm-colored eyes flickered open, wandering
briefly before fixing upon her, focusing there
with concentrated effort. She offered a neutral
smile. He wet his lips to speak, his first words
an accusation.

"You're a woman."

Garnet glanced down at her masculine garb, understanding his confusion. Wondering why she suddenly wished for the cinch of a crinoline, she answered a bit defensively. "My name is Garnet Davis. You're on my father's farm."

"Where is he?"

"He'll be back soon."

He didn't seem to notice the vagueness of her reply. Or at least, he didn't question it.

"You're here alone?"

Alarm bells jangled through her, prompting her to lie. "No. No, I'm not alone. Who are you, and who shot you?"

"Shot me . . . ?" He blinked, clearly struggling to retain his focus.

"You've been shot. I brought you inside and bound your wound. I need to know who shot you. Are we in any danger I should know about?"

But his eyes had closed upon her questions.

Garnet sighed in disappointment as her visitor slipped off to sleep. Her answers would have to wait until he was stronger, but did the delay put them in danger?

She rose and went to the front window, gazing out upon the undisturbed landscape. Was his assailant even now watching the house, waiting for a good time to finish what he'd started? She let the curtain drop and shot the bolt on the door. For the first time, her isolation caused her worry. Who would know if something bad befell her? How long would it be before a neighbor thought to check upon William Davis's daughter? If someone came for the soldier sleeping before her fireplace, could she—should she—fight them off?

Be careful what you wish for . . .

She grimaced and clutched the old rifle to her chest. Too late for caution in this case.

Her troubles were already here.

Chapter 2

Harp music.
I really am dead.

The sweet tones soothed his initial panic. Gentle sounds, plucking at emotions of regret and wonder and a strangely disassociated relief. He drifted upon the strains of wistful melody, his memories floating, entwined with the heavenly score. Images of long ago, of childhood dreams and adolescent longings never realized. Of the family he would never see again. Of the family he would never have. So sad. So unfair. So . . . unacceptable.

He had work to finish.

He couldn't die and abandon those who depended upon him. But the music was so beautiful, so pure. How could he surrender it to return to the harshness of living?

And then there was that face. That heavenly beauty with the tempting mouth and dark, soulful eyes. How could he let her go without exploring the sweet mystery of those lips?

As if in answer, he felt the moist touch of that kiss upon his cheek, cool against his fevered skin, an irresistible invitation. Opening his eyes to catch a glimpse of his angel, he turned toward the kiss and was met by a wet black nose and flaring nostrils.

"What the—?"

The music stopped.

"Boone, get away from him!"

Remembrance returned as Deacon jerked back upon a wash of fresh pain. His movement startled the lanky dog into leaping back as well, setting up a din of barking that pounded through Deacon's head. He squeezed his eyes shut, fighting the returning swells of sickness.

Dog toenails scrabbled against wood flooring followed by a baleful yip, a rush of cold air, and blissful silence. Then came his angel's voice.

"I'm sorry. He doesn't like strangers."

Deacon slit his eyes to gaze up at the figure who was both stranger and strangely familiar. The baggy clothing, the short black hair, and the easy movements belonged to the quarry he'd been studying all week.

But the soft voice—so like music itself—and the sinfully lovely features were those of a tempting siren. He stared, amazed that he could have made such a glaring error.

From a distance, the mannish clothes and cropped hair disguised what could never be questioned up close—that this was no man, no boy. The bulky shirts and trousers couldn't conceal a form so ripe with curves. The hair couldn't detract from the gentle contour of her wind-burned cheeks, the mysterious slant of dark eyes fringed with impossibly long lashes, the full lips pursed as if awaiting a man's attention.

Good God, what a beauty hidden away in this isolated hole in the mountains beneath the inappropriate garb. Such beauty was meant to be captured on canvas, in marble, or by some lucky aristocrat who would adorn her with silks and lace. The cruelty of fate distracted him long enough for her to grow concerned.

She bent to touch her work-roughened palm to his brow, to his unshaven cheek. Air sucked through his teeth in a noisy hiss.

"A fever's started," she pronounced in dismay. "I'd better check your wound again."

In his rapid reassessment, Deacon figured her to be Davis's wife or perhaps his sister, but when she reached out to peel back his shirt, he realized the truth. It was inexperience coloring her cheeks in fiery embarrassment. It was youth that made her hesitate before placing a hand upon his exposed torso. The maturity ripening her face and form had not yet touched her spirit. She was little more than a child in that regard. Yes, now he remembered. This must be Davis's daughter.

"It's not my wish to discomfort you, Miss Davis. You needn't compromise your delicate nature. I can tend myself."

Words meant to soothe her agitation instead braced her with a new determination.

"That's all right, Sergeant. I'm hardly delicate, and this war has left little room for modest sentiments."

Sergeant? He was about to correct her when she pulled the crude dressing away, tearing at the edges of his wound, making him gasp. The shock of hurt restored his clear thinking. Sergeant. Yes, of course. He remembered the rank sewn upon his stolen coat. He'd almost betrayed himself in his rare distraction over a pretty girl.

He'd have to be careful.

The girl chewed her lip as she surveyed the wound. "It's still bleeding something fierce. I'm afraid I don't know what else to do. You can scarce afford to lose any more blood if you're going to pull through."

That was quite the comfort.

Deacon ground his teeth as he came up on his elbows. He blinked hard into the watery waves of sickness, forcing them to ebb back to a manageable level. One look down told him everything she said was true. He wouldn't last until morning unless something drastic was done.

"Miss Davis—it's Miss Davis, right?" At her jerky, wide-eyed nod, he continued in a tight voice. "If you'd be so kind as to hand me that stick of kindling . . . "

She followed his gaze to the fireplace, but not his reasoning. With a frown of confusion, she drew out the slender piece of glowing oak and delivered it into his unsteady hand. She waited, expecting some explanation.

"Miss Davis, you might want to step outside for just a minute."

She absorbed the quiet caution in his tone while searching his gaze for answers. He could tell the moment she arrived at the correct one. Her face lost all color.

"Oh, my. Surely, you don't mean to—"

"It'll cauterize the wound and stop the bleeding. If you can think of another way, I'd be glad to hear it."

Breathing in quick agitated snatches, she thought long and hard, then reluctantly shook her head. "I'm sorry."

"Leave now, Miss Davis."

She looked wistfully toward the door and its offer of escape from what was to come, but after forcing a hard swallow, she said, "No. I think I should remain, in case . . . in case you should need me for anything."

He paused, unable to phrase his admiration. Such courage for a young creature! His voice gentled.

"At least look away."

Garnet turned her head, steeling herself for the worst.

Coward! Do something!

Chiding herself for being unable to aid him in the horrible deed, she vowed not to behave squeamishly, even as her stomach ached with anticipation of his screams . . . screams that never came. A sudden sickly sweet smell reached her.

She clamped her lips together when she realized it was the scent of burning flesh.

A quiet thump sounded as he fell back into unconsciousness.

Still fighting nausea as the scorched scent overwhelmed her, Garnet looked back, then quickly snatched up the discarded bit of kindling as it singed the wool of his uniform jacket. She tossed it into the fire, then forced herself to examine the grisly injury.

No bleeding escaped the seared edges of the wound. She let her breath go in a rattly gush. In the face of his incredible bravery, she couldn't excuse her own hesitation. Controlling her breathing into a practiced rhythm, she also conquered her panic. She could do this.

By the time the soldier came to again, Garnet had washed around the wound and redressed his side with clean linens. She smiled at him as his eyes blinked open, unable to conceal her awe. When he put a hand to his ribs, she answered his unspoken question.

"The wound is closed. Hopefully, there'll be no problem now with its healing."

His hand fell away as he breathed a sigh of relief.

"Do you think you could stand with my help? I'd like to get you in bed." A fierce blush suffused her face when she considered what she'd said. With a stammer, she amended, "You'll be more comfortable than here on the floor."

"Don't go to any trouble on my account, Miss Davis."

"It's no trouble."

It would be a blessing to get him out of the front room, where she was constantly distracted by his presence.

With her assistance, he was able to sit up. With an arm looped about her shoulders, he struggled to get his feet under him, while she hauled back and steadied him. She'd guessed at his height before but had been unprepared for the way he dwarfed her. Lean and long-limbed, he was nonetheless solidly made. That she discovered as she slipped her arm tentatively about his middle. His fingers bit into her upper arms as he swayed.

"Give me . . . a minute."

Don't let him swoon!

She didn't know how she'd manage to keep him on his feet if he fainted, let alone wrangle him into the bedroom. She angled under his arm, letting him drape over her shoulder with a soul-shocking familiarity. His breath pulsed hard and fast against the side of her face, quickening her own heartbeats in response.

"Are you all right, Sergeant?"

She felt him nod. Then slowly, to prove it, he began to straighten, relieving her of most of the burden of support.

"Where to?"

She directed him to the curtained doorway, pushing it aside with her free hand and guiding him within the cozy dimness. Heavy drapes at the windows sealed out both the chill and the thin daylight. Once he'd targeted the bed, he let momentum carry him to it. The springs groaned under his abrupt descent and Garnet found herself pulled across his lap. Startled by the contact, she tried to lever back, but his arms remained about her, anchoring her there upon his knees. She sat stiff and still, engulfed by his size, by his heat, by his intimate proximity. For a long moment, neither of them moved. He was merely gathering his strength, she told herself. There was no reason to be alarmed—or to be charged with anticipation.

Finally he leaned back, allowing her to slip from the circle of his arms. Thankfully, his eyes were closed, so he didn't witness the way her knees knocked together when she stood away from him. Taking a deep breath, she returned to the matter of making him comfortable.

To turn down the bed, she had to reach behind him. Awareness of him overwhelmed her once more. She'd been around so few men, and this one, by virtue of his courage alone, was enough to make her giddy.

She jumped slightly as his uniform jacket hit the bed. Nervously she edged back to see him unbuttoning his long underwear. Her gaze riveted to the expanse of lightly furred chest revealed with the release of each fastening.

"Could you help me with this?"

"Oh . . . yes, of course."

She was slowly able to draw off the blood-stained garment, leaving him bare from the trouser band up except for the white swatch of her crude bandaging. Her gaze fixed itself upon his knees.

"What else?" Was that tight-throated little voice really her own?

When he didn't reply, she was forced to glance upward. A small smile etched upon his weary features.

"Just my boots, if you don't mind."

A nervous smile released some of her tension. Just his boots. She bent to wrestle them off one at a time.

When she stood, his figure slumped. His head bowed, his eyes closed, his exhaustion was plain in the droop of his shoulders. Garnet's tender heart melted.

"You rest, now. Get your strength back."

He needed only that gentle encouragement. When he started to lie back, the movement caused a grimace to twist his features. Garnet slipped her arm behind his back to support and guide him to the sheets. His eyes never opened, but as she pulled the covers up around him, he murmured a soft, "Thank you."

Feeling as though she should withdraw but unable to make herself take the first step away, Garnet watched him sink into a healing slumber. Only then did an important thought occur to her.

"Your name? What's your name?"

She needed something to call him other than the impersonal moniker of "Sergeant." Especially within the privacy of her own dreams.

When he remained unmoving, she figured him to be asleep. Disappointed, she turned toward the curtained doorway.

"Deacon. Deacon Sinclair."

Deacon.

She smiled to herself, liking the way it settled familiarly within her mind.

"Rest, Sergeant Sinclair."

She stepped outside the room and closed the drape. A sigh escaped her.

Deacon.

But he didn't rest. Sleep couldn't overtake the rapid turnings of Deacon's mind. He glanced at the Union jacket she'd hung so respectfully on the bedpost. He was in and she didn't suspect a thing.

Once he'd gotten over his surprise that the occupant of the farm was a woman, he busied himself thinking how to use the fact to his best advantage. She was just a girl, really. A girl full of modest blushes and curiosity. A girl whose heart had beaten with untested passion as he'd purposefully held her near. The way to win her over was no mystery. He was halfway there already. This was her bed. There was no mistaking the herbal scent that clung to the pillows. The same fresh fragrance was in her ridiculously short hair.

Soft hair, soft lips, soft shape easily molded to his own.

He jerked his transgressing thoughts back to task.

But, providing his intelligence was correct and that he was in the right place, could she tell him what he needed to know?

That was the important thing, the only thing. All that mattered was the information. Information he was to get from any available source, by any means necessary.

From the other room, the music started up again, sweet remembered tones played so poignantly. As he closed his eyes and listened, wondering from what instrument she coaxed those winsome melodies, a peaceful sleep stole over him, his first for a very long time.

And in the gentle dreams that followed, a beautiful angel beckoned to him with a harp of gold. Calling to a soul he no longer believed he possessed.

Later, from the doorway, Garnet watched him sleep. She knew it was wrong to spy upon him. Telling herself she was checking his condition didn't excuse the amount of time she'd lingered there to follow the gentle rise and fall of her covers.

There was a man in her bed.

The notion alone had her jumpy as a cat inside. Of course, this man was injured and a stranger.

But my, he was handsome.

Though lacking in comparisons, Garnet knew what appealed to her: *he* did. Everything about him did. The long, lean look of him. The slated stare so stormy with intelligence and intensity. The generous shape of his lower lip and the angles of his unshaven cheeks. She bet he was something to behold when all cleaned up. Though he was wearing Federal blue, his accent held neither clipped Northern syllables nor an exaggerated Southern drawl. She heard a middle states softening to his words. His manner was genteel and his hands bore no burr of the working class.

What was an obviously well-learned and clever man doing in a lowly sergeant's uniform?

Her thoughts were disrupted as he shifted beneath her sheets, growing restless in his slumber. The covers lowered, gifting her with a superb view of his upper body. Lamplight from the main room gleamed with bronze highlight and shadow along broad shoulders and well-made arms and muted upon the hair-dusted chest. Goodness, but he was nicely put together.

Brave, smart, and an appealing eyeful.

The answer to prayer.

Until he began to mutter in his sleep. Of the words she could comprehend, one of them was another woman's name. That woke her like a slap.

Chiding herself for getting so carried away, Garnet left the doorway, turning from her every dream. He wasn't here to fill the void in her empty hours. This was simply an unexpected stop for a stranger on his way from one place to another. He had a past that didn't include her and a future she would never know. All she had were the hours or days he would remain in her care; then her name and face would fade from his memory.

Knowing she would make no lasting impression only emphasized her isolation.

A sudden scratching at the front door startled her from her brooding. Boone! She'd forgotten all about him. Made hasty by guilt, she opened the door, welcoming a snowy fury. After making a quick circle near the fireplace, the dog picked up the scent and dashed, snarling fiercely, through the curtained opening to her room.

"Boone, no!"

By the time she reached the bedroom, the gangly pup, now all protective dynamo, stood with forepaws planted on her guest's chest. Deacon had the dog by either side of the ruff, holding his snapping jaws only inches away from his face.

"Boone!"

She dragged the bristled animal from the bed and admonished him from the room with a boot to the hindquarters. The pup huddled on the other side of the draped door, peering under the curtain woefully.

Deacon was struggling to sit up.

"Oh, Sergeant, I'm so sorry."

Before she thought of what she was doing, Garnet sat on the edge of the mattress. With palms pressed to either bared shoulder, she urged him to lie back before the exertion reopened his wound. Even after he'd complied, her hands remained where they were for another long minute, lost to the feel of warm skin stretched over hard muscle. The sense of breathlessness returned.

"I can see why your father feels safe leaving you here alone with that hell hound to guard you."

The sound of his voice woke her from her reverie. She sat back, rubbing her palms on the rough nap of her trousers. Though flustered, she had the presence of mind to remember her earlier fabrication.

"I'm not alone."

Sinking back into the pillows, he chided her with a look.

"Well, not for long. I expect him back at any moment."

He closed his eyes. She couldn't tell if he believed her or not. She took advantage of the silence to place a tentative hand upon his brow.

"Your fever's no better," she stated unhappily. "Perhaps if you took some nourishment. Do you think you could eat something? I can make some broth."

He shook his head in vague disinterest. "Maybe later."

Thinking it was probably rest he needed more

than anything, Garnet was about to withdraw when he said, "Miss Davis, I'm sorry for the trouble I've caused you." His gaze was fixed upon her, somber and sincere. His unblinking focus brought back her bout of nerves. Her smile trembled.

"It's no trouble. You needn't worry that you'll not return home to your wife in one piece."

His brow puckered. Garnet bit her lower lip as if she could take back those impulsive words.

"Wife? I have no wife."

She flushed. "You were calling a name in your sleep. I assumed—"

His frown deepened. "What did I say?"

"You said the name Patrice, and I thought—"

He relaxed with a faint smile. "Patrice is my sister. She and my mother are the only ones worrying about my fate."

"Oh." She clenched her teeth so as not to grin at that welcome bit of news. No wife. No sweetheart waiting. "They must be frantic with concern," she murmured, walking to the window and looking out into the snowy darkness so he couldn't see her disconcertedness.

His gaze lowered, as did the pitch of his voice. "I haven't seen them for six months, not since my father and I went to join up. I was on my way home on hardship leave when—when you offered your hospitality. Now I'm bringing them the news of my father's death."

She turned to him, the last of her caution and

wariness melting away at the sound of his sorrow. "I'm so sorry."

He accepted her words with a slight nod. "I only wish I could stay with them for more than a couple of weeks. I hate the thought of leaving them there alone."

She understood his dilemma very personally and sought to reassure him. "They'll be fine, Sergeant. We women are a lot stronger than you men give us credit for."

His mouth took a slight bend. "You certainly are. Now, tell me the truth. How long have you been here alone?"

She couldn't pretend with him, not now. "Months. And I've managed quite well."

"And your family?"

"There's just me and my father."

"Is he a soldier?"

"A telegraph operator."

Deacon took the news like a swallow of raw whiskey. He breathed into it for a moment before he could catch his wind. Then he smiled at the unsuspecting girl, no longer feeling the twinge of conscience at spinning such pitiful lies.

"An important job."

"One that keeps him on the move more than either of us would like."

He made a sympathetic sound.

Garnet approached, but only to draw the covers up around his shoulders. The movement was quick and efficient, as if she found it distasteful. Or distracting.

"You'd better rest. I'll make sure Boone doesn't disturb your sleep again. I think he's just put out because he usually sleeps in bed with me." Realizing what she'd just confessed, she turned a bright crimson. Deacon took advantage of her embarrassment, releasing a slow, ungentlemanly smile.

"I can understand his annoyance."

"He'll survive it," she said gruffly, trying to survive her own sense of humiliation. And the insinuation. Would he really envy another her company in bed? She backed hurriedly from the room, afraid to linger over that tempting thought. "Good night, Sergeant."

"Good night, Miss Davis."

And Deacon smiled to himself, satisfied with his progress. He was in the right place, and time was on his side.

Chapter 3

~~~⌒⌒~~~

At first, Garnet thought her restlessness was from the discomfort of sleeping on a pallet before the fire. Clad in her warm woolen nightgown and curled upon the bearskin, which at first seemed cozy but now seemed no insulation at all between her and the hard floor, she'd been dozing fitfully when all at once she came fully awake.

Boone straightened at her side to issue a low, threatening growl. Something had woken him as well.

"Oh, hush, Boone," she muttered irritably, thinking that their visitor might be moving about. Then she again heard what had awakened her.

A soft, intrusive sound . . . from outside.

Placing a silencing hand on Boone's muzzle, she reached for her scattergun. Whoever was creeping about in the night was more likely foe than friend. Her first thought was of some vagrant bent on stealing her stock. Pulling on her heavy coat, she muttered about the unlikeliness of her letting that happen. Then, at the door, she paused and considered her guest.

What if the intruder . . . or intruders . . . were looking for him?

She took a stabilizing breath. She wasn't about to surrender up Deacon Sinclair any more than she'd let anyone make off with the horses.

Peeping out from behind the front curtain, she could see only a peaceful scene of fresh-powdered snow washed by moonlight. Then the setting took on a sinister twist with the discovery of hoofprints—two sets. She faded back against the wall, fighting to control the sudden quivering of her knees. *Trouble.* Her first real trouble. Time to make good on all the blustery promises she'd made to her father about holding their homestead against all comers.

First, she'd have to find out where they were. Then she'd find out what they wanted.

Hands shaking almost too much for her to do the job, she tugged on heavy boots and clapped on a hat. She thought of waking Deacon and returning his gun, but hesitated. What help would he be, weak and wounded? What did she know about him? Her mind took a practical step away. He still hadn't told her why he'd been shot or who might be after him.

And as stealthy footsteps sounded on the porch boards, the opportunity to ask slipped away.

Time to act.

Jerking open the front door, she came face to

face with a single bearded man. A startled gaze fixed upon the greeting end of her gun, then lifted slowly to meet her own.

"What is it you want, mister?" she growled in her best threatening manner.

When he smiled, not intimidated at all, the word "trouble" came home with heart-thumping consequence.

"You all by yourself, a pretty little thing like you?" He glanced over her shoulder, scanning what he could see of her main room with a quick, cold assessment. "Or you got somebody in there with you, willing to hide behind your skirts?"

So they *were* looking for Deacon. She bristled up as protectively as Boone in his defense.

"That's my business. I believe I asked you to state yours."

She'd clearly seen two sets of tracks. Where was the other one? It was too much to hope that this one had been leading a pack animal.

She glanced away for an instant to check the shadows of the porch briefly, but it was long enough. She gave a dismayed gasp as his hand shot out, closing about the barrel of her shotgun. With a fierce yank, he had it.

Shoving the flat of his hand against her coat, he pushed her into the house and followed. Then the other one appeared behind him. His features had been badly scarred by fire, making his smile into a hideous sneer. He came in and closed the door.

They were inside and she was unarmed.

She couldn't let panic get the better of her. She searched her mind for options.

"Nice place you got here. All cozy and warm. Bet you could make it real hospitable, if you was of a mind to," Bearded Face said.

With the muzzle of her own gun, he nudged back the drape of her coat, exposing the unmistakable curve of her breast beneath modest flannel. The sudden heat flaring in his gaze filled her with a primal fear, but she stood fast against it.

Stall. Think.

"Who are you men?" She studied their clothing; she saw no sign that their allegiance was either with the North or South. "Deserters?"

The scarred one laughed. "You'd have to belong to one side or the other to desert from it. We makes our living on what they leaves behind."

Scavengers. Her stomach tightened. The worst kind of threat. She'd find no honor or mercy in them . . . and unless she thought of something fast, no escape from whatever they intended.

That intention grew more apparent when Bearded Face ordered silkily, "Take that there coat off, missy. Get yourself comfortable."

As she eased out of the bulky folds under his watchful and appreciative eye, Garnet's mind flew ahead. Where was Boone? The dog's absence and silence meant what?

"Cale, set the girl to making up some grub,"

Scarred Cheek grumbled. "I ain't eaten nothin' home cooked for months."

The bearded Cale grinned. "What she's gonna be cookin' up ain't gonna be your supper, Bronson. If you're hungry, you can rustle up your own vittles whilst me and the little lady gets to know each other better."

Over my dead body. Garnet carefully folded her coat and laid it upon the seat of her father's favorite chair. Her hand slipped beneath the cushion, brushing against metal, coming up with the sergeant's pistol from where she'd hidden it. Concealing it in the loose fabric of her gown, she steeled herself for whatever action it would take to save herself and her home.

And her guest.

"Bronson, check out them other rooms so we don't get no surprises."

Bronson lifted his disfigured face away from the pot where Garnet had broth simmering. "If she'd had company, we'd have seen 'em by now."

"Do it," Cale snapped, having no patience for the other's moaning. He gestured to the ladder and asked Garnet, "What's up there?"

"My father's room." Anxiously her covert gaze followed the shuffling Bronson as he went to her bedroom. There was nothing she could do to prevent Deacon's discovery.

She swallowed hard as time tickled away.

"Where is your daddy?"

Her eyes narrowed, allowing her contempt for the men to show. "Off doing his duty to his country."

"Quite the patriot, leaving a tasty little thing like you behind. Bronson, what'd you find in there?" After a long beat of silence, he glanced toward the curtained doorway. "Brons?" The gun barrel jerked up, jabbing into Garnet's throat. "What's in there?"

"My room."

"How come he ain't answering?"

Wondering the same thing, she drawled, "Maybe he's trying on my clothes."

The force of his hard-knuckled blow sent her reeling back against the chair. She clung to it for balance as the world tottered.

"An' maybe you got a surprise waiting for us back there, huh?"

His hand fisted in the front of her nightdress. He dragged her across the room toward the ominously still curtain. Her face ached. Pin dots of blackness obscured her vision as she stumbled after him. She tightened her grip on the pistol, afraid it would slip from her damp fingers. She wanted to call out a warning to Deacon, but her jaw felt broken.

Cale parted the curtain cautiously with the barrel of her gun, giving them a view of the bed and a pair of motionless boots of the man lying upon it.

Then a hand clamped down on the rifle barrel.

"Surprise."

Before Cale could react, Deacon angled the weapon upward and drove the butt of it into his bearded face, pulping his nose.

The scavenger fell back with a gurgling sound, dragging Garnet with him. He didn't release the gun. Stunned by the pain of her knees hitting the floorboards, Garnet lost the grip on her revolver and watched it spin just out of reach.

As Cale and Deacon wrestled for possession of the scattergun, she fought the tangle of flannel holding her prisoner, until a telling rip gave her the freedom needed to lunge those few extra feet. Her hand closed upon the smooth grip.

Finding himself in possession of a loose length of fabric, Cale let go, needing both hands to combat his unexpectedly strong opponent. Garnet rolled up into a crouch, vaguely aware that half her nightgown hung down to her waist as she brought the revolver up into play. But the two men tussled on the floor, struggling for the shotgun, giving her no clear target—until Cale smashed his knee into Deacon's injured side, causing him to double up over the site in fresh agony.

Cale staggered to his feet, his heavy beard streaked with crimson, his breath laboring. He worked his ravaged features and grimaced. Then, with a cold purpose, he fit the muzzle of the gun against the back of Deacon's head.

"You're going to die for ruining my pretty face, mister."

"No."

He turned at the sound of Garnet's soft cry. His eyes widened at the sight of her in her near-nakedness, appreciation rather than apprehension bringing a smile even as she brandished the revolver.

"Wait your turn, missy. I'll get to you in a minute."

He didn't believe she was a threat.

He was wrong.

She heard the click of the hammer as he thumbed it back. Forced to act without hesitation, she pulled the trigger.

Cale dropped without a sound. Deacon caught the shotgun before it hit the floor, and once he'd crawled over to make sure the man was dead, he turned to where Garnet stood frozen in shock.

"Nice shot."

The pistol wavered wildly in her hand. "I—I couldn't just let him shoot you."

"I appreciate that."

Her unblinking gaze remained upon the man whose life she'd taken. She was unable to look away, unable to erase the memory of the brief flicker in Cale's eyes just before she'd killed him, a look of horror as he saw his own death approach on a .45-grain slug. A look she'd instilled there just before she'd put out the light of life forever.

Then the awful sight was blocked by Deacon, who'd managed to regain his feet. Before she could lift her wounded gaze to his, he drew her up against him, his hand closing over the pistol and gently removing it from her grasp. He pressed her cheek into the soft furring of his chest.

For a long moment, she remained there immobile, until a quiet shuddering began in her soul and spread relentlessly outward until her whole form quaked with the consequence of what she'd done. She squeezed her eyes closed, knowing the image could never be shut off that easily.

"I've never—"

"Shhh. It's all right. It's over."

As sobs claimed her, he held her in silent support, knowing there was nothing he could say to lessen the grief and guilt she suffered. Her hands came up slowly to clutch at the hard swells of his upper arms, clinging to him as her knees weakened and her courage fled. She felt the warm brush of his lips upon her brow and the movement of his hand up her arm as he restored the torn half of her gown to her shoulder. Then she felt nothing beyond comfort in the surrounding safety of his embrace, a sensation so unique, so necessary to that moment of shattering circumstance, that she could do nothing but linger, limp and listless, against him. Until a soft whimpering intruded.

"Boone."

She pushed off his chest shakily and glanced about.

"What happened to Boone?"

"I couldn't have him giving me away."

She frowned up at him. "What did you do?"

Before he could answer, she tottered into the bedroom, to be momentarily taken aback by the sight of the scar-faced Bronson stretched out on her covers growing cold. There was no sign of violence to the body. Deacon answered her unasked question with the brutally frank facts.

"I broke his neck. I didn't want him giving the other one any warning, either."

Broke his neck . . .

The power and skill necessary to accomplish such a gruesome task without sound . . .

Garnet shuddered and quickly averted her eyes. Her attention caught upon a mysteriously rocking clothes chest. Deacon crossed to it and lifted the heavy lid. Boone was huddled inside. His dark eyes fixed upon Garnet in a forlorn plea above the muzzling wrap of one of her stockings. She released his jowls and was rewarded by his slobbering affection as she hoisted his gangly form from the trunk. When she set him down, he backed up against her legs to whine uneasily, scenting death in the air.

"Maybe you should put him outside while we take care of our unwanted company."

We. Our. He said the words casually as if he wasn't a stranger under her roof. For the moment, he wasn't. The circumstance bound them together with something as strong as intimacy.

"I guess we could put them in the cold cellar for now."

"Perhaps you should, umm, get dressed first."

A downward glance revealed her immodest

state. Her flannel gown was rent to the waist. The gap of fabric framed the inner curve of her bosom and a sleek length of bare midriff. Garnet clutched the halves together with a horrified gasp.

Picking up his uniform jacket, he said in a slightly growly rumble, "I'll wait in the other room."

She acknowledged his offer of gallantry with a mortified nod. The moment the curtains closed behind him, she cast off the shredded gown before Bronson's unseeing stare and pulled on drawers, trousers, and a heavy shirt over a thin chemise. Even with the coarse wool against her skin, she feared she'd never feel warm again.

With Boone whimpering at her heels, she bundled the dead man up in the sheets she knew she could never use again for her own purpose. His body made a dreadful thump when it hit the floor. She paused to swallow down her sickness before dragging him into the front room.

Deacon had already rolled Cale into a patchwork coverlet. To her dismay, Garnet recognized it as one of the few things left her made by her mother's hands. But it was too late to reclaim the piece of handiwork. Blood already seeped through the carefully joined squares.

Deacon leaned against the back of a chair, his elbow tucked up into his side like a bird nursing a broken wing. Pale skin slick with sweat betrayed his pain. Garnet forgot her own agonies in the face of his.

"Are you all right? Are you sure you're up to this? Maybe I'd better check your wound."

He shook his head. "Let's get this done."

She was all for ridding her home of the evidence, if not the consequence, of her deed.

Once the bodies were locked in the storage cellar just behind the house, Garnet busied herself in scouring the stained floorboards. Deacon watched from the impersonal distance of the dining table as she worked frantically to scrub away the source of her guilt. He could have told her that men such as those weren't worth a single tear, but that wouldn't have lessened her remorse.

Perhaps there was some way he could both ease her conscience and serve himself.

"I wasn't sure at first, but now I am."

She paused in her cleaning but didn't look up. "Sure about what?"

"Those two were the ones who ambushed me. The scarred one grabbed my reins and the other shot me when I wouldn't give them my horse. So this is my fault. I brought them here to terrorize you. After all your kindnesses, I've been nothing but trouble to you."

She rocked back on her heels, considering his words but not commenting on them.

With a heavy sigh, he pushed himself up out of the chair. "I'm going to turn in and get some sleep so I can be out of here at first light."

She was at his side before he had a chance to grimace, supporting him with her quickly offered shoulder and her quiet statement. "It's too soon. You shouldn't be riding until your wound begins to knit together."

"But—"

"It's no trouble."

He let her guide his arm across the unyielding line of her shoulders. He marveled at their steadiness after all that had happened, and at their strength. Instead of releasing him, she continued to hold onto his hand, curling her fingers into his palm in a gesture so filled with trust it brought an unevenness to his breathing. Such a mix of courage and vulnerability. He wasn't sure how to respond to her or the effect she was having on him.

He knew he shouldn't respond at all. It wasn't his business to admire her for her spirit and resilience. But he did. And that was dangerous. Emotions were always dangerous, but he couldn't seem to get his in check. He was tired, that was the reason. Tired and hurting, and strangely receptive to the tender care of this backwoods girl who seemed ready to forgive him anything.

Now, how was he going to forgive himself for what he had to do?

Chapter 4

❧

Deacon leaned against the doorway while Garnet covered the bed with fresh sheets. Her movements were quick and efficient, and she avoided any eye contact. He recognized that she was operating on raw energy to keep reality at bay, knowing the instant she stopped her busy work, all the ugliness would be right there waiting.

Smoothing out the blankets, she paused to suck a deep breath, then turned back the covers. Only then did she meet his stare. Her features were drawn with exhaustion. Panic flickered at the edges of her gaze.

"Let's hope we have no more excitement this evening." She attempted a smile, the result a failure.

He crossed to the bed, his movements halting as the full brunt of overexertion hit hard. Shrugging out of the jacket, he eased down upon the mattress, working to catch his wind. Shards of pain stabbed out from his wound with each breath, no matter how shallow and controlled.

Seeing his distress, Garnet knelt between his knees and without a word, gently peeled back his bandages. Satisfied that all was holding together, she rewrapped his side only to glance up in question as his hand settled on her shoulder. He let his expression soften in gratitude. And something else—something deeper, more disguised—slipped through as well.

"That's twice that you've saved my life today. I only hope I'm worthy of your efforts."

"I—"

He hushed her with the touch of his forefinger to her lips. While she remained still, her gaze lost within the intensity of his, that fingertip sketched the full curve of her upper lip and stroked down to her chin, nocking beneath it.

As he slowly bent toward her, the sound of her inhalation seemed inordinately loud. Almost as loud as the sudden thunder of her heartbeats.

She knew what he meant to do, and knew as well that she shouldn't allow it, not from a stranger. But they didn't seem like strangers, not now, not after all they'd shared.

Her eyes drifted shut as she awaited the first touch of experience.

He made it sinfully sweet, her first taste of passion, pressed upon her awe-slackened lips with lingering attention to each dip and tender swell. Warm as a summer's eve and soft as a whispered secret, it played upon her quivering senses. Finally realizing her hands hung wooden at her sides, she lifted one to fit the beard-roughened line of his cheek and let the other move with an awkward intimacy along his shoulder, shy encouragements that should have tamed his doubts, but instead, let loose a wild rush of urgency.

In his mind's eye, he saw not the impersonal target of his carefully laid plans, but the courageous figure binding his wound, the fierce warrior bracing a threat to them both with his pistol in hand while her torn nightdress revealed charms meant to stop a man just as effectively. A killing combination—innocent strength and unintentional allure. For the moment, he had no power to resist.

Fueled by her tentative response, he curled his hand in her bobbed hair, angling her head so their kiss could mature. He'd meant to tease her with just a sample, then found he himself was too hungry to leave that feast unsatisfied. She was made for kissing, her mouth ripe and sensually shaped, her reactions both refreshingly modest and unashamedly eager. And because the need to take advantage of both those things overwhelmed all but the last fragment of his reason, he hung onto that saving shard and forced his passions to abate.

He'd accomplished what he'd meant to. There was no need to pursue his point so fervently that both of them let the moment get the better of their judgment.

She trembled against him as he traced his mouth from the willing part of hers down the tempting curve of her throat. He could feel her confusion, her frustration, in her rapid swallowing, and his own in his unwillingness to lean away. Instead, he pillowed his head upon her shoulder and let a heavy sigh express the depth of his exhaustion.

"I'm sorry. That was a little more than thank you."

Now he would discover if he'd pushed too far, too fast. He waited for her reply, then shut his eyes in relief as her fingers combed lightly through his hair. He was forgiven. Again.

"Rest now," she told him, with a calm she was far from feeling. She stood unsteadily and helped him lie back upon the mattress. Her own emotions winced at his involuntary gasp. Quickly, she brought his feet up on the bed, then waited anxiously for his fingers to unclench from the sheets.

She knew she should leave him then, should return to the other room, where she'd find no relief from the torment of memories.

As if understanding her reluctance to face her deed, Deacon caught her hand and drew her slowly, with a nonthreatening strength, down to the mattress beside him. As his arm formed a protective curl about her, he closed his eyes in search of needed sleep.

Garnet lay unmoving. Maidenly shock wasn't quite strong enough to overcome the appeal his closeness had upon her strained senses. She found comfort and compassion in his offer, not compromise. True, he'd kissed her with a shattering familiarity, but he'd stopped before taking any real advantage and he'd apologized for those brief liberties. She could have protested at any time . . . but hadn't.

And her sensibilities didn't protest now.

After levering out of her boots and pulling the covers up over them, Garnet placated her chafing morals by rolling away from him, as if the denying line of her back and backside presented an insurmountable barrier to any wrongdoings. But she continued to hug to the arm he'd wrapped about her, her fingers clutching to his for the sense of safety it gave her. And surprisingly, she slept, demons at bay on the night that she'd experienced two things that forever changed her life.

She'd killed one man and kissed another.

If Garnet had gone to sleep blissfully surrounded by the sense of security, she awoke to the shock of encompassing sin. Darkness blanketed the room, but she didn't need light to get a clear picture of her situation.

She was tangled with Deacon Sinclair under her bed covers.

Sometime during the night, she'd pressed herself close to the nearly naked sergeant. Her head was cozily cradled in the lea of his shoulder, where his soft breaths stirred her hair. Though she was fully clothed, she met the long line of him inch for inch, her breasts cushioned against his ribs, her knee casually riding his thigh, her toes brushing along the calf of his leg.

The contact reinforced her awareness of him as a man, hard where she was soft, lean where she was rounded, furred where she was smooth. Those differences excited in ways both foreign and frightening. Frightening because she had no desire to correct the impropriety by easing away from him.

Her arms lay in a circle about his shoulders. The back of his head rested in her palms. Instead of releasing him as modesty dictated, she tightened that loop possessively.

And she wondered what she would have to do to wake up entwined with this man for the rest of her days. And nights.

She wasn't ignorant enough to think that a simple kiss would do it. Though no small matter for her, she was certain he'd kissed his share of women without ever thinking of marriage. What could she offer that would make him want to return after this conflict was over? She'd saved his life by his own admission. Would that provide bonds strong enough to hold him, or would her sacrifices be forgotten the minute he rode out of her yard?

All she knew at this moment they fit together, was how quickly he'd filled all the empty corners of her existence. What she didn't know about his life in details, she'd learned by example. He'd shown her fearlessness when she'd been desperate and tenderness when she'd been needy. And his kiss . . . his kiss had shown her the dormant power of her own desires. How could she ever quiet what he'd awakened in her? How could she be satisfied with solitude when she'd known the completing warmth of his body lying next to hers?

How was she ever going to let him ride away and out of her life?

"What's wrong?"

The low caress of his voice startled her from her anxious thoughts but not from their purpose.

"Just thinking."

"Bad dreams?" His hand fell upon the back of her neck to begin a light massage. At his touch, her bones went to butter.

"No, not bad dreams."

"Then what?"

She took a small breath and forged ahead. "Just thinking how nice it is not to be alone."

He was motionless for a long moment and she feared she said too much. Then his cheek rubbed the top of her head.

"It is nice. I've been alone for a long time, too."

Was that an encouragement, or a simple statement of fact? She didn't know. Cursing her naïveté, she proceeded with care. "This should feel all wrong, but it doesn't."

She felt his nod. "It feels comfortable."

"Comfortable?" She rose up, frowning slightly. "Comfortable like with a sister?"

She could just make out the slightly crooked

smile that shaped his mouth in the dimness.
"No. Not like with my sister."

"Oh." Mollified, she snuggled back against
him, then ventured, "Like a friend?"

The kneading movement of his hand stilled.
"I don't usually kiss my friends."

"Oh."

Not sister, not friend. What did that leave, if
not lovers? A chill of anticipation swept her,
making her burrow in closer to his heat.

What would that mean, lovers? She was
thinking soul mates, of complementing partners
in life, of courtship upon the promise of his
return. What was he thinking? She wished she
dared question him.

Instead she asked, "Do you think I'm pretty?"

"How old are you?"

Not exactly the reply she wanted. "How old
are *you*?"

"Old beyond my years. Positively ancient. Too
old for a young girl like you."

"I'm not all *that* young."

A chuckle vibrated beneath her cheek. The
sound was husky and intimate, and she went
weak inside.

"You didn't answer my question."

"No, I don't think you're pretty."

As she swallowed down that disappointment,
he added, "I think you're beautiful. And brave.
And too desirable for us to be having this conversation. Go back to sleep."

Sleep? How could she sleep now? Beautiful,

brave . . . and desirable! She couldn't stop, now that she'd gone this far. Concealing darkness gave her the courage to continue.

"Have you ever been in love?"

He was silent for a long moment, then said, "I thought so, once, but that was many years ago. Why do you ask?"

"I've never had anyone else to ask. Do you mind?" she added shyly.

"I guess not."

Encouraged, Garnet smiled dreamily. "It must have been very wonderful."

"As I recall, a tooth extraction would have been less painful."

Hearing the hurt covered quickly by his quiet laughter, she pressed, "Did she break your heart?"

"No . . . yes . . . I don't know. I was young. Younger than you are now. I should have known better than to start something I couldn't finish. It was my fault if we both got hurt."

How romantic it sounded, the way he drew a slow breath and let it out upon a sigh.

"What happened?"

"She was beneath my station. My family didn't approve. I had to give her up."

"Did they force you to?"

"It doesn't matter now."

But it did. From the tone of his voice, it mattered very much.

"What was her name?"

"Jassy."

"Was she a neighbor?"

"No. She worked for my family. As I said, it was a long time ago."

And best forgotten, his tone intimated. She obeyed his wish for once, lying quietly within the curve of his arm while mulling over his words and what they didn't say. Finally, he asked, "And you? Have you some handsome beau picked out?"

She almost swallowed her tongue. If he only knew . . .

After a moment to cool her agitation, she said, "No one yet. But then, as you pointed out, I'm still a child, and not so very old as you."

He chuckled, then winced at the pain it caused him. She could feel his smile against her hair. She would have liked very much to see it, for she guessed he didn't smile often. She wondered if the loss of his young love had cast his life in a somber shape. At that moment, she wished ardently that she was clever enough or woman enough to fill that void in him. But being neither, she stayed silent, feeling his melancholy and aching for those long-ago lovers.

But if that first love had not been fated to fail, he wouldn't be here in her arms.

If only there was a way to keep him from leaving them.

Garnet woke to find the warmth she'd snuggled up to belonged to a large snoring dog.

The room showed no sign that Deacon Sinclair had ever been there. For one brief moment, she wondered if last night had been some cruel sort of dream.

Then the unmistakable scent of coffee reached her.

Poor exhausted Boone never so much as twitched when she slipped out of bed and quickly changed her clothes. As she hitched a belt up to secure the baggy trousers about her waist, a sense of wistfulness overcame her.

How long had it been since she'd owned a new dress? How long since she'd felt the feminine sway of lacy petticoats? How could she get Deacon to see her as a woman if she didn't even look like one? She touched a hand to her home-cropped hair, feeling the thick curl of it at the nape of her neck. What would it be like to have the heavy weight of long tresses pinned up in a sophisticated knot instead of in this loose boyish tangle?

Then would Deacon see her as a woman and not a girl?

There was no help for her lack of wardrobe or length of hair, so she would have to make the best of it.

She pushed aside the curtain and was greeted by the inviting picture of Deacon Sinclair at her stove, scrambling something delicious-smelling in her skillet. She paused for a moment to simply absorb the sight. Unfortunately, he noticed her almost immediately. He smiled in welcome, waving a fork toward the table preset for two.

"Good morning. I made myself useful. I hope you don't mind."

"You've been busy." Her gaze touched on the snowy prints by the door.

"I thought you could use the sleep."

"Not so much as you," she protested, both liking and disturbed by the idea of him taking over her daily chores.

"I'm feeling much better, thanks to you, and I'm hungry. I figured you wouldn't mind sharing the food so much if I prepared it."

"I wouldn't have minded at all."

He grinned at her prickly answer and the gesture made him so heart-stoppingly handsome, she hurt inside just looking at him. This was a man she could lose herself to every morning of her life.

"Sit. This is almost ready. How do you like your coffee?"

"With sugar." She took the seat, somewhat dazed by the service and the server. He presented her with a steamy cup of hearty brew and a plate of questionable ingredients.

Noting her arched brow, he told her, "It's mostly eggs and anything else I could find that was edible. Don't worry. It won't poison you."

"I wasn't worried." She met his gaze for a long beat, then said, "You clean up nicely."

He touched the fresh-boiled shirt and looked

sheepish. "I hope you don't mind. I borrowed this from your father."

"And his razor, too, I see."

He put fingertips to his smooth cheek. "I should have waited to ask."

"The improvement outweighs the impropriety," she told him with a smile. "Join me."

For the simple pleasure of having another at the table, she would have forgiven him anything. The thought of him going through her father's clothes cupboard and plying his straight edge were the least of her concerns. It was the fact of his apparent recovery that had her close to weeping. She could see in the way he moved that he would be gone much sooner than she'd hoped.

"You said your father was with the Union telegraphers. Was that his profession before the war?"

Glad for the casual conversation to distract her from the way her heart pounded so painfully, Garnet said, "No, he's a farmer."

"I wondered . . . seeing as how you're so far from any town." He took a sip of coffee, his features relaxed, his gaze upon hers in genuine interest.

Flattered to have him show curiosity about her life, she answered freely. "My father wanted to do something for the Union cause. Unfortunately, his poor eyesight and breathing troubles made him a poor candidate for the field. It broke his heart to think they couldn't use him in some capacity."

"Providing food for the troops is a noteworthy contribution."

Garnet smiled gratefully but shook her head. "That wasn't enough for him. You see, he was born in this valley, in this house. He wanted to make his mark on the outside of these hills." Her wistful tone said she envied him that opportunity.

"So, how does a farmer become a telegraph operator?"

Garnet blushed slightly and focused on her plate. "Well, actually, it was my doing. I could see how much he wanted to give, but no one wanted what he had to offer. So I found something that they would want." She glanced up to catch his encouraging half smile.

"And what was that?"

"I've always been good with numbers. There were no schools nearby, so my mother taught me to read and write and cipher. She said it was a natural gift, the way I took to mathematics. I'd been reading about the use of coded messages in the field, so one evening, I came up with my own series of coded dots and dashes for him to take to the federal command."

He stared at her for a long moment without blinking. "You invented a code."

"I adapted it from what had already been in use. The Union officers were impressed enough to bring my father into the telegraph corps. We'd made a deal, you see, I'd give him the code and he'd let me stay here to keep the farm going."

"Very clever of you."

She wasn't sure the soft spoken statement was a compliment. The warm admiration was gone from his slate-colored stare. In its place was the steely intensity, as unreadable as it was unbending. Was he censuring her for bargaining with her father to get what she wanted? Color climbed into her cheeks when she considered how calculating it must have sounded.

"This is my family's farm, Sergeant. It's all we have to pass from generation to generation. Just this land and what sits upon it. If I'd followed my father's edicts and had gone docilely to some big city where I would be safe and cared for as befitting my female gender, how long do you think this place would stand? What do you think the chances would be that there would be anything for us to come home to?"

"I wasn't being critical of the choices you made, Garnet. I admire you for them."

It was the way he said her name as much as the content of his phrase that fired her blood like heat lightning.

"Oh."

"I was marveling that a girl—a *woman*—like you could best the best of Confederate intelligence with a code they've found to be unbreakable."

Her awkward blush returned along with a

fluttering heartbeat. "You won't tell anyone, will you?"

He made the sign of an X over his heart.

"Oh, I'm sure someone will figure out the combinations sooner or later, but until they do, my father is the unit's darling and I've given him his chance to live a dream."

"Show me."

"What?"

Deacon reached out to slip his hand over the top of hers. His thumb stroked along its sensitive valley in devastating circles. As he held her gaze transfixed within the smoky mystery of his own, he gave a small, coaxing smile that set her budding passions ablaze.

"Show me how you did it," he urged silkily. "Teach me your code."

Chapter 5

S he studied him for so long and so hard, Deacon panicked. She suspected. She might not have known for sure, but she intuited that something was wrong about his interest.

He shouldn't have searched through her father's belongings under the guise of finding clean clothes. Perhaps that alerted her. But the opportunity presented itself, too choice to ignore. And now all his plans teetered near ruin.

"Is something wrong?" His voice betrayed nothing of his inner alarm.

Garnet hesitated, then gave a funny little laugh. "It's just that I'm not supposed to talk to anyone about it."

He nearly sagged in relief. Embarrassment. That was what had her acting so strangely. She was embarrassed about not being able to tell him. Smiling easily, he pressed her hand.

"I understand. It's a government secret, after all. You can't give that information to just anyone." He emphasized "anyone" ever so slightly, then began to withdraw his hand. Hers seized up around it. Slowly she turned his palm up and used her forefinger to tap out a series of stops and starts. His pulse beats were equally irregular.

"What did you say?"

Her smile was pure feminine mystery. "I can teach you. It's a simple mathematical progression."

"I don't want you to get in any trouble."

She shrugged. "Even if you knew the code, the secret's safe. Only my father can use it."

"Why's that?"

"Those he contacts recognize his 'fist,' his manner of keying. It's as individual as a signature. It's a way to protect his value to the Union cipher corps."

He smiled and again vowed, "Very clever."

Her features brightened. "So I guess it couldn't hurt to teach you."

His smile widened. "I guess not."

So he listened, and he learned, and soon he had all the information he'd been sent to discover, told to him with a sweet naïveté by a girl who trusted strangers. All he had to do was take what he knew back to the Confederate line.

But leaving was no simple matter.

He told himself it was a slight recurrence of his fever that forced him to seek a few hours' rest. His head did ache. Not a fit of conscience. No, it was far too late in his life for him to experience a pause of reluctance. He'd done far worse things than tarnish the illusions of one lonely girl—far worse. So why couldn't he think of any instances that made him writhe quite so uncomfortably as this one?

As he lay in the darkened room, on sheets redolent with her herbal scent, listening to the soul-plucking sounds of her harp, he asked himself one question.

When had he become such a loathsome creature?

He could argue that the job demanded it. That the times commanded it of him. But he knew the truth. The truth was, there remained no scrap of decency in his soul, no sense of remorse. That's what made him the perfect spy. No action was too abhorrent, no consequence too dire. The problems of others were not his, and he didn't trouble himself over them. One had to look above and beyond the miserable coil of life if one was to be successful. Hadn't he learned that at an early age? And he was always successful. Always.

So why did he feel so empty? Why could no action, no accomplishment, fill him up?

Why did the sum of all his victories fall so painfully shy of the satisfaction he found in one country girl's admiring smile?

He was tired. That was all.

After he turned in his report, he would go home for a while to refresh his spirit and renew his dedication. Viewing the vast fields at Sinclair Manor never failed to instill him with pride and purpose. Then he would forget this one brave girl whose life he would inexorably change under the guise of duty.

But not today.

Today he wallowed in the murky swamp of ethics that made him question the right and wrongs of what should not be questioned.

And the sooner he left, the better off he'd be.

There was no mistaking the anguish in her gaze when he emerged from the bedroom in full uniform. She knew good-bye was coming, and the pain of it shone with guileless brilliance in her beautiful dark eyes. There was nothing he could do about that. He owed her nothing but his thanks—for the hospitality, for the selfless care, for the secrets she'd sworn not to tell another soul.

"I'll pack you some food for your journey home."

That was all she said. Her simple acceptance of the situation upset his balance more than any feminine plea could have. She didn't have to say it. She was sorry to see him go.

And the hell of it was, he was sorry to be leaving.

"You don't—"

Her smile disarmed him. "It's no trouble."

So he stood there in the cozy room, watching her in her ridiculous men's clothing, preparing him a repast when soon she would be cursing his very existence. From under the table, Boone regarded him with wary hostility. The dog knew better than the master that he was not what he seemed. Perhaps it could smell a rotten core.

Garnet brought him a carefully wrapped parcel, offered with a frozen smile. She wasn't as successful at keeping the emotions from her uplifted gaze. Unshed tears shimmered there, and he was the cause.

"This should see you for a couple of days." Her words fractured slightly. She hid the failing of her voice with a pretended cough.

Deacon took the generous gift. "You've been more than kind, considering the inconvenience I've caused you."

"The excitement, you mean." Her small smile sent another spear to prick his conscience. "You certainly managed to shake up my daily routine, Sergeant."

He wanted to correct her, to have her call him by his given name, but it was better that she didn't. Better that she remind him of the pretense and his reason for being here in her cheery home. It wasn't to get personal with her.

"Before I go, I'll help you bury those two men. It's the least I can I do," he concluded quietly.

Her reluctance was clear, but she nodded. "Yes, that's probably a good idea. I'll get the shovels."

So they dug into the hard soil a distance from the house while Boone sniffed happily about the trees. When one large hole was ready to receive the morbid evidence of what they'd done, they

hauled the stiffened bodies out of the storage cellar, leaving twin trails through the snow. They
were dumped unceremoniously one next to the
other.

"Should we say something over them?"

"I say good riddance."

He regretted the wry sentiment the instant he
saw her expression. His callousness horrified
her. She didn't deserve the additional distress.

"Whatever you feel would be appropriate,"
he amended.

With her eyes actually tearing over the fate of
the two vermin, Garnet murmured, "Lord,
accept these unfortunate souls into Your forgiving embrace. We cannot commend them for any
of their good qualities, having known them only
as thieves, but I'm sure You are aware of them,
whatever they might be. Forgive us for sending
them into Your care. Amen."

"Amen," he echoed half-heartedly.

Would she speak as charitably at his own
graveside, he wondered, casting the first spade-
ful of dirt atop the deceased. He winced as pain
jumped in his side but continued to backfill the
hole with steady repetitions. Once the villains
were covered, he hoped Garnet could forget
they'd ever shadowed her idyllic valley. As if
sins of the past could be so easily buried.

Despite the chill, he was soon running with
sweat and favoring his injured ribs. He didn't
look over at Garnet for fear that she'd read the
discomfort in his eyes and force him to quit

before the unpleasant job was done. He refused to quit on her in this one thing.

But it was something altogether different that made him pause in his laboring. An odd sound. A wheezy rattle.

Garnet had bent over double, clutching at her knees. Her lovely face was flushed and running wet as she struggled to catch her breath. She did not struggle as if tuckered out by effort, but actually fought to fill her lungs with any degree of relief.

"Garnet?"

She glanced up.

One look at her fear-rounded gaze and he let the shovel drop. His hands slipped beneath her elbows for support. Up close, the sounds were worse. Panic knifed through him. Was she suffocating? Choking?

She clutched at his forearms, fighting to say the words. "Must get inside. The cold. Can't breathe."

He didn't wait to hear more. He scooped her up and jogged toward the house, alarming Boone into following on his heels, barking frantically. He found it easy to ignore the agony in his side because the sudden shock to his heart was ten times worse.

The attack was a bad one. If she hadn't been so distracted by the pain of Deacon leaving, she would have felt the symptoms coming on.

She hadn't had one of her spells for several

years, but there was no mistaking the way it gripped her chest with crushing savagery. The more she battled for breath, the tighter the constriction grew. Helpless and immobilized, she never would have made it back to the house if not for Deacon's quick action. He whisked her back into the cabin's warmth, where he heeded her objection to the bedroom over an upright position in a rocker. After tearing off her damp overcoat, he knelt before her.

He looks terrified.

The observation bemused her. He hadn't displayed a flicker of dismay when fighting against Cale for his life, nor when he'd pressed a burning brand into his own flesh. But her distress scared him. She put a calming hand to his cheek, letting her fingertips trail down his neck to rest upon his shoulder.

"It's not as bad as it seems," she wheezed, speaking the lie to reassure him. Fear almost at once muted to concern.

"What is it? Do you know? Has this happened before?"

At her jerky nod, he became a man of purpose.

"Tell me what I can do to help you."

She fought to bring out the words. "Steam helps."

He was up and gone. She heard pots banging and the splash of water. Then he was back, crouching down to open the first few buttons of her shirt, then blotting her face and neck dry. His touch was gentle, his manner comforting in its control. When he said, "You'll be all right," she believed without question.

Even Boone seemed convinced of his sincerity, for the pup lay beside the chair soundlessly.

When the kettle he'd put on to boil reached a roiling intensity, Deacon carried her carefully to a high stool angled in front of the stove. While he held her in the curl of one arm, she leaned forward into the hot, wet steam, getting as close as she could stand. He draped a towel over her head to capture and contain the moist air so it could work its magic against the swelling in her throat and lungs. And for the next hour, Deacon held her in an easy circle, massaging her back and shoulders, soothing her panic with his wordless encouragement.

Gradually, relief came.

She knew the crisis had passed when the first cough spasmed through her. With each violent seizure, more saving air was allowed to pass. Deacon carried her back to the rocking chair. She looked like a drowned kitten; the steam plastered her hair to her head in wet strings. Her shoulders convulsed with the force of each harsh, yet productive cough.

She glanced up wearily when he held a cup to her lips.

"Drink," he ordered. "It will ease your throat."

She drank, tasting honey and a sear of her father's celebration whiskey, which was only taken out for a sip or two on holidays or occasions. She guessed this qualified. Then she made no protest as he slipped off her heavy woolen shirt, now dampened and clinging unpleasantly to her skin, and restored her to his lap. As the coughing spells dwindled down to raspy sputters, he rocked her slowly, letting her sag upon his chest until the attack was at an end. She barely noticed when he moved into the bedroom to lay her down upon the sheet they'd shared that past evening. All she knew was that when he straightened away from her, she wanted to share that same comfortable closeness again.

"Don't go."

Her voice rasped like sand on a wood floor, the plea so soft, her look so vulnerable, Deacon could deny her nothing. First, he removed her wet boots, then his own, followed by his ruined Yankee uniform jacket and pistol belt. Then he eased down gingerly and stretched out beside her, opening his arm wide to invite her up against him. The fit of her along his form seemed so familiar, so right, he would have been disturbed by it if he'd not been so drained by worry and fatigue. His own wound ached as if ravenous teeth chomped down on his ribs. The only thing making it bearable was Garnet, who even now was dead to the world in slumber.

He touched her hair. A mistake, he knew, but the gesture came unbidden, not to comfort her, but rather himself. How would she look with it long and luxurious about her shoulders? What would an evening gown of finest silk do for her glorious figure? The image of her in torn flannel flamed across his memory.

Reminding himself that she was barely a woman couldn't dissuade a bodily response. His first in longer than he could remember, and as inopportune as it was ill fated. Pleasures of the flesh were among those other enjoyable vices he denied himself by virtue of his station. If he were to be an example, he could not corrupt himself with worldly distractions. He didn't smoke. He drank rarely, and then in moderation. He gambled when the social situation demanded it, and then only if he was winning. His language was governed by a control he almost never surrendered. And like any well-bred planter's son, he took his rare ease, when necessary, upon the women in Louisville who made it their business to entertain those on business in the city.

He would have to marry. It was his duty as heir to Sinclair Manor, one he intended to pursue as soon as this war was over. Since he had no opinion on the matter, he would defer to his parents' wisdom. His father would consider the financial benefit and his mother the practical in steering him toward the proper mate.

He pictured this unnamed female with indifference and disinterest. She would be pretty table dressing, as finely weaned as a show pony and trained as to her function—which was not to interfere with his life. He would give her whatever material goods she wanted, and she would give him a son. Beyond that, he saw a

wife's position in his household as little different from the staff whose job it was to serve him
invisibly.

Of course, he'd see that the position of being
his bride was tolerable and prestigious. He
would be considerate and kind and would even
converse with the mother of his children, should
the need arise. He knew how to be civil, though
he found few instances in which to practice
those skills. He wouldn't burden his bride with
his passions or his presence. He would model
his relationship upon what he'd observed at
home: his father ruling the roost, his mother
quietly controlling the home.

It never occurred to him that he might like the
woman he would wed. He had little admiration
for females, aside from their physical appeal,
which he preferred to observe like fine art—
from a distance. They were shallow and flighty
and given to irrational fits that could only be
appeased by bribery. They were a necessary
inconvenience when one needed a dancing partner or to procreate. He found them unpre-
dictable and unreliable, a threat to a man's
well-being.

How often had some hare-brained scheme of
his sister's brought a whisper of disharmony to
their home? Dramatic and temperamental, she
was often more trouble than she was worth. He
was anxious to push her out from under their
roof under the control of some unfortunate fool
who believed he could rule her. There were

times when he was genuinely fond of Patrice. She could be amusing in her own way, and a fierce loyalty lay behind her merciless teasing. He could almost concede that she was a rarity within the gender—until he met Garnet.

Despite their different upbringings, Garnet was in some ways similar to Patrice. They both spoke their minds—evidence that they actually had minds—and they displayed fortitude more often than feigned delicacy. He found their company . . . less than objectionable.

He closed his eyes, letting his mind wander in a dangerous direction.

What would married life be like if he were wed to a woman like Garnet? As soon as he posed that question of himself, a seditious whisper undercut it. Not a woman *like* Garnet. *Garnet*. Forget for a moment that that was impossible. Consider instead coming home to her conversation at dinner. Seeking out a mutual bed for more than just the obligatory heir. Enjoying the company of someone who was caring and clever, rather than self-absorbed and cunning. A novel idea. A damned attractive idea. One as disconcerting as the woman in question. Would he really want his life confused by emotions he couldn't control?

Would he really want to commit his heart at the risk of it being broken?

His hand stilled atop her head.

No.

No.

He closed down his mind, guarding his feelings against the possibility. It was his duty to place property and profits before any personal pleasures. A woman like Garnet would disrupt his priorities. Never mind that he was about to betray everything that she held sacred. This wasn't the time, this wasn't the woman, and he'd be courting disaster to think otherwise.

Even as he shut her out of his thoughts, his body was aware of the contentment found in cuddling her closer. Hers was a form created for such a task—soft on the surface, steel underneath. And he yearned to embrace those pleasures. Pleasures that teased through a fitful sleep and roared to life upon waking.

He was still there.

Garnet lay unmoving, studying the relaxed features of the man beside her.

He hadn't left her.

Hope quivered through her as she considered the way he'd cared for her, had comforted and encouraged her during her attack. The vulnerable embarrassment she might have felt was offset by the magnitude of his actions. She remembered the tenderness in the stroke of his hand, the gentle strength in his voice. That, combined with the way he'd kissed her, proved his intent was more than Samaritan.

Didn't it?

She recalled the anxiety steeped in his eyes and the way he'd rocked her upon his lap. Could it be that he did have feelings for her?

Could the man beside her hold the secret to her future happiness? Or was she setting herself up for heart break at his hands?

It was early. Sunlight had yet to penetrate the winter gloom. Shadow softened the lines of Deacon's face, making him seem more approachable, more attainable. Until his eyes opened with a snap, his body instantly alert.

"Good morning."

At her soft greeting, some of the stiffness left his posture. Some, but not all. There was an edge of wariness to him she hadn't noticed before.

"How do you feel?"

She took a sample breath and pronounced, "Fine. My chest hurts a little, but that's to be expected."

At the mention of her discomfort, the air of remoteness ebbed. His knuckles brushed her cheek. "I was worried."

Humbled by his honest admission, she gave a shaky smile. "It's scary. I've had spells for years, but they never fail to frighten my father witless."

"You said he had breathing troubles, too. This same sort of thing?"

She nodded.

"And there's no name for it? No cure?"

She shrugged philosophically. "The steam helps, so do some of the local folk remedies. It's worse in the winter when it's cold, or when I get very upset about something." She avoided his intent stare, focusing instead upon the light thatch of hair escaping the opening of his long johns.

"You've had a rough couple of days," he agreed. "Good thing I'll be leaving so you can get back to your normal pace."

"Good thing." Her voice trembled. She didn't think it was a good thing at all.

She held her breath as his hand slipped beneath her chin to tilt her head up, forcing her gaze to return to his.

"I have to go."

Was it her he was trying to convince, or himself?

"I know you do."

"Is there anything you need before I leave?"

She could think of several things, actually. She nudged her cheek into his palm, feeling his fingers widen to cup the side of her face. "This is nice," she said softly.

He didn't answer, but he didn't withdraw his hand, either. She felt his muscles tighten as her palm traveled up his arm, then heard his sharp inhalation as it glided across the sculpted terrain of his chest. The hard beat of his heart made her think of the campaign drum he followed . . . and would follow again once he left her bed.

But would he have to leave her life forever?

Give him a reason to return.

Because she couldn't comfortably phrase her wants in words, she stretched up to touch her lips to his. His remained cool and unresponsive, so she pulled away in sudden shame. He regarded her unblinkingly, his gaze unreadable.

Had she read his interest wrong?

"I'm sorry," she blurted out, hot with humiliation. "I didn't mean to obligate you—"

He shushed her awkward speech with the press of his fingertips. "No, I'm sorry. A gentleman should never place a lady in such a compromising position."

Her gaze rose to his, wide and innocent in its appeal. "Even when she wants him to?"

A flicker of need crossed his steady stare, an expression so surprisingly revealing, she could read it as easily as her own heart. She saw loneliness in that stark and hungry gaze, a need for companionship as deep and fierce as her own. It was something neither of them would have acted upon had the circumstance been different. But at this moment, in this place, the time felt so very right.

Her eyes drifted shut in anticipation as he bent to kiss her.

Chapter 6

J ust a kiss . . .

He should have known the moment her soft lips parted beneath his that it would be more than just that.

Much more.

At her invitation, he slipped his tongue inside to taste the sweetness of her offer. She stiffened slightly, whether in shock or surprise it soon didn't matter, not when she was ripe for new experiences. She opened wider. And when her own tongue danced silkily around his, Deacon knew he was lost. Purpose faded. There was nothing beyond this warm, willing creature who sought so eagerly to fulfill what had been missing within him for so very long.

One kiss chased another, each varying in expression and design. This one a deep plunging hunger, the next a tender nibble, then a wet tangle that encouraged their hands into play. Her fingers raked through his hair, shifting, kneading, finally fisting as desire shivered through her, hot and out of control. His palms slid down the undersides of her arms, revolving slowly to encompass and reverently claim the fullness of her breasts. Such lush, tempting bounty. His head dipped down. His mouth fastened over one pebbled peak. Even through a layer of cotton, the sensation made her gasp in awe and unexpected arousal.

She needed to feel him closer.

Her fingers trembled over the small buttons of her chemise, then peeled the fabric away so the next covering would be the surprising heat of his hands. He thumbed an even tighter welcome before bending to taste and tease and torment with the pull of his lips. Having never realized such delights, Garnet moaned wantonly and arched into his suckling kisses. A strange new yearning began to knot low in her belly, the sensation so disturbing, so raw, she sought a way to alleviate it. Moving against him in anxious little pulses seemed to help at first, then only made matters worse when he leaned back to give them both a saving space.

"We can stop now," he told her. "We *should* stop now."

But his eyes said different, and so did her quivering soul.

"No, we can't. It's too late, isn't it?"

The storm brewing in his gaze broke with lightning intensity. "It was too late the first time I saw you and thought I'd gone to heaven." Then he concluded with a husky, "I was right.

You're my angel, and this is the only heaven I'm ever going to know."

She pulled him to her, into her urgent kiss.

It was too late. Deacon surrendered to that fact with both reluctance and relief. He shut his mind to circumstance and consequence and opened his heart to this woman who deserved no less from him. He'd never wanted anything quite so badly as this brief chance to explore happiness in her arms, to have his sense of wonder reborn each time she gasped in discovery.

Awash in the first pink of dawn, he undressed them both. To overcome her awkwardness, he murmured whatever came to mind, praising her beauty, her femininity, her softness, her desirability in words that made her quake and all wooingly warm—because she'd never heard those things before, had never truly believed them until he'd made them so. She opened to him without hesitation, opened her heart, her eyes, her inhibitions, and then her knees, so he could settle between them.

"Don't be afraid," he crooned in a tight-throated voice, struggling to slow and control the moment so she'd have no reason for fear.

"I'm not," she assured him with a shaky bravado, then confessed, "I don't know what to do with my hands."

Charmed by her naïveté, Deacon pressed kisses to her palms, then fit them over the swells of his shoulders. She grabbed on tight, sensing the moment was at hand when mystery would be replaced by knowledge. Then there'd be no going back.

She felt him push hard and alarmingly huge against her. Modesty bade her to recoil, but instinct whispered for her to relax and trust him. The instant she let down her anxious guard, he breeched the last secret of womanhood with one swift, sure stroke. Innocence and her sense of isolation were both torn away at the same time. This was belonging, this wonderful, foreign fullness that spread all the way to her soul.

"Oh, Deacon," she sighed, her eyes going misty with emotion. "Surely this must be heaven."

He dropped a fierce kiss of agreement upon her lips and began to move within her. Slow and easy, with regard to her inexperience and his own healing injury. Slow and easy, to contain his raging passions. The degree of effort shook along his limbs but rewarded him at last with her sudden explosive cry of revelation. He drank up the sound and let himself go, riding out the same satisfying spasms that left her limp and smiling in sated lethargy beneath him.

Breathing hard and drained of all vitality, he rolled onto his side and continued to cuddle her close. And somehow that was as fulfilling as the act itself. He'd never lingered after the fact before, seeing no reason to remain nor feeling the desire. But this was a moment he never wished to end. He wanted to bask in the thrall of passions well met. He wanted to preen with accomplishment and hear flattering claims of his prowess. He wanted to hold her tight and love her all over again, in case there was some small delight he might have missed during their first humbling encounter.

Lord, she was a treasure, a heaven-sent, earthy dream.

And he could enjoy her every night for the rest of his life if he made her his bride.

But even as that notion staggered him with awesome potential, the remaining truth hit and hit squarely.

He could have her only if he relinquished the duty that had brought him to her door.

Garnet watched the frown lines gather on Deacon's brow, and because of her inexperience, guessed that the event that had shaken her spiritual foundation had somehow disappointed him. At a loss, she shyly traced her fingertips along the hard contour of his upper arm and waited for him to reveal the source of his displeasure. Instead, he captured her wandering hand and held it curled within his own above the relentless thunder of his heartbeats.

"Have I done something wrong?" she ventured with a wavering bravery.

He shook his head, then glanced at her. His gaze was convincingly tender. "No. You've done everything right."

Then she saw the truth. It was regret coloring his mood.

"I know you have to leave. It's all right. I understand."

He smiled somewhat wryly at her heroic claim. "No, you don't, angel. You don't understand anything about it at all. Or about me."

"I know that you are courageous and kind." His soft snort of disagreement interrupted but did end her statement. She concluded with a quiet dignity. "And I know I'm not the type of woman your family would approve of, either."

His gaze jumped to hers, all stark misery. "This isn't about you, Garnet. It's me."

Of course. He didn't care for her. That was it. She lowered her eyes and took a stabilizing breath. She would pretend that knowledge didn't devastate her.

His kisses started at her brow and worked their way down to her pursed lips. Once there, she allowed him to convince her that she was wrong in that belief, too. When he lifted away at last, she regarded him through a teary, adoring gaze that proved a killing stroke to his conscience.

How could he intentionally shatter the guileless illusions held in those lovely dark eyes? She saw him as both saint and savior, and he found he wanted to be those things for her. He'd surrendered up every good thing in his life in the name of duty, in the cause of loyalty to the land, and what had it gotten him? A lifetime of loneliness, a future void of happiness. Endless servitude to someone else's ideals. He'd been taught all his life that that was the best he could strive for, but in these past few days, with this honest, endearing young woman, those rigid tenets had been proven false.

Here was his ideal, a woman who demanded nothing and made him want to surrender all. A connection so basic, so pure, it surpassed anything he'd known and everything he could have hoped for. In the past hours, he'd seen another future for himself, one stripped of regiment and lies, one borne of simple passions and no regrets.

This was what he wanted, this woman, this feeling of satisfaction, this sense of contentment. What else could possibly be waiting outside this valley to equal what he'd discovered about himself in Garnet's reflective gaze?

He wanted to be what she saw in him.

Her mouth opened sweetly beneath his, accepting him without reservation. A clever girl, she'd figured out what to do with her hands and used them to coax him to new heights of urgency. Her shyness gave way to a healthy curiosity about all things involved in what made man and woman different. Her discoveries were his delights, delights shared equally and abundantly as he moved above her, inside her, to the brink of paradise and beyond. Delights shared quietly as they lay curled together afterward in exhausted bliss.

About then Boone began to whine, his whip tail thumping the floorboards.

"I think somebody wants out," Deacon murmured sleepily.

Garnet pressed a kiss on his mouth as she levered up off the bed. "Don't go away."

His laugh was a low rumble. "Don't worry."

He closed his eyes, giving her the opportunity to observe him unnoticed while she slipped into her clothes. He was glorious: sleek, naked, and unashamed. And in her bed, filling it from end to end with his long form, from side to side with the outflung reach of his arms.

And for the moment, he was hers.

It took the cold air of the new day to wake Garnet to the realities of what had occurred.

As she stood shivering in the doorway while Boone sniffed his rounds, consequence sank deep.

She'd given herself to a man without the benefit of marriage. A terrible sin. Perhaps an unforgivable one. Unless that man became her husband. But there had been no commitments spoken between their hurried kisses. Was she a fool for not waiting to hear them?

Or was she twice the fool for thinking he meant to say them at all?

No matter what he said within the next few minutes, she had a picture to hold close in her dreams, the glorious picture he made all tall and lean in Union blue, every inch the handsome hero.

Her throat tightened as she made herself smile. His parting impression of her was not going to be one of a petulant little girl weeping for what was never offered.

"How far do you have to travel?" she asked, as she shut the door.

"Pride County. A day's ride, if I leave now."

She nodded at that wisdom. "There's the look of some serious weather coming in. You probably shouldn't waste too much time."

She tried to read his expression but found she couldn't. It was closed down tight around an impassive stare as he watched her pretend to be unconcerned. As if they'd spent the night reading scripture, rather than violating it.

"I'll make you breakfast—"

"No."

She paused with a smile. "It's no trouble."

"It's better that I go now. Sharing breakfast won't make our good-byes any easier."

Hope leapt in her heart. Did that mean he was finding it difficult to walk away? She turned toward the stove, afraid of what he might see in her naked gaze.

"I won't send you off without some coffee. Beans are hard to come by, but I've been hoarding them for . . . special occasions."

She caught her breath as his hands skimmed up from elbows to shoulders where they rested with a welcomed weight. She couldn't help leaning back against him as his mouth lightly brushed her temple. She held herself still. If she turned toward him, it would be to drag him off to bed again. And that wouldn't make things any easier, either.

"What unit is your father with? I'd enjoy meeting up with him if we're in the same neck of the woods. I can tell him that I've seen you and that you're all right. He'd probably like to hear that."

"Yes, I'm sure he would." Garnet thought nothing of relaying the information.

"Anything you'd like me to tell him?"

"Just that I miss him and to hurry home."

Thinking of his long absence brought a burning to her eyes. Instead of giving way to the welling tears, she continued to put the water on to boil, trying to ignore the way Deacon's nearness similarly heated her blood. To distract herself, she spoke of a neutral topic.

"What's your family like, Sergeant?" She chose to call him by his rank to keep the suggestion of distance. He didn't help matters by nuzzling against her neck.

"My mother's soft-spoken and elegant, the perfect hostess. My sister Patrice will be quite the lady if she ever decides to stop playing the hellion. You'd like her, Garnet."

She swallowed hard. As if they'd ever meet . . .

"And your father? What was he like?"

Deacon paused for so long, she began to regret reminding him of the fresh pain of loss. Then he spoke with an atonal respectfulness, as if discussing a stranger. "He was a firm, sometimes even hard man when he had to be. He taught me all the lessons I'd need to survive in life . . . but he never showed me how to enjoy it. You did." His hand tightened on her shoulders to bring her around to face him. He still wore the impenetrable look, but the husky quality of his voice woke a shiver inside her. "I've never known anyone like you. I've never had anyone express an interest in what I felt."

"Surely, your friends—"

"I never had time for friends. I never even had a dog. No wonder yours dislikes me so. I've no idea how to act around him, just as I've no notion on how to behave with you."

"But you're a gentleman—"

"Who knows how to be gallant and flattering and shallow and shut off to the things that really matter. I haven't a clue about what I'm feeling inside right now. I don't know what to do about it. I don't know what to say to you."

She placed tentative fingertips upon his chest to sample the tension and thunder there. Quietly, she advised, "Say what's in your heart."

He made an uncharitable sound. "Have you ever tried to read in the dark? I'm blind to what's in there."

"Then what is it you want to do? Not what's expected of you, but what *you* want to do?"

He seized her upturned face between his palms and bent to snatch her lips in a bruising kiss, one that echoed the angry frustration she'd heard in his tone. One that gentled to a heart-tearing tenderness when she swept her fingers through his hair and melted against him.

"I want this," he told her with a soft savagery. "I want to feel like this forever."

"You can," she encouraged, with words, with

her quick reinforcing kisses. But his hands were lowering, dropping back to her shoulders to push her away.

"But I have to leave."

"And I'm not going anywhere."

He searched her expression intently. "You'd wait for me."

"Forever. I want to keep this feeling, too."

He drew a shallow breath, indecision on some mighty scale warring behind his suddenly shuttered gaze. He touched her cheek and toyed with the awful homemade crop of her hair. And then a smile softened his sober features and Garnet felt her heart give way.

"I'll be back as soon as I'm able."

Not trusting her words to escape the thickening in her throat, she simply nodded.

She sent him off after a final cup of coffee with a day's supplies and a scorching kiss. And then she settled in to wait. For however long it took him to return to offer her the future she desired.

He rode hard and fast, but no amount of speed, no degree of cold or exhaustion, could tether the lightness in his heart or erase the scent of her from his nose or the taste of her from his mouth. It was madness, he knew. Craziness, he was certain.

It was treason.

He reached the Confederate camp early the second day. Still wearing the federal uniform, he put up his hands as if in surrender so the sentries wouldn't shoot him. He asked to be taken to Brigadier General Hobbs. After some amount of discussion, he was able to convince the wary corporal that he wasn't a Union assassin seeking a chance at their Intelligence leader and was taken to the brigadier's tent.

The general lifted a brow at the sight of the perforated Union coat and waved the enlisted man out. Without asking leave, Deacon crossed to the general's sideboard to pour himself a healthy glass of whiskey, another action that peaked Hobbs's curiosity.

"Are you all right, Reverend?"

"Fine, Joe. I'll be glad to get out of this particular color and home to see my family."

Joe Hobbs regarded his Intelligence agent with a grim impassivity. Sinclair was perhaps the best man he had in the field: quick minded, coldly unscrupled, and totally reliable. He worked under the code name "Reverend," since those involved in espionage seldom cared to use their own names at the risk of endangering their families. Sinclair was close to his, but Hobbs didn't relish the idea of losing his services.

"After I've heard your report, I've some news for you."

Deacon froze, his expression blanking. "Good or bad?"

"News. First, tell me yours."

This was the part Deacon dreaded. As skilled as he was in deceit, he hated to lie to those who counted upon him for his loyalty. Here in

Hobbs's tent, smelling the familiar odor of the general's favorite rancid cigars and enjoying the luxury of a relaxed code of conduct, the decisions Deacon made on the trail seemed less compelling, his reasonings less sure. He would be betraying more than just a commander who believed his word implicitly. He'd be turning upon his whole way of life, for the sake of a woman who several short days ago was nothing more than mission to him.

But now she was much more.

Enough to make him calmly give out an inaccurate account of what he'd been sent to discover.

"I infiltrated the Davis farm. Only the daughter was there, and she didn't know anything about her father's business. It was a dry run, I'm afraid."

Hobbs sighed in disappointment. "Sorry you had to waste your time, especially now. We'll find another way."

Deacon waited for him to say more, alerted and growing alarmed by his superior's unusual silence. Normally, Hobbs was full of ribald jokes and off-color anecdotes.

"You said you had some news for me."

"Sit down."

He braced himself. "Tell me."

"We got the latest casualty reports. Your father's name was on the list."

He received the information without a blink. "They're sure?"

"As sure as anything can be these days. I'm

sorry. You'll want some time to be with your family. They should hear it from you."

"Thank you, sir." He exited the tent with that wooden formality.

Hobbs frowned and clipped a fresh cigar. From behind him, a figure slipped through the rear flap and came to stand at his back.

"He's lying to you, Joe."

"Why would you say that, Hermes? He's got no reason."

"I don't know why, but I know a lie when I hear one. Comes from telling so many of my own."

Hobbs glanced back at his second-best spy, indecision playing briefly upon his features. True, Sinclair was his best man, but in their business, truth sometimes was shaded by the higher price.

"Maybe it's the woman."

"Deacon Sinclair?" In his astonishment, Hobbs blurted out his operative's full name. "Not likely."

"It's something. I'll guarantee it. Can you afford not to check up on him?"

The general chewed his cigar for a moment, thinking past the individual to the whole network of those who worked beneath him. One thing he couldn't afford to make was a wrong assumption.

"See what you can find out about this Davis person and his daughter. Visit that farm. If there's a reason for me to distrust the Reverend,

I want to know it before I send him out again. And Hermes, be discreet. I don't want him to think that I don't trust him. He's the best man I have."

"Yessir."

And the shadowy figure faded from sight, his scowl becoming a grin that flashed briefly as the tent flapped closed behind him.

Chapter 7

After taking about a dozen steps from the tent, the numbness gave before a shock of reality.

His father was dead.

Suddenly too wobbly to continue, Deacon dropped into a crouch, bending low and lacing his hands behind his head. He bit down hard on the swells of disbelief and sorrow.

It had to be a mistake.

Men like Avery Sinclair rode through the thick of things and came out without a scratch, medals displayed on their chests. They went home to their families, to their wives, to their land, and went on as before. They didn't just . . . die.

He took a tight breath and let it out in a noisy shiver.

How could he take the news home to his mama? Imagining her pain increased his own tenfold. He dug his elbows into his ribs in an effort to contain it. That fresh hurt only combined with the other, making it more impossible to control as grief and a surprising anger spasmed through him.

Gone, just like that. A man of his father's status and power, cut down like the lowliest infantry-man. How could such a thing have happened?

How could Avery Sinclair just up and die, dumping the weight of his responsibilities and expectations upon his son's shoulders?

Just when he'd decided to walk away from them.

The irony brought bitter tears to his eyes and a hoarse laugh that strangled in his throat.

While he was flirting with happiness in the arms of his enemy, his father was on some nameless field, dying to keep him from ever attaining it. He'd been so close to escaping. But that door had closed on him, shutting him in with the future that had already been prescribed for him to follow.

Leave it to his father to find such a damned dramatic way to remind him of who and what he was.

A Sinclair.

And a Sinclair never let unimportant things like happiness interfere with a duty to be done.

He took a breath, then another. The third came easier as a quiet sense of purpose settled over him, stilling the pain of all he'd lost.

For a moment, he'd allowed a gentle smile and a wooing taste of freedom to lure him from his path. He'd let himself believe that he could be what Garnet had wanted to see. His father's death denied that illusion.

He was the heir to Sinclair Manor and a soldier to the South. He'd let himself forget that, an unforgivable breech of the rules of war. A failure of character that shamed his father's teachings and now, his memory.

It was time to get back to duty, time to put dreams back in their place and do what was expected of him.

Hobbs looked up through a wreath of smoke to see Deacon Sinclair in his doorway.

"Reverend? Something else on your mind?"

Deacon stepped in and brought down the tent flap. "I'd like to finish my report, sir. I wasn't completely truthful with you before."

"Oh? And why was that?"

"Davis's daughter. She made me forget my priorities for a moment but that moment's gone. She got me thinking about civilized things that have no place in war. The only civilized thing to do is get this whole mess over with as soon as possible. The only way I can do that is to do my job, unpleasant as it is at times."

"This entire business is unpleasant, but we can save the lives of those men out there on the battlefield by doing some of the more unsavory aspects of warfare behind the scenes. That's our job. It's not glamorous. It may not seem patriotic or palatable at times, but that's how wars are won."

"Yes, sir."

Hobbs eyed him critically. This was the man he was used to seeing; all steely-eyed and unemotional. Whatever fit of conscience colored his earlier abbreviated statement was gone. And good riddance. There was no room for compassion or conscience in the game of espionage.

"I'm listening."

"I've managed to learn the Federal code."

Hobbs stared at him for an incredulous moment, then broke into a grin. "Good man. Get busy teaching it to our operators. We can flood the lines with false information on troops size and movement."

Deacon hesitated, just for an instant, but it was long enough to alert his superior to caution. "Yes, sir. Right away."

What wasn't his operative telling him?

"What about your family?"

Deacon's dispassionate stare said plainly, *What about them?*

"I'll write them."

Damn, Sinclair was a cold piece of work, but Hobbs couldn't ignore something that worked so well in his favor. "Set it up."

Without a word, his man was gone. But the feeling of uneasiness lingered as the general pulled at his cigar. Better to cover all points carefully. A lapse in judgement on Sinclair's part might be a symptom of some greater weakness.

Just to be on the safe side, he wouldn't call back Hermes. If Deacon wasn't forthcoming with all he knew, Hermes would fill in the blanks.

That's how wars were won.

Once Confederate ciphers were busy at the Teletype key relaying false information to enemy troops, Deacon took his long overdue leave. He'd head for home, perhaps arriving before his tersely penned message to deliver the news in person.

But first he had a stop to make.

He meant to take Garnet with him.

The hows of convincing her to go weren't important. He was quick when it came to hatching convenient lies.

But he had to get her away from the farm. It wouldn't matter to the Union army that Davis hadn't betrayed them. They'd only see treason and view Davis as the easiest scapegoat. And traitors and their families were treated harshly by both sides.

His anticipation grew with every mile. His desire to see Garnet, to hold her, to surround himself in her comforting care became a driving force. He'd wanted nothing else quite so much since learning of his father's death. A strange yearning, as he wasn't one to take his woes to another living being. Something about Garnet Davis encouraged him to bare his heart, to unburden his blackened soul. Maybe she would understand . . . and forgive him in time. She knew about patriotism, about duty. She'd realize he was just doing what they called him to do.

God, he hoped so.

If she only knew what this compromise had cost him. He rode with the weight of his father's displeasure pressing down on his shoulders, but it was a weight he would bear. For her.

His horse wheezing, his side seething with misery, Deacon crested the final hill leading down into the Davis's valley. And there he reined in to simply stare in dismay at the smoldering ruin below.

The house, the barn, his peaceful haven . . . gone. A Confederate detail still sifted through the rubble, hoping to find something of value in the ashes. Deacon struggled with a wild desire to draw his rifle and to ride down upon them like a vengeful angel of death. *His angel* . . . Where was Garnet? The need to know enabled him to control his rage as he cantered down into the center of devastation.

One of the men spotted him and warily straightened, his rifle ready to defend against the intrusion.

"The woman who lived here, where is she?"

"Who wants to know?"

"A superior officer. Answer me!"

"There weren't no sign of the Yankee bitch when we got here, so we went ahead with our orders."

Relief washed over him, tempering his fury. "And what were your orders, Private?"

"We was to confiscate the property and anything of value upon it."

Deacon looked over the smoking remains of the house and barn. Picturing the cozy fireplace, the rocking chair, the big bed where he'd found such paradise, he was sick inside at its senseless destruction.

"Who gave the order?"

"Sorry . . . sir. I ain't at liberty to say."

It didn't really matter who gave it. *He* was behind it. *He'd* brought this plague down upon the head of the woman whose only crime was to help him, to trust him, and to love him. He'd betrayed her goodness with the ruin of all she held dear. He thought of her pride in holding this property for her father. Gone because she believed his deception.

At least she'd escaped.

That was the one good thing he held in his heart through the remaining years of war. Even as he numbed himself to the atrocities he'd condoned, to the sins he'd committed, he was one step above damnation because she was somewhere safe, and hopefully, would someday be happy. It was punishment enough to savor that sliver of contentment he'd found in her arms knowing he'd never have it back or see her again.

Until she showed up in his front hall five years later to brutally end his dreams, just as he'd once crushed hers.

*   *   *

William Davis was a happy man.

In his counting of blessings, he was careful to ask forgiveness for the daily ruse he played with his superiors. Using his clever daughter's code, he'd made a niche for himself in the Union forces where he could be of service, and that ability made him a fortunate man.

A lucky man blessed with a plucky daughter whose unshakable belief in him allowed him to live out his dreams.

He was thinking of her as he made his way out to the latrines on the cold, starless night, hoping she was well, wishing he knew for sure.

"Captain Davis?"

He turned to see a figure silhouetted against the distant campfires.

"Yes. Who is it?"

"Let's say someone who has your daughter's best interests at heart."

A terrible tightness seized his chest, making it difficult for him to draw his next breath. "Garnet? Have you some news of her?"

He heard a soft, sinister chuckle that had the hair prickling at his nape.

"Let's just say from this point on, I'll make the news you'll hear regarding her health and safety."

"Who are you?"

"That's not important. What's important is that you listen very, very carefully to what I'm going to tell you and that you believe each and every word."

Davis was silent, his heart banging against his ribs, his breath shivering in the cold night air.

"I'd hate to have something happen to your little girl. It's up to you to see nothing does."

"What are you talking about? What is it you want?"

"A few days ago your daughter took in a wounded Union soldier and nursed him back to health. Only she didn't know that he was actually a Confederate spy sent to learn your code."

"If he hurt her—"

The threat dangled impotently as the stranger chuckled. "Oh, he didn't hurt her. He romanced her. And she happily gave him everything he wanted. Everything, including the code."

Davis was silent, his mind whirling with the consequence of what was being said. He could feel the other man's smile.

"I see you understand. The only problem is, the code is useless to us without the man behind it. A little detail forgotten by my sneaky friend, but I know that sometimes *who* sends the message is just as important as what it says. I need you to send some messages for me."

Davis gave a hoarse sound of objection. "No. I won't."

"I can make you, Captain. How would you like to see your precious daughter jailed for collaborating with the enemy?"

"H-how do I know this isn't all a lie?" Even as he asked, Davis knew a sinking terror. Then he stared at the bound book the shadowed figure extended to him. He recognized it at once, even in the poor light. It was his daughter's diary.

"You might want to read the last few entries. Very instructive. Very incriminating. I took the liberty of removing several of the more . . . damning references. Imagine what I could do with them?"

Davis could imagine, and he knew at that moment there was nothing he wouldn't sacrifice to keep his daughter safe. "What do you want?" His voice was gritty with helplessness.

"I want you to send this information. And from time to time, I'll be back with other messages for you to code. And as long as you cooperate, your little girl will be just fine. And if you don't, I'll see she suffers hellfire for your indifference."

"I'll do it . . . just leave her alone."

"I knew you'd be sensible. After all, what's a war compared to family?"

"What kind of man are you that you could do such a thing?"

"I'm a man who's never had the luxury of having what you have. I never had a daughter to protect, or parents who'd do anything to keep me from harm. So while I can understand your distress, I can't sympathize with it. Don't mistake me for a man of mercy. I have none. Now . . . you've some messages to send, don't you? I won't keep you from your duty any longer."

And he was gone, just like a cloud skimming the pale moon. Leaving William Davis with the weight of his daughter's dreams in his hands and her fate on his conscience.

And in that unyielding darkness, the shadowy figure allowed a brief smile. By the time the fool discovered that his daughter had escaped capture, he would have already condemned himself by transmitting treasonous falsehoods to his own troops.

And the success would not go to Deacon Sinclair.

It would go to the man who was fast moving up to replace him as the best.

Chapter 8

Five years later
1866

For an instant, it was as if no time had passed at all.

She looked unbelievably good to him. For a moment, nothing else mattered, not the mortgage in her hand, not the husband at her side. Beneath the coiffed hair and frilly hat, behind the frosty smile, above the gaudy elegance of her gown, were the dark, soulful eyes that had once begged for his love.

But it was too late.

He knew it as he watched the light of longing extinguish in those eyes.

Tyler Fairfax laughed as he looked between the two of them. "I jus' love happy reunions. I thought you'd appreciate knowing the place was passing into the hands of someone who wasn't a stranger."

Fairfax's drawl shocked Deacon back to the reality of the situation. Garnet Davis may have been his onetime lover, but she was here before him now as Garnet Prior to purposefully strip away his pride.

And he'd be damned if he was going to let her.

"Why this place?" His eyes skewered Garnet's, demanding she tell the truth. "I'm sure there were many other homes of far finer quality from which you could evict their owners."

He learned something about Garnet Davis Prior when she smiled in answer. She was no longer a naive little girl.

"I wanted this place because it feels so familiar, almost as if I'm already family."

He wanted to tell her the incredible irony of the situation: that if he'd found her, she would have been family—part of *his* family. This would have been her home—theirs, together. But that wasn't how things had happened, so he said nothing.

It was too late.

"Do we discuss business here in the hallway, Sergeant? Or should I call you Colonel Sinclair?"

"It's Mister, now," he corrected, wondering how much she knew about the details of his deception. Enough. Enough to want to hurt him and his family as deeply as possible. By pulling their home out from under them, she was going to succeed.

"Won't you come with me into the parlor? I'm sure you're thirsty after your travels."

"Mother, they are not our guests."

Hannah Sinclair gave him a reproving glance.

"Deacon, your manners, please." Then she smiled at the couple and even at Tyler Fairfax. "Please forgive my son. He was not raised to behave so badly. If you'll follow me."

Deacon trailed behind them, movements stiff and angry. Why was his mother shaming him in front of these people? They didn't deserve any courtesy. They deserved to be driven off his land. They were like Tyler's sneaking night riders, who terrorized under the cover of darkness. Only these robbers were bolder, coming out in daylight to do their dirty deeds. And his mother was treating them like welcomed visitors. His hands clenched at his sides. He thought he was showing extremely good manners by refraining from throwing them out into the muddy drive like dirty dishwater.

"You've a lovely home, Mrs. Sinclair," the Englishman was saying. "It seems to have survived your war quite nicely."

Only to surrender to this new British invasion. Deacon's teeth ground.

Hannah smiled and tilted her head proudly. "That was Deacon's doing. I'm afraid, in truth, it weathered the war rather poorly, but he restored everything to its prior glory with his own hands."

Deacon looked away, bitterness closing up his chest. Not with his own hands. He'd gone to Fairfax, allowing pride to take precedence over common sense. He'd bargained with a devil, and now the devil was here to claim his due.

"We shall be very comfortable here. Perhaps we should thank your son for his industry."

Deacon glared at Garnet. His voice was a low, lethal purr. "Don't thank me, Mrs. Prior. Believe me, I didn't do any of it with your comfort in mind."

Liar. What a liar he was. He'd replaced every rotten board foot, restored every ornately carved section of molding, while in his heart and mind he'd pictured her living as hostess in these rooms—as *his* hostess. As his *wife*. While he sweated and toiled, he'd held the image of her awed pleasure as he showed her from room to room, inviting her to make it her home. A wry smile shaped his lips. Well, she'd done just that, hadn't she?

Clever girl.

His eyes narrowed.

After the obligatory drink in the parlor, not his first of the day by any means, Tyler thanked Hannah prettily for her hospitality and enjoyed a moment of complete satisfaction as he bowed to the Priors. "It's been a pleasure doing business with you folks. I wish you all the best in settling into your new home. I'll have everything sent out to you."

Garnet nodded. "You've been very . . . helpful, Mr. Fairfax, and I thank you."

He grinned. "As I said, my pleasure." And his grin faded into a thin smirk as he met Deacon's glare. He held it for a long moment, long enough to convey his contempt and a sense of sweet vengeance for what he considered Deacon's betrayal. If Sinclair had just gone along with things the way he'd promised, it never would have had to have come to this. The planter's vanity was at fault for his family's circumstance, and not Tyler's for simply doing good business. His grin broke wide again. "Good day to you all."

With just the four of them in the parlor, an awkward tension settled beneath the civility. Hannah was the consummate hostess, but even her innate gentility couldn't overcome the fact that she and her son were being pushed from their home. And she wasn't such a fool as not to see something looming, dark and dangerous, in the history between her son and this woman.

"So," Deacon drawled, with deceiving nonchalance, "Fairfax is having your things sent over. All ready to occupy enemy territory, then?"

"We wouldn't want to put you out," Prior vowed, with what seemed to be sincerity.

"I thought that was your intention . . . wasn't it, Mrs. Prior?" When Garnet wouldn't answer with more than an impenetrable stare, he concluded tightly, "Don't concern yourself with our welfare."

Prior cleared his throat uncomfortably. "I know this is rather bad form to be discussing such things, but Mr. Fairfax confided that you were without funds."

"That's none of Mr. Fairfax's or your business, sir."

"I would not wish to be accused of tossing a widow from her only shelter."

Deacon smiled thinly. "Then you'll return our property?"

"No." Garnet's flat statement was followed by a more benign intention. "What we had in mind was an offer of employment."

Deacon went white with rage. "You want my mother to become your servant? You can go to hell, Mrs. Prior."

He was surprised by the feel of his mother's hand upon his sleeve.

"Deacon, mind your language. I would like to hear the offer."

"Mother—"

She regarded him with a calm censure. "There is no shame to be found in honest work. And I would rather support myself than be a burden to my children."

"But Mama—"

She turned from his dismayed look to smile at Garnet. "What is it that you have in mind, Mrs. Prior?"

"I would like you to stay on, Mrs. Sinclair, in your own rooms, of course, to act as our housekeeper. It's a role you are well familiar with, and it would not be taxing . . . except to your son's pride, perhaps." She slid Deacon a cool glance, observing the way his lean features sharpened with compressed fury.

Hannah thought for a moment, then nodded. "I think I should find that satisfactory. I've no desire to leave this place, and I would take pleasure in teaching you its history."

"*Our* history, Mother. Why would the Priors be interested in that?"

"Of course I'm interested," Garnet corrected. "I'm interested in discovering everything I can about the things I'm involved with. Ignorance is one's own worst enemy, I've learned."

Though Deacon didn't wince outwardly, inside he cringed at her flat summation. She'd had the best of teachers, hadn't she?

"And you, Mr. Sinclair? Have you any plans?"

Deacon met Prior's polite inquiry with a dismembering stare. "Do you mean to offer me a position in your household, as well? Blacking your shoes, snipping the ends off your cigars, putting a crease in your trousers?"

"Nothing so insulting as that, dear fellow."

"It's all insulting, sir. Your presence here, your smug charity, every bit of it."

Prior drew back, nonplussed by the fierce verbal attack, but Garnet took it in stride, saying smoothly, "Don't aristocrats work, Mr. Sinclair? Is it an insult to do whatever needs to be done in order to survive? I hadn't thought your sensibilities would be so delicate."

Deacon said nothing, so she continued.

"Believe me, Mr. Sinclair, I am well aware of your talents and would not waste them employing you as a valet. I've something else in mind, something that would involve you with the growth of your properties."

"My *former* properties, you mean." But he was listening now, very carefully.

Her gaze chilled. "Exactly."

"So, Mrs. Prior, how exactly do I fit into your plans? I assume you have plans."

"Oh yes, carefully laid plans. For the properties."

And, obviously, for him.

"And they are?"

"I understand your acreage used to be put toward hemp production. Since the bottom has fallen from the cotton market, that is no longer a profitable endeavor. I—that is, *we*—plan to turn the majority of the acres over into planting rye. We've made an arrangement with Mr. Fairfax—"

"Fairfax?" He spat out the name. "Dealing with Fairfax is how I ended up with nothing but the shirt on my back. You're a fool if you think you can do business with the likes of him."

Her stare cut through him. "I'm not interested in hearing your advice, Mr. Sinclair. It hasn't served you particularly well, after all."

He clamped his jaw shut. Let her learn the hard way, then.

When it was clear he had no more to say, Garnet went on with her vision for Sinclair Manor. "The remaining acres we'll share out, collecting off a portion of the crops."

"So I'm to scratch in the dirt for a living while you live off my toil like a fat tick?"

"Charming illustration. But no. I daresay you would not make a tolerable farmer. We plan to

set up a store in town where those who work
our lands can obtain supplies and necessaries on
credit against their harvests."

"Another means to suck off them," he murmured dryly. She ignored him.

"I—we should like you to run that store for us.
I already know you have a talent for mathematics
and have seen proof of your merciless business
dealings. In return, you can earn a decent wage
to apply toward repurchasing some of your
acreage, if you choose, and you can continue to
live here. I want to be in close communication
with those who work under me."

"So you are in charge?" He glanced over at
Prior, who seemed more interested in the carved
molding on the fireplace than in matters of
finance.

"Yes, I am. What is your answer? Are you too
proud to work for a woman?"

He wasn't thinking about that at the moment.
He was calculating rapidly. The offer was no
longer an insult, but an opportunity. "I could
buy back my lands."

"An acre at a time, Mr. Sinclair. Have you that
kind of patience?"

"I can wait forever for something that I want."

She looked away quickly, as if hiding something in her expression. Before he could wonder
what it was, a familiar sound came from the
foyer: dog toenails scrabbling for traction on the
polished hardwood floors.

Boone burst into the parlor, skidding halfway

across the room on the first rug he came to. He'd grown from a gangly pup to half the size of a horse, and all of it muscle. He scrambled up, focusing on Deacon with a remembered ire. In two great leaps, he'd crossed the room, and with a single lunge, knocked Deacon to the floor. As he grabbed the massive head to hold the snapping jaws away from his face, he heard a small childish voice intrude.

"I'm sorry, Mama. I tried to keep him outside, but he gots loose."

"Get back, Boone." Garnet was hauling on the animal's collar. "As you can see, Boone has fond memories of you, too, Mr. Sinclair."

The moment he was freed from the dog's weight, Deacon rolled to his feet in search of the child who'd called Garnet "Mama." The boy stood just inside the door, shyly regarding him. A terrible pain twisted through Deacon's insides, for here was evidence of Garnet's relationship with the much older Brit. The fragile-looking boy studied him through Garnet's dark eyes beneath a shock of tawny hair inherited from Prior.

This was the child they'd made between them.

But in looking at the boy, Hannah Sinclair saw something totally different.

She saw the boy her son had once been.

She knew.
Garnet watched Hannah Sinclair's features

purse with confusion, then brighten with recognition.

But would she say something and spoil all Garnet's plans?

"William, please take Boone back outside." As the boy came to grab onto the leather collar with both hands, she admonished, "Go with William, you big ox."

Boy dragging dog exited the room, leaving a new tension behind.

"William," Hannah whispered. "Is that his name?"

"After my father."

"How *is* your father?" Deacon asked, dreading the answer.

Garnet stared at him through emotionless eyes. "He died in a federal prison. Thank you for asking."

If he took that information like a double-barreled blast to the gut, he absorbed the impact without flinching.

"How old is your son, Mrs. Prior?"

She met Hannah's soft gaze without betraying her inner panic. "He's four." She watched the woman doing the math before sliding a look at her son to see if he'd done the same figuring.

But no questions crossed Deacon's tight expression. His stare was deadened.

"A handsome boy."

"Thank you, Mrs. Sinclair. We're very proud of him."

"There's a room on the west side of the stairs

just right for a child. Plenty of shelves where the sun won't wake him. It was Deacon's when he was a boy."

Garnet forced a smile. "I'm sure it will do nicely." Anxious to turn the topic elsewhere, she asked, "Mr. Sinclair, have you decided upon the job?"

He was silent for so long, she felt sure the answer would be no. Then he surprised her by saying tonelessly, "I'll move my belongings back into my room."

"Would that be the master suite?" At his nod, she supplied a taut smile. "I think it's only fitting that that room belong to my husband and me, don't you? I'm sure there are other suitable quarters."

"Perhaps one of the old slave cabins would appeal to your sense of fairness."

"Whatever you feel appropriate, Mr. Sinclair." His sense of pride still moved her.

Everything about him still moved her.

Had she expected any different? If she had, she wouldn't have gone through the elaborate lengths it had taken to reach this point in her plans for the future. She couldn't afford to forget what a dangerous man Deacon Sinclair was, because of his former profession and because of the way he still acted upon her heart.

And because of the innocent life that hung in the balance between them.

Her heart had nearly stopped beating when she'd first seen Deacon again. Her every memory sharpened, her every sense cried out. And for a brief instant, when he'd met her gaze, she thought she'd seen a hungry longing clouding his gray-eyed stare. She'd almost given it all away right then and there . . . except for a little boy playing out in the yard. She had to put him before all else. He was the reason she'd come to find this man who'd deceived and betrayed her.

Was *this* the real Deacon, so cold, so distant and contained? Was this the same man who'd rocked her in his arms and made love to her so sweetly? The one who'd made her want to believe so desperately that all had not been a lie? She saw no evidence of that man here before her. True, he was shocked and angered by the way she'd come back into his life, but it was more than that.

If the man who'd come to her door five years ago was tough, this one was cut from stone. All emotions that would have softened the edges of his facade—qualities of understanding, forgiveness, regret, or even guilt—were absent. If she'd been drawn to the glimpses of tenderness he'd shown her, she'd no proof that those feelings existed any more. If they ever had at all.

Had it all been pretense? Could any man be so good at spinning lies? Or had she just been too young, too gullible, to know the difference?

That's what she'd come to discover. And what she'd seen so far was more intimidating than encouraging.

How was she going to get to know the true

man behind the granite bearing and impenetrable stare? Her future depended upon it—hers and William's.

She could afford this man no mercy. She knew she was being heartless, and she hated herself for it. But she needed him to see that she wasn't some simple country girl who could be manipulated by a kiss . . . at least, not anymore. What could he accuse her of that could be worse than what he'd laid upon her?

If he expected her to show any sympathy for what he suffered now, he was mistaken. The past few years had wrung the naïveté from her. The memory of her father wrung all charity from her. Her father, who had never intentionally harmed a soul. Her father who had died an agonizing death in a prison run by those to whom he'd remained unwaveringly loyal.

And Deacon Sinclair had put him there to suffer for what he hadn't done, and to die for it.

But, oh, Deacon was nice to look at. And oh, how easy it would be to let go of the desires yet simmering beneath the surface. But one thing she'd been taught since he'd left her, other than what a terrible price trust could exact, was control—control of her actions, control of her thinking, control of her life. Seeing him, however, proved there was no controlling her heart.

If she couldn't control it, she would have to contain it. Just as he contained whatever else moved behind the lean, hard lines of his expressionless face. He'd taught her a degree of toughness she'd never attained on her own. Heart-break and disillusionment shored up her resolve. So she would be careful. She would betray nothing of her true intent. And she would learn what she'd come to Pride County to discover.

The kind of man Deacon Sinclair really was.

"Mama, whose child is that on the porch?"

They all turned as Patrice Sinclair Garrett lumbered into the room. Despite the chill outside, she was flushed becomingly and slightly breathless. And huge with child. Seeing the company, she drew up short in surprise, then embarrassment.

"Please, excuse me. I didn't know you were entertaining." Her hands went to her burgeoning middle as if she could hide her pregnancy behind the spread of her palms. She knew how sensitive her mother was to her displaying her "delicate" condition in public. An annoyance to Patrice who felt as healthy as one of her husband's brood mares and just about as delicate.

"They're not company, Patrice. They're the new owners of the Manor."

Her animation faded. She glanced to her brother, seeking some reason for the odd tension in his tone that went far beyond the sentiments he'd expressed thus far. But Deacon was closed down tight, his posture rigidly correct, his features shuttered. At his sides, his hands fisted, his knuckles shifting restlessly. Perplexed, she focused on the interlopers who were there to steal their home.

"Forgive me if I don't say 'Welcome' under the circumstances."

"Patrice," Hannah scolded, mortified by her children's sudden lapse of manners.

"So, you're Patrice." The dark-haired woman advanced with hand extended. Patrice took it gingerly as she studied the other through a critical eye.

What she saw was a voluptuously shaped creature with boldly sensual lips, snapping black eyes, and enviably flawless skin. And money. That was obvious from her Paris clothes. But money and lineage were two different things. One could possess money these days without any claim to pedigree. She guessed this was the case with the woman before her, not because of anything she didn't do—she was elegant and genteel—but a little too eager to convey the bored sophistication of a true Southern aristocrat. Who was she, then? Northern carpetbagger trash? If that was so, why couldn't her brother take his eyes off her? Deacon Sinclair wasn't one to stare at a woman just because she displayed more curves than the hourglass-shaped vase in their foyer.

"Should I know you?" Patrice asked, puzzled by the woman's familiarity with her.

"No, of course not." She pressed Patrice's hand firmly, then smiled. "You've no reason ever to have heard of me. I'm Garnet Prior. My husband and I will be your new neighbors. The child outside is ours. His name is William. And when is yours due?"

Patrice raised a russet-colored brow at the directness of the question. She could imagine her mother's gasp of horror. So she smiled. "In about a month."

"And you're up and about?" Her dark gaze said clearly, "Good for you," and reluctantly, Patrice liked her for her unconventional stand. "Perhaps you should sit down and rest a moment."

"I feel fine, just big. I'm not here for a visit. That will have to wait for another time." Her mood cooled. "My husband and I have come to collect my mother and her belongings."

"Then you might as well visit, because she's staying here."

While Patrice stood in confusion, Deacon explained the situation stoically.

"Mother and I will be remaining on in the generous employ of the Priors."

Reeve Garrett strode in, coming to place supporting palms beneath his wife's elbows. Having heard that last, he remarked, "A decent day's work won't harm you, Deacon . . . you arrogant bastard." That last was added for his wife's hearing alone. Her elbow jabbed back, making him suck air before continuing. "So all the trunks in the hall get toted back upstairs, then."

"I can show you where they go," Hannah offered, anxious to escape the room to gain some perspective on what she now suspected.

"Lead the way, Miz Hannah." He touched a kiss to Patrice's temple. "Are you all right, 'Trice?"

"Quit asking. I'm fine. I'm not about to have this baby in the middle of my brother's parlor." Then her attention shifted to the invading couple. "Or should I say, the Priors' parlor."

Garnet betrayed nothing, an equal for Deacon in keeping an impassive front. "As long as you're going up, perhaps you can show us where our rooms will be. I'd like to freshen up a bit."

"Yes, of course, Mrs. Prior." Hannah gestured toward the stairs. "Follow me."

Once alone in the parlor with her brother, Patrice dropped all vestiges of what was proper to demand. "She's the one, isn't she?"

He never so much as blinked. "The one, what?"

Damn him for his secrets and his bland lies. He wasn't going to slip the truth so easily this time. "The woman you were in love with."

He recoiled as if she'd slapped him. No denial he could speak would outweigh the brief flickerings of pain and loss crossing his expression. At the first sign of his distress, Patrice forgot her annoyance and went to him, hugging him tight, even though she knew he'd hate the show of overt affection. Surprisingly, he didn't shrink from contact. In fact, he laid his head atop hers for the duration of an unsteady breath. Then he moved away.

"Don't, Patrice. Don't interfere."

It wasn't a warning as much as it was a request. That in itself startled her enough to warrant worry. "Deacon, who is she?"

"Penance for past sins. Please, Patrice, leave it alone."

She touched his taut cheek with her fingertips. "Can you? Can you leave it alone?"

He turned away from her gentle gesture and from her look of empathy. "There's not much I can do. I made my choices five years ago. Now, I have to find a way to sleep with them at night."

While the only woman he'd ever wanted was living under his roof . . . sleeping with another man, as his wife.

The room was heavily masculine: dark draperies, dark wood, dark paper on the walls. And Garnet could feel Deacon's presence like a physical force. Its austerity suited the somber man she'd met downstairs: repressed, closed up tight, and steeped in isolating dignity. In a defiant move, she jerked open the curtains so sunlight could flood inside, spilling across the bare floor and over the textured counterpane.

Deacon's bed. Her hand caressed the smooth wood, then followed along the length of the mattress to where he would have lain his head at night. To where he would have laid a bride to conceive his lawful children. A covetous ache built within her breast. Oh, to have been that woman.

"Garnet?"

She pulled her hand back and just as quickly, reined in her imaginings to give Montgomery Prior a strained smile. "Well, we're here."

"Yes, lovey, we are. Is it all that you'd hoped for?"

Her smile took a bittersweet bend. "I'm not sure yet."

"He's a hard piece of work, your Deacon Sinclair. He doesn't strike me as a man who surrenders easily."

"I think he's just beginning to realize that."

"The look on his face must have given your dear father some sense of satisfaction."

That glaze of recognition when he'd realized just who it was who'd snatched away his destiny . . . her conscience quavered, but she ignored it to say, "I'm sure it did."

But it hadn't given her the satisfaction she'd desired. She'd wanted to feel a fierce vindication, a sense of justice done—for herself and for her father. She'd wanted to take pleasure in Deacon Sinclair's dismay and anticipate the downfall of his pride. She'd expected face-to-face proof of his misery to lessen her own.

But none of that had happened. The confrontation lacked the drama she'd imagined. Deacon had betrayed nothing. How could she revel in the evidence of his distress when he'd shown none? And how could she find any gratification in causing a gracious woman pain? She'd lost her own home. She couldn't take enjoyment in stripping Hannah Sinclair of hers when her only crime was bearing a son of indifferent morals.

No, the moment hadn't brought her the release she'd desired. In fact, seeing Deacon again only confirmed her worst fear—she was still in love with him.

And that made her furious.

"If Deacon Sinclair thinks I'm through with him, that's another mistake on his part. I want him to squirm. I want him to feel all the indignity and wretchedness my father must have felt while unfairly imprisoned." Her expression hardened, causing the mild Montgomery to frown in alarm. "I want to rip the pride from him and see him choke on regret." Then she looked to the older man in question. "Is that too much to hope for, after all he's done to me?"

Montgomery embraced her with a fond indulgence. "No, child, not at all. I'll help you see he gets everything he deserves. And then some."

Chapter 9

Her father had died in a Union prison.
Deacon took in the facts like hard-packed
soil slowly soaking up rainwater. Only these
truths didn't quench his thirst for absolution.
They brought a further parching to his soul.

He'd never tried to find out what had happened to William Davis. Why not? He wondered
that now as he stood working his way through a
bottle of bourbon even as unwelcome strangers
settled into the room that had been his, and his
parents' before him. If his feelings for Garnet
had been genuine, wouldn't he have wanted to
discover the fate of her only living relative?
Wouldn't he have done what he could to see the
man freed once he'd served his purpose? A good
man would have seen it as his responsibility. A
decent man would have made it a priority. But
what had he done? He'd looked down upon
those dead ashes where he'd found such fleeting
happiness and he'd deliberately extinguished all
further thought of Garnet Davis.

Or he'd tried.

He'd ridden back to camp without ever going to see his family. He'd thrown himself back into the field, taking the first available assignment.

A decent man wouldn't have slept nights.

He slept fine. It was the waking hours that tormented him.

He looked forward to the nights because they brought him dreams of Garnet. But when he was awake, reality soured the serenity of those dreams. In the daylight, his conscience was stalked by the deeds he'd done.

William Davis was just another ghost.

She'd lost her father. His own actions had taken the man from her.

How would she ever forgive him for such a thing—if forgiveness was something he could ever hope to attain?

He was tipping up the bottom of his third glass, trying not to think of the couple settling into his bedroom, when his gaze happened upon the little boy and the gigantic dog racing about the side yard. He tracked the boy without being aware of it, watching the long, spindly legs pumping determinedly to keep up with the galloping hound. He wasn't aware of the smile shaping his lips.

Garnet's son.

Garnet and Montgomery Prior's son, he corrected. But that truth couldn't quite erase the poignant emotions curling about his heart.

Had he made different choices, he could have

fathered that boy. He could be settling down in that room upstairs with Garnet as his bride.

What were the chances that he'd ever watch his own child play? An heir . . . an heir to what? Running a sharecroppers' store for a pittance wouldn't make him the catch of Pride County. Where he'd been slow in picking a bride before, now there wasn't a prayer that one would have him. Not that he cared for the lack of companionship . . . just the lack of tender feeling swelling inside as he watched another man's son.

And as he watched, Boone gave a boisterous leap, colliding forcefully with the oncoming little boy. William fell back into the remains of Hannah Sinclair's garden. And at the sound of his first wail, Deacon was out the door.

The child sat whimpering in the middle of a ruined English rosebush. Great teary eyes lifted as Deacon knelt down to the boy's level.

"I got a pricker," William sniveled, extending his thumb for Deacon to see. When Deacon took the small hand in his, William started blubbering in earnest, anticipating the hurt to come.

"Stop that."

The boy blinked at the cut of Deacon's tone. He'd never had anyone speak to him harshly before. Tears froze and shimmered on his flushed cheeks.

"A man doesn't cry over such piddling things."

The boy's lip quivered, but he bit back further wails. His eyes grew large as he met the other man's serious stare. And he took the sober instruction to heart.

"A man doesn't cry, no matter how much it hurts. Not ever."

"Is that all men, or just heartless ones like you?"

With that said, Garnet pushed Deacon aside and bent down in a pooling of silk. Her voice grew tender. Deacon tensed, remembering the sound of her compassion.

"Let me see, darling." She took up the soft hand between her own to inspect the tiny wound. The boy's eyes welled up in response to her sympathy, but after a quick glance at Deacon, he blinked them manfully away.

"It's just a thorn, Mama. Just a piddling thing."

"It'll have to come out."

Deacon reached to take the boy's hand from hers. He didn't look at her, even when he heard her sharp inhalation.

"Let me. I've fallen into these bushes more times than I care to remember. And have taken thorns in worse places then a thumb."

William smiled, shakily.

Squeezing the meaty pad of the little thumb between two fingers, Deacon gave the boy a stern look. "This is going to hurt. Don't yell."

"Yell if you want, baby," Garnet contradicted, but the boy's gaze was fixed in Deacon's as he nodded bravely.

Moving quickly, Deacon brought the injury up to his mouth, biting down, then spitting the barb out to one side. William swallowed hard but didn't make a sound. He inspected the reddened thumb proudly, then showed the wound to his mother.

"It wasn't that bad at all."

Garnet smiled narrowly at his smug proclamation. "Then go play, dear. And stay away from the rosebushes."

He bounded off happily, leaving the two adults kneeling together in the garden. Flushing angrily, Garnet gathered her skirts and began to stand. To her irritation, Deacon was quick to offer assistance—she was irritated because of the way her pulse leapt at the simplest touch.

"Don't cry. Don't yell. For heaven's sake, he's just four years old."

"Old enough to be taught to take what comes without—"

"Without what?" She shook off his hands and brushed down her crumpled skirt. "Genuine emotion?"

"Without flinching. That's what my father taught me."

She glared at him. "Well, you're not in a position to teach my son anything. I'll decide what lessons I want him to learn."

He'd gone cold and distant. "Yes, of course. Forgive me for intruding. I'm sure you're doing an excellent job turning him into a dandified sissy like that man you married."

"Don't you speak like that about Monty," she hissed. "He's a fine man who's done his best for me and William. And he's taught my son what you never could—honesty. Or isn't that something you consider as important for a real man? Good day, Mr. Sinclair."

As she spun away, intent on sweeping from him in indignant righteousness, he foiled her plans by catching her hand. The shock of contact blanked her mind like a sudden lightning surge. She looked up at him in flustered alarm.

"I'm sorry about your father, Garnet. I didn't know."

No other words could so efficiently cut through her daze of conflicting feelings. Her lips thinned.

"I don't want your sympathy."

"Then what do you want from me?"

She freed her hand with a jerk. "I want you on your knees."

He let her go then. The moment she was freed, she hurried toward the house. He could almost imagine the girl with man's trousers, bobbed hair, and coltish stride.

On his knees.

So that was the way it was going to be.

A Sinclair never humbled himself before anyone. Especially to some backwoods girl who'd suddenly taken on aristocratic airs and a wealthy husband. Even though he was genuinely sorry, he wouldn't go so far to make amends. War was war, not something personal for which he should be forever apologetic.

However, Garnet's parting glare let him know to her it wasn't about a war or duty . . . it was about a very personal betrayal. And amnesty for the South and all its soldiers wouldn't excuse him for what he'd done in that peaceful Cumberland valley.

The Priors wasted no time in their occupation of the Sinclair home. By late day, a wagon filled with trunks and boxes arrived under the escort of a half dozen house servants. Garnet directed them to Hannah, who took control with practiced ease—happily, Deacon noted in chagrin. She was always at her best when in the middle of domestic chaos—even if she was managing it for someone else.

With nothing to occupy his time, Deacon stood aside, as thrilled with the proceedings as he would be if it were a plague of locusts settling into his fields. Not his fields. Not anymore. Nothing here was his anymore.

"Be careful with that!"

Garnet hovered anxiously as two burly men struggled beneath the weight of an upright parlor piano, easing it from the back of the wagon, then pushing it up the planks laid down to make a ramp up the front stairs. And as she dealt with the laborers, her fancy husband lingered in the dormant flower garden, studying the bare branches of Hannah's ornamental bushes with more interest than he showed his property. Such an attitude provoked contempt from a man who'd spent his entire life devoted to an estate rather than its frivolous decorations.

Garnet, however, quickened in him nothing as safe as contempt. What she stirred in Deacon defied categorizing. Longing wasn't big enough, jealousy was too narrow, desire too one dimensional. Regret came closest to describing the want, the sense of loss and emptiness inside.

She was glorious. But then, he'd thought her spectacular even before she knew anything about female graces. With her lush figure hugged by expensive silk and her glossy hair twisted up in a sophisticated style, none would guess she had once tended livestock while dressed in oversized galoshes. Or that she'd killed a man in the front room of her cabin. Or made wild love to him in her virgin's bed. Traces of that country girl were all but lost beneath the elegant trappings of affluence. Deacon would have believed them gone for good if not for the way she met his intent gaze with a glare like a double-barreled scattergun. The wildcat was still there, swaddled in exotic finery but no less the scraper.

That knowledge both pleased and distressed him: pleased him because he admired her for her uniqueness, disturbed him because she'd allowed the man she'd married to make her over into something not as valuable as what she'd been before. Part of what had charmed him was the fact that she was so different from the women he was used to; a breath of fresh air after the stuffy society parlors. One of the things that had made the loss of her more bearable was the fact that she wouldn't have fit into his world. He would have hated breaking her to fit the rigid mold of his peers, fearing that in doing so, he would destroy the naïveté that had attracted him in the first place. Seeing her now, all primped and powdered and pressed with that snap of vinegar still intact intrigued him all the more. Why had he ever doubted her ability to move in his same circles? She had him revolving in them with scarcely any effort at all. And he didn't like the way it left him dizzy and off-balance.

But then again, he did.

It made him feel alive. And at the same time, in hell, knowing that what he gave up was now being enjoyed by another. In his room. In his bed. On this very night, while he awaited an impossible slumber only four doors down.

The poignancy of tucking her son into bed in Deacon's childhood room became unbearable as Garnet listened to the boy recite his prayers. Always touched by the child's somber intonations as he asked God to bestow his blessings, her heart constricted when William added, "And bless Mr. Sinclair for taking the thorn out of my thumb, 'cause he's not as scary as I thought he was at first. Amen."

He looked up at her in expectation when she failed to murmur the echoing "Amen." She could only mouth the word. The heaviness in her throat forbade sound. Satisfied, the boy slipped between the covers. He sighed happily in this new setting, closing his eyes as his mother bent to kiss his brow.

" 'Night, Mama."

"G'night, darling," she whispered, turning down the light. The minute the room darkened, she heard the sound of Boone creeping up along the other side of the bed. The instant she was out the door, she knew the big dog would be up under the covers. Tonight she didn't mind.

She turned and started slightly to find Hannah Sinclair framed in the doorway. Were those tears shimmering in the older woman's eyes, or just a trick of the fast fading light?

It was the moment Garnet had feared all day, a one-on-one meeting with the woman who could, with a single claim, destroy everything. She hadn't expected complications so soon. She hadn't been prepared for them, mentally or emotionally. If Hannah didn't know for sure, she certainly suspected. And time spent with William would only convince her more.

Self-preservation brought a solution to mind. Get rid of her. Send her away, from the house, from the child, from the truth. Though she'd said nothing to Deacon yet, there was no guarantee she would remain silent for long. Perhaps she was just waiting until she had proof positive. Allowing her to keep close company with William was dangerous to that end. But seeing the dampness on her cheeks made Garnet realize something else that swayed her from taking drastic action.

This was William's grandmother. No matter

what had occurred between Garnet and Deacon, was it fair that this kind and gentle woman should suffer for it by being denied access to the child? Garnet thought of her own lonely upbringing. She'd heard only vague stories about her mother's past—a past she left behind to wed a man beneath her standing. She'd never voiced regret, but the pain of loss was ever present in her occasional bouts of sadness. When she died, Garnet clung to her father all the more as her only link to that family she desired. Could she isolate William from those who would love and comfort him?

Though it would endanger her plans, Garnet could not drive the other woman away. All she could hope for was the other woman's wisdom, and that Hannah would stay quiet for the sake of the boy.

"I didn't mean to intrude, Mrs. Prior. I was just wondering if you needed anything else this evening. Otherwise, I'll retire for the night."

"I'm fine, Mrs. Sinclair. Thank you for being so helpful today. It could have been very difficult had you not been so generous with your acceptance."

Hannah smiled faintly. "We've all gone through enough difficult times, don't you think?" And then, when she could have said so much more, she cast a tender glance toward the now slumbering child and murmured, "Good night, Mrs. Prior."

Garnet watched the other woman retreat,

relief weakening her knees, and gratitude softening her heart. This was the family she'd wanted: Hannah with her knowing empathy filling a mother's void, Patrice, with her outspoken candor, a sister to share secrets and sorrows with.

But they were not her family. They were Deacon's. And suddenly she felt very much the intruder within the elegant walls.

Sinclair Manor. It was more beautiful than she could have ever dreamed. The endless acres of rich land, the stately brick home steeped in tradition and pride. The sense of affluence, of society at the very pinnacle.

Though she could buy her way in, she couldn't make herself belong. Not to the house and its history, nor to the man who should have held them both.

She didn't care if the wealthy of Pride County didn't take to her. She had enough money now to assure her acceptance if not their approval. She didn't care if they liked her means of taking over the Manor or the progressive use of parceling out its fallow lands. Their opinions meant little to nothing to her. Only one man mattered—the one who shouldn't have held sway over her emotions.

She wanted to impress Deacon Sinclair. To make him realize that in using and betraying her, he'd made the miscalculation of his life.

Montgomery sat upon the foot of Deacon's big bed, sketch pad across his knees. He diligently worked to capture the twists and intricacies of the design of a side table centerpiece, failing to notice that Garnet was in the room until he was satisfied with his shading. Then he glanced up and smiled, proudly showing his pencil rendition.

"Very nice. Needs more shadow there."

He noted the area with a frown, then nodded. "You're right. You've a discerning eye."

"Considering I have no ability, you mean."

"Now, I would never say something so cruel as that."

"No, of course you wouldn't." She sighed and walked to the long windows. Looking out over the lawn, the sense of pretense returned. The fact that all was hers still escaped her.

"You appear worse for wear, lovey. Perhaps I should let you retire."

"I would appreciate that . . . Monty."

Without another word, he folded his drawing pad and slid from the bed, pausing only long enough to press a fond kiss to her temple. Then he adjourned into the attached sitting room where a day bed had been prepared, "for his bouts of insomnia," he'd told the staff. In truth, Monty slept like a stone. But he didn't sleep with his wife. The story had been created to quell gossip.

That she and Monty slept in separate beds was a story Garnet didn't want to get back to Deacon on their first night under this new roof.

With a soft, "Good night, dear," Monty shut the door between their rooms, leaving Garnet to her privacy and her troubled thoughts.

Was she doing the right thing? she asked herself again, as she stretched out across the same mattress where Deacon had spent his recent nights in slumber. She was right to want retribution for what her father had suffered. She was right to demand compensation for Deacon's lies. But was she right in placing herself and her son in this house, with the one man who could hurt them both beyond reparation?

It wasn't for her father that she was here. It wasn't for her own injured heart. It was for William. And it was William that she would protect, no matter what the cost to her own emotions.

He was her future, her hope.

And it was up to her to decide if Deacon Sinclair had a place with them in it.

Whether he wanted that place or not could wait until she'd determined if he was worthy.

Worthy of being her son's father.

Chapter 10

C oming downstairs to find himself in the hub of bustling industry shocked Deacon. This was how his house had once been, before the war, before his father's death. Prosperous. Smelling of beeswax and humming with the murmuring of servants. Under his own reign those scents had turned to decay and those voices had been silent. It wasn't his fault, he knew even as he thought it, but the mind couldn't dismiss the blame settling deep in his spirit.

He'd brought ruin to his household and left it to others to restore.

Not sure what he should be doing or where he should go, he lingered in the front hall, stepping out of the way as several housemaids hurried by without halting in their chatter. They didn't recognize him as anyone important. It surprised him still to realize that they were right. That sat ill with him; the sense of having no purpose adding to his melancholy. Until a small voice interrupted his brooding.

"Lookee, Mr. Sinclair. It's all better this morning."

Obligingly, Deacon bent down to survey somberly the stubby little thumb held up to him. "Yes, indeed, it does look better. The reward for your bravery, young man."

Pleased with that, William grabbed onto Deacon's hand and began towing him toward the dining room, chattering happily as he went. In his childish innocence, he didn't notice the way Deacon reacted to the impulsive contact—with startlement and alarm.

"Mama's having her coffee. She said you was driving us into town this morning."

"Really? So my status has been upgraded to driver."

"Do you like horses, Mr. Sinclair? I do. Mama promised me a pony when I get bigger. Did you have a pony?"

Recalling the temperamental creature, as broad as it was tall, that his sister had misnamed Princess, Deacon smiled. He still had a scar on the back of his thigh from where the surly beast had bitten him.

"Yes, I did."

"Where is he now?"

"He died. A long time ago." Strange, how thinking of that nasty animal filled him with such a flood of memory. Had he really been as full of animation and blissful eagerness as the boy tugging on his hand? It was a past he'd lost touch with long ago—like the tears he'd shed when he'd heard of that vicious pony's death. Then the sound of his father's voice slashed through his memory.

Men don't cry. Wipe your eyes and stop disgracing me.

Even after all the years, the echo made him stand up straighter.

"Where are the rest of your horses?" the boy continued. "Boone and me was out to the barn and it's as empty as a church on Monday."

"All our horses were sold." Before the little inquisitor could ask, he added, "To make room for the ones you'll buy." No sense in confusing the child with the truth, that the horses were sacrificed to buy legal aid that proved as empty of success as the stalls now stood.

He hadn't been able to find a way to break Tyler's hold on his properties, and now they were his no longer.

"William, are you bothering Mr. Sinclair?"

"No, Mama. We was talking about horses. Mr. Sinclair had a pony just like the one I want to get."

Deacon smiled to himself. Not just like dear departed Princess, he hoped. Then he looked up from the glowing little face to the impeccably garbed Garnet Prior and his smile thinned.

"He's no bother. He was telling me about the schedule you'd made for my time today."

She didn't blush at the mild censure in his tone. "Good. We'll be leaving in an hour. I'm checking on several properties in town and I want your escort."

"Isn't that what you have a husband for? Where is his lordship this morning?" He glanced around the empty dining room, noting the feast set out upon his family's newly polished silver.

"Monty prefers to start his day at what he calls a civilized hour."

"Obviously not born to a plantation or farm schedule."

"No." She allowed a small smile that set Deacon's senses shivering. He thought of the long ride to town—just the two of them.

"If it's an escort you need, I see plenty of able souls about this morning."

Her mood froze along with her smile. "It's not a request. I want you with me because I'm looking at possible store properties. I assumed you'd be interested."

She'd assumed wrong. "If you say so."

She crossed to the sideboard, cup in hand, then waited, longer than she should have had to, for him to come and pour for her.

"After I decide on a property, we'll meet with Mr. Fairfax for lunch."

"Mr. Fairfax? Cole or Tyler?"

"Tyler."

"I'll pass."

"Again, it's not a request. He specifically asked that you be there."

To taunt him, the maggot. "Then he'll have to be disappointed."

Garnet leveled an impatient stare. "Perhaps

you don't understand. You *will* accompany me to lunch with Mr. Fairfax."

Silence stretched out between them with a tension thick enough for William to notice. He pulled at Deacon's sleeve.

"You'll go, won't you? Then I can have somebody to talk to."

Deacon's gaze dropped to the boy. He gave a narrow smile. "I guess I can't refuse, then, can I?" His stare returned to Garnet's, conveying his answer like a slap. Because the boy asked, not because she demanded. She set down her untouched coffee.

"It's settled, then. An hour, Mr. Sinclair."

"I'll be counting the minutes, Mrs. Prior."

After she'd exited the room with a regal toss of her head, Garnet collapsed back against the hallway wall. Her knees were shaking and her palms made damp marks where they clutched the bell of her skirt.

Her first confrontation with Deacon was not exactly the success she'd hoped it would be. She'd ordered and he'd balked. What would she have done if William hadn't been there to earn Deacon's compliance? How would she have backed up her command? With threats? By throwing him out of the house he'd been born in? Though she was grateful the moment was over, it had taught her a valuable lesson: never issue ultimatums unless she could back them up with something stronger than a little boy's wishes.

Deacon Sinclair was not going to submit

gracefully to her rule. How to gain leverage over him would be her next order of business. Because if he ever guessed how flustered she was just being in the same room with him, her tenuous control would be broken.

Just as he'd already broken her heart.

The drive into Pride wasn't as awkward as it could have been, mainly because of William. With his mother bundled up in the back of the open carriage, he stood with arms crossed on the back of the front seat, chattering to Deacon as he handled the reins. The two adults never exchanged a word.

Garnet took advantage of the time to observe her surroundings. Raised on a farm, she knew how to gauge the lay of the land and estimate its productivity. How her father would have loved the chance to coax crops from this dark bluegrass country. She admired the remaining plantation homes that sat back from the road in queenly elegance. She cringed at the sight of the scorched chimneys rising out of rubbled dreams, well remembering what she'd left behind.

And she covertly watched her son and Deacon together. His patience with the boy surprised her. For a regimented man who'd shown little tolerance since her arrival, he set aside his hostility where the child was concerned. And William blossomed under the attention.

Monty was good to the boy, but he still saw William in the traditional manner of "should be seen and not heard," with instruction coming from paid tutors rather than indulgent parents who were free to shoo him away when his questions grew tiresome. But Deacon, even as a captive audience, answered the endless stream of curiosity, speaking to him not as a bothersome child but as a small adult. And the potential she saw there confused the feelings of disloyalty and desire already volleying for dominance within her.

Then they reached the outskirts of Pride and she could see Deacon withdraw into a stony silence.

"William, sit here with me, darling."

The boy pouted but did as instructed, obviously preferring Deacon's inattention to his mother's doting.

He was growing up too fast.

Pride. Deacon's home. Though she'd seen many bustling cities since she'd once dreamed of visiting here, the sight of the small but growing town touched a chord in her heart. This was the place she'd envisioned when she'd thought of a home and a place to raise her family, a place where there were more churches than saloons. A place where tradition remained untouched even as progress had its way along the wide main street. A setting intimate enough to be run by neighbors who all knew one another, yet reluctantly opening to outside influences.

She and Monty were classed among those intruders flooding in with money and changes in mind. Only her plan wasn't to dominate and alter the harmonious blend of past and present in a mad, greedy rush toward the future. Hers was to become an accepted part of all she saw—family to the businesses just now opening their doors to a crisp new morning and to the people who greeted Deacon with a recognizing nod and her with undisguised suspicion.

In belonging to Pride, she'd be one step closer to Deacon.

"Go to the bank," she called to the back of Deacon's head. "Mr. Dodge was going to show me what was available."

He made no move to show that he'd heard her but did pull the carriage up in front of the new bank building. Deacon alighted with a fluid bound and tied off the horses. He then caught William, who launched himself trustingly into his arms. Garnet stood, and after again waiting for an insulting length of time, took the hand Deacon finally offered up to her.

If Pride's banker, Hamilton Dodge, thought it strange that the former and current owners of Sinclair Manor stepped into his office together, he betrayed no sign of it. He came up out of his chair, smiling broadly, depending slightly upon a gold-headed cane as he made his way around the huge desk.

"Good morning, Mrs. Prior. Right on time. Have a seat, ma'am. Deacon, some coffee? Hasn't been sitting long enough to require a knife and fork."

"No. Thank you."

Garnet settled into the chair the amiable Northerner proffered. She'd never had dealings with the banker directly, but Tyler Fairfax intimated that he was shrewd and trustworthy, high praise from one who seemed to trust no one. She had wondered where Dodge stood in her purchasing of the Sinclair properties, but Dodge wordlessly answered that question with a squeeze of his hand upon Deacon's shoulder.

"How you holding up?" he asked with a quiet concern. Deacon only nodded, his expression stoic, his mood remote. Dodge didn't pursue it. Instead, he returned to his seat to find William had climbed up into it.

"Hello. Who's this?"

"My son, William. William, get down from there. I'm sorry, Mr. Dodge—"

"No need for apologies, ma'am. Got one about the same age, myself. Hell on wheels, if you don't mind me saying so." He lifted William, then settled into his chair with the boy on his lap in the easy manner of a father. He located some blank sheets of paper and a pen. "Here you go, William. Why don't you draw me something while I talk to your mama and Mr. Sinclair?"

As William set happily to the task, Dodge regarded his customers with a bit more curiosity. "I've found several properties that could serve your needs, ma'am. Be happy to show them to you. Just what's your interest here, Dea-

con?" At least he didn't hem and haw but came
straight to the point.

"Mr. Sinclair is going to run my store for me,
so I'd like his input as well."

Dodge arched a brow. "That so? I didn't know
you had mercantile leanings, Deke."

"A newfound passion," Deacon drawled,
"prompted by the need to survive."

To her credit, Garnet let that pass without
comment.

Dodge looked between the two of them, probably seeing more than either wanted him to. But
before he could say anything, the door burst
open to emit a pint-sized tornado.

"Papa, Miz Sadie's cat had its kittens and she
said I could have one if—" The boy drew up,
taking in the sight of another child occupying
his place on his step-father's knee. Green eyes
narrowed as he assessed the possible threat.

"Speaking of hell on wheels, this is Christien.
Chris, this is Mrs. Prior and her son, William."

The boy bowed properly to Garnet and murmured a polite, "Pleased to meet you." She stared
at the handsome child, wondering why he looked
so familiar, until Dodge answered her musings.

"My wife, Starla, is Tyler Fairfax's sister. The
boy favors his uncle, don't you think?"

"Uncannily."

"In looks alone, if you're lucky," Deacon
added in a soft aside.

"Chris, why don't you take William here and
show him those kittens? He can help you pick one

out. Then it'll be up to your mama to say yes or no." He grinned, knowing Starla would deny the boy nothing. "If that's all right with you, ma'am."

The two boys eyed each other for a moment, then Christien decided for them both. "C'mon, Willy. One of 'em's got seven toes."

"Seven toes?" That was all it took to coax William from his shyness. He jumped down, then paused, looking hopefully to his mother.

"Don't catch cold," she warned. "And don't overtire yourself."

The boy was already racing to the door when he promised, "I won't, Mama."

Dodge stood. "Let's go look at some storefront property, shall we?"

The first place they went all agreed was unsuitable: too small, no room for expansion. The second was next to the livery on the far end of town: too far from the flow of commerce and too close to the smell of manure. The third was a soon-to-be-abandoned building originally constructed with the traditional two-storied square front of a mercantile. Deacon remembered the storekeeper, a Jewish immigrant named Rosen. He'd begun his trade from a humble peddler's pack, traversing the muddy roads at first on foot, then in a one-horse wagon to reach potential customers. Deacon recalled the excitement of gathering around as the strange little man with his funny accent who unlaced the awning-striped cover of his pack, opening a tantalizing world to them with a flourish. Out came the rush of scents: soaps, leather goods, cheap perfume, sachets and spices. How they looked forward to his visits until the day he'd earned enough to put his sway-backed horse out to pasture with the opening of his own store.

When in town as a boy, Deacon headed straight for the square box front, with its narrow front porch, rusting sign and pungent smells reminiscent of childhood. He'd lost himself amongst the cluttered countertops, awed by the stacks of merchandise and lured by the tall jars filled with striped candy. He'd bought his first pair of long pants from Rosen's, had posted his first letter there. He'd stood for long minutes reading the notices of pending auctions and camp meetings, funeral handbills, and the intriguing "Dead or Alive" posters. Now among that bristle of nails and tack heads studding the wood siding, a "For Sale" sign hung proclaiming hard times. Imagining the large room emptied of all but dust and memories left an odd ache inside him. When had the old man decided to close his doors?

And if Rosen had failed in business, what would keep them from doing the same?

The heavy double doors were still shut and locked, the shutters bolted behind vertical bars. Dodge withdrew a massive key and opened the store for their inspection.

It was just as Deacon remembered, with the post office off to the right behind its homemade bars, only there was no postmaster now. Beyond stretched the heavy sectional counter locally fashioned from heart-pine paneling that was built to last for centuries. It housed tilt-out bins for flour, rice, and seeds and rows of heavy drawers with sturdy pulls, and across the aisle taking up the front half of the store were glass showcases displaying fancy merchandise. Only the cases stood nearly bare.

The back half of the store was for the storage of barrels and dry goods. It, too, was sadly undersupplied. The center aisle which should have been crowded with the harbingers of spring: plows, horse collars and onion starts, were all but vacant. Even the aromas Deacon recalled so fondly; those heady smells of apples, cheeses, tobacco, salt mackerel, axle grease, soap and kerosene, were muted into an indistinguishable blend.

"This is wonderful," Garnet commented, unaware in her enthusiasm of the history she overlooked. "What's off to the side?"

"Feed rooms," Deacon murmured, remembering how his father and Rosen would slip back into them to whisper of crop predictions and chuckle over ribald jokes not meant for delicate ears.

"And upstairs?"

Dodge rifled through an untidy stack of overalls, then conscientiously straightened them. "It used to house meetings of the Masonic lodges, but it's vacant now. You could let the space out to any number of endeavors."

"What happened to Mr. Rosen?"

"Who?" Garnet gave Deacon a puzzled glance.

"Herschel Rosen. He started this store from the goods in his peddler's wagon when I was just a boy. What happened to him? Did he fall ill?"

"More like he fell prey to overextended credit," Dodge said. He wouldn't give the particulars to betray client privilege.

"Probably didn't have Mrs. Prior's deep pockets."

Dodge ignored the wry observation. "The bank took his mortgage last month and he's been trying to move the remaining inventory to cover some of his losses. I'm sure he'd let you buy it up for next to nothing."

Garnet wound up and down the aisles, trailing her fingertips along the dusty display cases. Calculating possible profits with that mathematical mind of hers, Deacon surmised, from the concentration furrowing her brow.

"How much to get us in business, Mr. Dodge, building, back taxes, stock, and all?"

Dodge nodded toward the door. "C'mon back to the bank and I'll run some figures by you. Deacon, you coming?"

"I think I'll poke around here a bit longer."

He caught the heavy key Dodge tossed him.

"Lock up when you're done."

In the ensuing silence, Deacon could almost hear the past return in echoed whispers from where yarn spinners gathered around the huge pot-bellied stove, whittling and spitting and making up bigger and more fantastic tales. He half-expected to see Rosen standing behind the long counter. Deacon could picture him clearly trimming off a nickel's worth of cheese with a snick of the mechanical cutter, then dipping into the twenty-four-pound box for a handful measure of crackers as customers filled bowls from a selection of cove oysters, sardines, and link sausages, disguising the taste of cottonseed oil with liberal dashes of pepper sauce, catsup, and vinegar. The cutter was now quiet, the cracked bowls sitting in forgotten stacks.

And Deacon was struck anew by how easily a man's dream died.

The two boys left Sadie's boardinghouse comparing scratches left by needlelike claws.

"I like that little gray one. How 'bout you, Willy? You think your mama will let you get one, too?"

William sucked at the back of his hand before answering. "I like the black one with all the toes." And he was hoping.

"Think of all them claws!"

William just smiled, then said, "We had best be getting back."

Christien caught at his sleeve. His tone lowered. "Hey, you want to see a dead squirrel?"

His childish curiosity warring with a strong sense of dread, William balked. "I don't know. I'm supposed to go right back. My mama worries."

"You chicken? Gotta do everything your mama tells you?"

The mocking challenge brought a prideful bristling. "Don't you?"

"Hell, no."

William's jaw dropped. "You swore!"

Christien just grinned. "Learned me all sorts a words from my uncle's friends." His voice became cajoling. "C'mon, William. Don't be a sissy-boy."

William hesitated, then said, "Well, maybe just a peek."

Wanting the companionship more than the morbid satisfaction of seeing his first really dead thing, William galloped after the other boy, following him to the end of the main street, then toward a large warehouse building. There, caution returned.

"Christien, what is this place? Are we supposed to be here?"

A flash of his charming grin. "Why, sure. It's my granddaddy's place."

"What's that smell?"

"They're making liquor." He leaned forward to intimate, "It tastes worse than it smells."

Shocked that his new friend not only knew and used bad words but had sampled the forbidden drink as well, William regarded him with a mix of respect and reluctance. Maybe his mother wouldn't want him to have a friend like this. But he'd met no other boys his age and he was desperately lonely.

"Where's the squirrel?"

With a victorious smile, Christien led the way

around to a rear loading dock. Sure enough, squished flat by a delivery wagon was the intriguing carcass. Stomach knotting up, William bent to get a closer look and was assaulted by a smell worse than anything he could have imagined. He turned just in time to chuck up his breakfast, then was mortified. Surely the other boy would ridicule him. But Christien observed him with a strange smile of sympathy and gratification.

"Pretty stinky, huh?"

William gave a weak nod.

Christien glanced about to make sure no one was looking, then fixed a bright green-eyed stare upon his friend. "What say we have some fun?"

Alerted by the gleam of mischief, William again held back. "I don't know. It's getting kinda late."

Scowling, Christien hissed, "You're no better'n a baby. Go on and run back to your mama."

Provoked by the taunt, William squared his shoulders. "I'm no baby."

The sly look returned. "Then you keep a lookout."

"What're you gonna do?" Both alarmed and fascinated by the dark turnings of Christien's mind, William began casting about for any sign of adults. Then he shuddered as Christien picked up the dead animal by the tail and slipped inside the building. Caught up in the skulduggery, William followed. He drew up in horror as Christien opened one of the big smelly vats and dropped the squirrel inside. It gave a rewarding splash.

"What'd you do that for?" William squeaked.

"For fun. Why else?"

Concerned now with consequence, William said, "Your daddy's gonna beat you but good when he finds out what you done."

"You mean what *we* done."

The emphasis wasn't lost on William.

Christien gave a cocky smile as he led the way back outside. "Besides, my daddy don't like my granddad anyways. And he ain't really my daddy. My daddy died a hero in the war."

Taking a deep breath to flush the strong fermenting stench and fear from his system, William was impressed. "A hero? Really?"

"Yep. How 'bout your daddy? He in the war?"

Hanging his head slightly, William mumbled, "Nope. My daddy's from England."

Christien's opinion definitely dropped by the way he said one word: "Oh."

Feeling like an outsider again, William shuffled back toward the bank, his heart heavy. After a moment, Christien trotted up beside him, his animation returned.

"Hey, wanna see a two-headed turtle?"

William brightened. "You bet!"

"Ain't you afraid of what your mama will say?"

"Hell, no."

Grinning, Christien gripped his elbow. "C'mon, then."

Chapter 11

After exacting Dodge's promise that he'd watch out for the boys upon their return, Garnet led a reluctant Deacon to the boarding-house restaurant to meet with Tyler Fairfax. Tyler's flattery was a balm after Deacon's acidic disapproval. He might have been a rogue but he was a charming one with his dazzling green eyes, sly smile and swarthy Creole coloring.

"Why, Mrs. Prior, you look lovely. How did your business venture go? Successfully, I trust?"

"I've decided to buy Rosen's Mercantile. Mr. Sinclair will run it for me."

Tyler grinned at the stoic aristocrat. "Clerking? An admirable profession. I understand that nine out of ten planters' sons are going into that business, making it a true gentleman's trade."

"More respectable than some things I could name."

Tyler's grin never faltered in recognition of that slur. He turned back to Garnet. "Is your fine husband coming into town to sign papers,

165

then? I should like the chance to renew our acquaintance."

"Monty's given me full authority to handle our business pursuits while he attends his own interests."

"And what might those be?"

"He enjoys sketching and dabbling in politics."

Tyler's eyes glittered like fresh-cut emeralds. "Really? How fortunate that I know of some very influential fellows in the political arena. Shall I make the necessary introductions?"

Noting Deacon's tension, Garnet graced Tyler with a nod. "That would be kind of you, Mr. Fairfax."

"Tyler, please. I like to think that we will become friends as well as associates."

Feeling the chill of Deacon's stare, Garnet smiled. "I would like that, too. Shall we discuss pricing for this coming year's crop?"

"Mixing business with pleasure has never been more rewarding." Tyler lifted his coffee cup in a salute to Garnet before sliding a glance in Deacon's direction.

And that look was pure venom.

If the Priors were aware of the impropriety of inviting their hired help to dine with them, they were equally ignorant of the strange looks from both staff and the Sinclairs as mother and son sat down at the big table. The extravagance of the meal emphasized the leanness of the past months as course after course was delivered and

generously served. Garnet spent her time cluck-
ing over her son, cutting his portions and
encouraging him to eat. Monty played the host,
his interest fixed upon Hannah, whose beauty
may have faded slightly with the years but
returned with a glow at the Englishman's flattery. He was plying her for information on her
formal gardens. Deacon sat stiff and silent, his
plate mostly untouched, his thoughts his own.

"Mama, can I have a kitty?"

Used to the surprises that came with mother-
hood, she answered with a smile and a gentle
cautioning. "Don't you think Boone would get
jealous?" She could imagine the havoc the big
dog and one small kitten could wreak upon the
hardwood floor and delicate furnishings in the
Manor. Seeing the child's lip begin to quiver in
distress, she scrambled for a solution. "I suppose we could keep it at the store. Every store
needs a cat. How would that be?"

"At the store? And I could go play with him
there?"

"As long as you didn't bother Mr. Sinclair."

"I wouldn't be no bother. Please say yes."

"I guess it would be up to Mr. Sinclair." She
deferred to Deacon to see how he would handle
the matter. The remote aristocrat had little more
success in holding firm against one little boy
than she herself did.

"If you promise to feed and clean up after it."

William beamed.

"It's a big responsibility," Deacon warned in

all seriousness. "One you should think about carefully."

"I have. I will."

"Have you? Have you thought about those days when you'd rather be playing or those days when you just don't want to, and what happens when the cute little creature becomes a big cat and is not nearly as much fun? You've thought about those things and you still say yes? A man doesn't commit to what he doesn't mean to carry through."

Garnet frowned. For heaven's sakes, it was just a pet! She didn't understand the weight Deacon put upon such an insignificant thing until William pondered somberly, then said, "I wouldn't want to do that, sir. Maybe you could help me a little."

A shadow of a smile touched Deacon's mouth. "Maybe I could."

In that brief exchange, Deacon changed a boyish impulse into an adult decision.

And Garnet simmered.

How dared he instruct her son? How dared he ignite an adoration in one small boy after destroying what he'd once similarly evoked in her?

Deacon Sinclair was nowhere to be found when she grew heavy with child and consequence. He wasn't there when William came squalling into the world after twenty-three hours of exhausting and agonizing labor on a cold New England night in October.

He hadn't shared the pleasure of the baby's

first real smile of recognition or the dreadfully long months ruled by noisy colic. He hadn't gone sleepless when the child suffered his first harsh breathing attack, weeping and praying in terror as coughing spasms threatened the life of one tiny frightened soul. Nor had he known the anxiety that had her cosseting the boy so he wouldn't fall ill again or fretting over every sniffle or sneeze.

Having done none of those things, having shared none of those burdens, how dared he step into her child's life and win instant affection without doing a darned thing to earn it?

It took more than paternity to make a man a father. She knew. She'd had a wonderful example in her own: a man of honor and involvement, of caring and dependability. Deacon Sinclair expressed none of those traits, yet William smiled up at him as if he were responsible for the sunrise each day.

And her father was dead.

She finished her meal in silence, chafing in jealousy and alarm. William was a little boy, too young to realize that men like Deacon Sinclair didn't know how to give affection. They only knew how to demand, not return.

She tried not to think of herself as an overindulgent mother. She loved her child. She would do anything for him—her arrival at the Manor proving that. If she fussed over him more than she should, if she protected him more than was warranted, it was because she cared so much and had reason to worry. He was a delicate boy, sensitive and sheltered from harshness.

He was all she had in the world.

The big house, the fancy clothing, the society nods meant nothing when compared to the happiness of her father's namesake. Which was why she'd gone through such extreme measures to keep him safe from a truth he couldn't know—not yet. Not until she was sure.

But how could she be sure, when she couldn't take an objective stand? She couldn't seem to distance herself from the sizzle of response whenever her first . . . her *only* lover was nearby.

She would have to be stronger. She would have to hold firm against the treacherous undertow of desires.

For William.

For Deacon Sinclair's son.

The music drew him.

Soft, sorrowful tones played not on a piano, as he at first had assumed it to be, but on a harpsichord.

As he stood in the doorway to the parlor, he closed his eyes, imagining himself back where and when the innocence of the melody still had the power to move heart and soul. And on a quiet sigh, he lost himself to the moment, to a sense of peace long missing in his life.

Abruptly the notes ended, jarring him from his musings by a discordant silence. Garnet stared at his reflection in the window behind the instrument. Her expression was too complex for even him to read.

"Did you want something?"

How to answer that. What did he want? He wanted to hold onto those precious seconds where the world felt right again. And he wanted to hold on to the only woman who had ever brought him such contented bliss.

Instead, he told her with a flat brusqueness, "I need to talk to you about Fairfax."

Garnet swivelled on the stool to regard him suspiciously.

"What about him?"

With her hands folded in her lap, she looked like a prettily composed daughter of the South awaiting praise for her recital, until one looked into her eyes. They held a maturity of experience and pain in sharp contrast to her serene appearance. Deacon knew who'd put the pain there, and thinking of where else she'd gained the experience, twisted a shaft of jealous envy through him.

"You'd be a fool to trust him."

"I've placed my trust foolishly once before. I am more cautious now. I know what Tyler Fairfax is."

Smarting under her accusation, he said, "I don't think you do. If you did, you wouldn't go into business with him. He's not what he seems on the surface."

"Oh, and you are an expert on that, I know."

Grinding his teeth, Deacon fought the urge to leave her to her fate. But if she failed, the Manor would fail. Neither of those scenarios was acceptable to him.

"Tyler Fairfax is a dangerous conniver. He's motivated by greed and hate and he doesn't care who he hurts."

"The pot casting slurs at the kettle, sir?"

Deacon crossed the room in long, angry strides. Taken by surprise, Garnet shrank back against the keyboard, the press of her elbows issuing a squawk of unpleasant sound. If he read her expression right, it wasn't a fear of him that had her alarmed, but rather her fear of her own reaction to him. And he meant to use that fear to its fullest.

He didn't touch her. He didn't need to. With palms gripping the polished wood on either side of the keyboard, he corralled her between the brace of his arms and intimidated with his proximity. He could hear her breaths hurry in short, jagged bursts even as her stare continued to challenge him.

God, he loved her bravery.

He leaned in close, his voice lowering to a threatening caress. "Pay attention to what I'm telling you. Pay close attention. If I hadn't fallen prey to Fairfax's scheming, you wouldn't be here to torment me."

He saw her swallow frantically, but there was no waver of distress in her words.

"My being here has nothing to do with Tyler Fairfax's ability to take advantage of the desperate. It has everything to do with your willingness to do exactly the same."

Being compared to Fairfax hit hard and with an astonishing truth. But Deacon pressed on relentlessly.

"He likes to play games with people's lives just for the enjoyment of seeing them ruined. If you think he'll honor any vows he's made to you, think again. If you put your future in his control, he will take everything you have just because he can, not because he needs it or even wants it. I made the mistake of taking him at his word and he stripped me of all I held dear. If you think he's going to allow you that same pleasure, you're wrong. He'll use you to get at me for as long as it amuses him, then he'll turn on you, too. I won't have my properties and my home wagered as pawns in his little dramas."

Her features went pale. Against that soft sea of white, her eyes were enormous, her lips even more luscious. "So that's behind your concern, the land, the house." She had been foolish to think, just for a moment, that it might have been concern for her. She pulled an anguished breath and let fire flare in her eyes. "Well, you need not worry about what is no longer yours."

She tried to stand, meaning to push him back so she could escape him, but he didn't move. She found herszlf imprisoned by the appeal of his nearness, drawn to his heat, his scent, to the havoc of memories he stirred inside her. She gasped slightly when his hands cuffed her elbows.

"Why are you here?" he hissed down upon her bowed head. She couldn't look up, terrified that he'd unmask her heart. "Is it revenge? Is it retribution? What?"

She spoke into the crisp whiteness of his shirt front, struggling to keep the emotion from quavering through her words. "You gave me a picture once, a dream to hold on to. I've come to claim it. You've only yourself to blame for the fact that you're no longer included in it."

"What's mine, I keep. Remember that."

Wildly disturbed by that fiercely issued claim, she whispered, "Please excuse me," shoving hard to win her release. Then she ran to the door without gauging his response.

Had she turned, she would have realized how close she was to her goal. For just that moment, she could have seen his soul stripped bare to all but longing and loss. She would have reaped the satisfaction of recognizing his defeat. But instead, suffering for her own, she could only run away from the source of her misery. From the dream she'd wanted so desperately.

And still wanted with all her heart. If only such things were possible.

Montgomery Prior wasn't the distracted fool he pretended to be. He saw right though Garnet's fragile greeting to the anguish beneath it.

"What has the bastard done, my darling?"

From the enveloping care of his embrace, Garnet fought to contain a scrap of dignity when the temptation to dissolve into tears wore mightily. "Nothing, Monty. Nothing."

"I told you, lovey. I warned you that it would not be easy to hold against his pretty face and cold manner. He's a harmful addiction to you, my girl, and I'll not allow him to hurt you again. Or am I too late, already?"

"Why am I so weak when I need to be strong? For my father, for William."

"For yourself, Garnet. Be strong for yourself, my girl, for the suffering he's forced upon you with his indifference."

"I'm trying, but it's . . . it's so hard." So hard not to give into her yearning for the same man who had betrayed her. Weakness wasn't the term to describe it. A helpless self-destruction came closer to naming her need to fall into the same flame that had already seared her once.

"Then step away, child. Put the means of your vengeance into the hands of another and come back to England with me. Isn't it enough knowing that he's humbled without having to be there to see the deed done in person?"

"No." Purpose steadied her voice. No, what was between her and Deacon was personal, very personal, and turned over to another, the effect was gone. She had to be there to judge the degree of his remorse, to bend him to the power of regret. Until she saw more than fleeting apology in his eyes, she had to exert all pressure possible to make him realize the error he'd made in playing fast and loose with her future.

"But darling, you're risking more than you know."

"What else could he take from me?"

Monty remained wisely silent, fearing the answer. It fortified his own role in her charade. "Garnet, my dear, I made a promise to your mother to see you lacked for nothing, to see you achieved happiness. I can't make good on that vow if you insist on staying here, taunting fate a second time."

"I'm not young and innocent any more, Uncle Monty."

"Perhaps not, dear one, but you are still a woman, a woman who has shared a bed and a child with the same man you now plan to ruin. Be careful that you do it for the right reasons."

The right reasons. Garnet considered them in a whirl of confusion. What were the reasons that had brought her into this deception, asking her mother's brother to play along in a deadly serious game?

To hit back hard for her losses: for that of her home, her happiness, her father, her dreams. That's what she'd claimed. But because she knew all Monty said was true, because she understood her own weaknesses too well, she'd been wise to place a barrier between her child and the man who'd made him with her upon a bed of lies.

Deacon Sinclair would never gain the knowledge to destroy her. He would never learn that William was his son.

Not unless he proved himself to be worthy.

Of her love and William's trust.

She'd had to tell her uncle her motive was revenge. That was something he could understand, something that would bind him to her quest. If he'd known her real reason, he would never have agreed. He would never have brought her here to court danger. She couldn't have gained control of Sinclair Manor on her own, not without a "husband" to give legitimacy to her plans. She wanted to place Deacon Sinclair in a position where his true spots would show, to pressure him into revealing his heart and mind. A woman from his past and a child with no legal name couldn't force him out from behind his cold facade.

The land, the house, those were the things Deacon held dear. Well, William was her soft spot, and she could not allow him to become a pawn. So she'd asked her uncle to play her husband to protect her child. And to make her less vulnerable. It was as simple as that. And with William safely removed from the struggle for truth, she could explore the depths of Deacon's character. A darker, more dangerous task, she'd never imagined. But what she would eventually find would make all the difference to the little boy who slept in the room across the hall, unaware of the conflict swirling about him.

And that's the way she would keep it, by keeping Deacon at arm's length.

If she could.

His fingers lingered over the keys, but the issuing sound was nothing like the poignant melodies Garnet coaxed from them.

Damn her. Why did she have to be the one to steal his future?

Against any other, he could have stood firm and acted ruthlessly. He could have treated any other with a cold ferociousness that had served him well in war. He would have sunk to any low, used any weakness to his full advantage. Without thought. Without hesitation. Had it been anyone else.

What was it about this one woman that so completely stymied reason? Her courage, her beauty, her resolve? Or was it the paradise they'd shared so briefly between them? Even now, her scent filled his head, muddling his mind, clouding his resources like fine drink.

She wanted to reduce him from manor-born gentry to menial store clerk. And he let her. He allowed her to step on his pride, to grind her heel and kick it aside like something without value. But then, perhaps his pride was no longer the issue.

He didn't have to stay under this roof with the minute-by-minute reminder of all that he'd lost. But he took a perverse pleasure in doing so, because it meant being close to her, to the one woman he would have taken as his own. He might tell himself it was to retain a foothold in his home, to restore his properties yard by yard, but that wasn't the truth. The truth was what Patrice had guessed.

He couldn't leave the past alone. He couldn't walk away from this woman he'd loved.

His splayed fingers wrought a wince of noise from the keyboard.

What were his choices now? He saw only two, since walking away was not one of them. He could surrender. Or he could turn to clever subterfuge.

No one had ever taught him the humility necessary to give up with good grace. So that left the one thing he was truly good at.

Deception.

He could bide his time, pretending to submit while watching for the best chance to reclaim what was his. And the first thing he could do while waiting was get to know his enemy better.

"I'd like to send a telegram."

Gates Hargrove glanced up from the game of solitaire he was playing. For a moment, indecision warred in his eyes. Deacon could read it plain. Was he or was he not someone who warranted quick attention?

In the past, the groveling Hargrove would have tripped over himself to be of service to a

Sinclair. But now there was a definite air of inso-
lence in the leisurely way he collected his cards,
gave them a shuffle, then set them aside.

"What can I do for you, Deacon?"

Deacon. Not Mr. Sinclair. Even politely said,
the omission of respect was obvious.

"Send this for me."

"You wanna wait for a reply?"

"No."

Gates scanned the message, then his eyes
bugged. "This is going to Washington, D.C."

"I know where it's going."

"Special Judge Advocate of the War Depart-
ment." He regarded Deacon with a renewed
awe. "You want I should send somebody out to
your place with the answer, Mr. Sinclair?"

Deacon smiled thinly. "No, that won't be
necessary. I'll be right across the street. At the
mercantile."

And as Deacon crossed the dusty road on his
way to his first day behind the counter, he was
filled with new hope.

Soon, he would know everything there was to
know about Montgomery Prior. And somewhere in that information, if there was a God,
would be the leverage he needed.

Chapter 12

It took Garnet one look to realize her mistake. Surroundings made no difference. Even on his knees, covered with dirt, shirt sleeves waded up to the elbows as he tore into a box of household notions, Deacon was every inch a gentleman. It wasn't circumstance, it was attitude. He attacked the job at hand with no less determination than he would in going over the ledgers at the Manor. How could she bring humility to such a man when he took pride in even small endeavors?

Why would she want to?

The instant he saw her, the guarded blankness covered his expression. She managed a tiny smile.

Deacon dusted his hands on his trousers as he stood. Her gaze followed the ascension with a detailing interest. Seeing it, his lips quirked in a wry bend.

"Come to see how the laboring class is progressing, Mrs. Prior?"

She ignored the barb. "Just making sure all my orders arrived."

He gestured wide to encompass the crates and boxes making a fortress of commerce around him. "Everything from garters to fish hooks. There's an inventory sheet in the office if you want to double-check my count."

"There's no need."

"Then why are you here, Mrs. Prior?"

There was no avoiding his question or his probing stare. What could she tell him? The truth—that she couldn't stay away? That the need to simply watch him sort merchandise on the floor held a lure she was powerless to resist? Hardly. Instead, she drew off her gloves, using the time the exaggerated movements gave her to compose her thoughts and calm her voice.

"As I told you, this store is my project. I plan to oversee its operation on a daily basis."

His features tightened. In dismay or disgust, she couldn't tell. "Then why do you need me here? Afraid it wouldn't look good for a lady of your newfound stature to be grubbing around in packing crates?"

"This is only one of my interests, so I won't have time to devote to it exclusively."

"Just time enough to keep your finger on the pulse of the community and your thumb on me?"

She allowed a grim, "Exactly." Then her tone softened. "Besides, William is bringing Ulysses to his new home this morning."

"Who?"

"The store's live-in mouser."

"Oh." Deacon's face relaxed into a small, genuine smile. That slight softening of his expression melted Garnet's heart to the consistency of the molasses now sitting on clumsy racks in the back. It brought home with an unfair punch how different he was now from the gentle man who'd courted her affections. Had the war wrought that change from sensitive to somber, or had he just been playing the part for her benefit before? Unable to answer, she turned away in frustration and began a visual inventory of the store's goods.

"Gracious. Where will we put everything?"

"In its place, Mrs. Prior, and everything has one."

The cut of his tone brought her around with fire in her eyes. "Everything, or everyone?"

He stared at her, refusing to reply.

"And just where is *my* place, Mr. Sinclair? Is that what galls you so much? That someone like me, someone from the hill country with no fancy pedigree, could come in and lay claim to what you overweened aristocrats prefer to hoard among yourselves? Would you be so angry, so fierce, if one of your own were standing in my place here today, holding your future in his hands?"

"No."

His honesty took her aback, then fanned the flames higher. "So it's your snobbery that upsets you, then, your inability to accept that someone of my station could intrude upon your genteel life."

"No," he said again with the same flat forcefulness. "It's you. It's the fact that it's you."

Without explaining himself further, he disappeared into the side office. She could see him shuffling through papers on the chest-high desktop. His head was bent so his expression remained a mystery—not that she could have read anything there anyway. Suddenly she had to know what was behind his words.

"What do you mean, it's me?"

He looked up from the paperwork as she stood in the framed doorway, her arms crossed, her mood challenging. Without a blink, he went back to his sorting.

"It would have been easier to lose everything to a stranger."

She refused to give the pity she felt a dangerous hold upon her heart. "Just as it would have been easier being betrayed by a stranger."

He didn't glance up, but she could tell by the tensing of his jaw that she had his full attention. After a long moment, he said, "Exactly. So this evens that score, then."

He spoke it blandly, as if he were referring to a card debt or an insignificant tit-for-a-tat. All the rage she'd been repressing since she'd gotten the telegram saying her father was dead surfaced in a blinding rush. All the fear and panic she'd experienced finding herself alone in the world, then alone and pregnant, returned to scald her senses.

"Deacon?"

He glanced up just in time to take the full impact of her palm across his face. The act surprised her, both with its violence and by the satisfaction that came with it. Before she could pull back, he caught her wrist and yanked her toward him. Off balance, she fell into him. Her bracing hand met hard abdomen. And because her first instinct was to yield along his long, tough lines, she tried to jerked away in a fury. He held tight to her wrist, a painless grasp that was no less unbreakable. His other arm made an imprisoning curl about her waist. Helpless to escape from his closeness or her own frantic desires, Garnet fought against both, but the more she resisted, the more determined his restraint became. Finally she saw the futility of her struggles and went still against him, her glare anything but submissive.

"Our score is nowhere close to even," came her hiss of conclusion.

"What will it take to settle it?"

Before she could reply, the bell over the front door jangled and the patter of light footfalls announced William even before his cry of, "Mama, come see!"

Deacon's grasp opened and she was quick to lunge away, hurrying into the main room. William was kneeling on the floor over the wiggling bundle of his jacket, too preoccupied to notice her high color. She pulled up short to take a composing breath, then was distracted from her own pounding pulsebeats.

"William! Were you outside without your coat on?"

He looked up guiltily. "But Mama, I couldn't let Ulysses get cold."

She came down beside him to observe the mewling kitten, immediately taken but adding a scolding aside. "Ulysses is already wearing a coat. You know what happens when you overexert yourself."

His excitement dimmed at the thought of causing her distress. "I'm sorry, Mama. I guess I wasn't thinking." The sight of his bowed head was more than Deacon could take.

"No harm was done," he interjected mildly, bending down next to the two of them. He could feel Garnet's censure as clearly as if she'd snarled for him to mind his own business. "Let's get a look at our new employee." He lifted the ball of black fluff and bared claws from its worsted swaddling. "Did you check his lineage to see if he comes from mouser stock?"

William blinked then, catching Deacon's slight wink, and broke into a wide grin. "Just look at all them claws. I'm sure he'll scare the whiskers off them critters."

Not mentioning that the sight of the tiny fur ball would probably send any self-respecting cheese stealer into gales of laughter, Deacon stood, casting about for an empty crate. "Let's make our friend a bed and get him a bowl of food, then you can help me sort shoestrings while he settles in . . . if that's all right with your mother."

When both looked up at her, William through great pleading eyes and Deacon with the glow of her hand print still fading, Garnet felt cornered into saying, "Just be a help and not a hindrance."

She watched them together, feeling both pleased and powerless. It was so unlike her shy son to warm so quickly to an adult, and the prickly Deacon Sinclair seemed such an unlikely subject for his admiration. But the two had formed a firm bond whether she was comfortable with it or not.

But William wasn't her concern. Her own reactions were.

Perhaps she'd been wrong to place her and Deacon into such close proximity. She'd underestimated the dangers that accompanied the rewards. They would be behind closed doors, often just the two of them together. Romance wasn't what worried her, it was retribution.

She'd struck him, for heaven's sake! Her own actions appalled and frightened her, making her as much a stranger to herself as he was to her.

She'd taken his heritage. She'd battered his pride. Now she was threatening his future. Was she naive to think he would accept all that without malice?

Watching him with William, those uncertainties fled and her answer was no. Here was a man of innate decency who was somehow, somewhere, led to stray into darkness. By his severe father? By the hardships of the war? She could only guess at this point. But she wanted to know. She had to know.

If only to see if he could be coaxed back.

Montgomery Prior leaned back with a good cigar and a glass of Fairfax bourbon warming in his hand. He smiled at his host's inquiry as to his comfort.

"I assure you, I am as content as a babe."

Tyler Fairfax exchanged a knowing glance with Judge Banning, who had opened his home and his box of fine Havanas for the occasion.

"I thought the two of you would get on well," Tyler boasted. "The judge, like yourself, sir, enjoys playing at politics. He can fill you in on the local climate much better than I."

"Are you a member of the legal community, Mr. Banning?"

The handsome older man chuckled. "An honorary name, I assure you. It comes from folks 'round here deferring to my advice. And you, Mr. Prior, are you looking to get your feet wet in our community pool?"

"I think one is obligated to take an interest in his surroundings."

"Well, we would more than welcome your input and influence, isn't that right, Tyler?"

Tyler smiled and swallowed the contents of his glass in a single gulp.

Monty chuckled modestly. "I'd be more than happy to lend you my opinions, but as for influence, I fear I'm just a stranger in a strange land."

The judge waved aside his misgivings. "Nonsense. You own Sinclair Manor and are now privy to their power in the community. And I assure you, it is considerable. If you speak, folks 'round here will listen."

Tyler stood up, wobbling slightly, a condition he'd arrived in. "Well, I'll leave the judge to acquaint you with the community issues. And if there's any other way I can be of assistance, you be sure an' call on me."

Monty gave him a hopeful look. "There is something you might do."

"I am at your service, sir."

"I need a knowledgeable fellow to oversee the management of my properties. I'm frightfully ignorant of such matters. My dear wife would like to believe herself capable of handling it all, but I hate to place such a burden on her."

Both men made agreeing sounds.

"What about Sinclair?"

Monty viewed Tyler's suggestion with disfavor. "I'm sure he is the best suited, but I prefer to distance him from the running of my estate. I'm sure you can understand the delicacy of the matter."

"Ummm, yes. He is a difficult man to . . . control, though I'd say your wife has brought him to heel quite nicely."

Monty's jovial features went still, his eyes growing steely. "My wife shouldn't have to handle Mr. Sinclair. I prefer to distance him there, as well."

Tyler arranged his hat carefully as he mused, "Could be I know just the man for you. He's clever and discreet. I had dealings with him during the war and found him . . . useful in many areas. Would you like me to set up a meeting, Mr. Prior?"

"You know the area and the men far better than I, Mr. Fairfax. I'd appreciate your intervention."

"Well, now, I'll see what I can do."

When he was gone, the two older men enjoyed the bourbon and the silence for a long while. Then Monty broached the subject.

"Tell me, Judge Banning, how can a man go about gaining influence in this town?"

The judge grinned wide. "Mr. Prior, you've come to the right man for advice."

The remainder of the workday was without incident. With William as a buffer between them, Garnet and Deacon whipped the mercantile into shape. There was absolutely no mention of what had happened earlier or trace of an apology from either side.

And in that practiced silence rose a tension to equal their explosive contact in the office. What touch didn't allow, imagination could provide, and it made for a restless afternoon.

Finally satisfied with her arrangement of the jeweled hatpins and fancy earbobs, Garnet announced, "I think we'll be ready for our grand opening tomorrow."

There was a fierce curse from the back that brought William's head up in wide-eyed alarm.

"You okay, Mr. Sinclair?"

A flurry of other soft oaths filtered out from behind a keg of nails, then Deacon stood, sucking at his thumb. The boy went bounding over.

"What happened? Did you get a splinter?"

"It's nothing," Deacon growled, then immediately amended his surly mood when the child's lip quivered with hurt. With a sigh, he held his injured thumb down for the boy's inspection.

"Mama, come quick! Mr. Sinclair's squished his finger."

As Garnet came hurrying toward them, Deacon withdrew his hand. "It's nothing. Really."

But Garnet was already reaching for him. "Let me see."

"It's fine. I just dropped the keg on it, is all."

"Let me see."

She was trying to make the gesture appear as one of natural concern, but the harder she tried, the more Deacon protested, and the more aggressive her concern became. Finally, she made a lunge forward to snag his rolled shirt sleeve, dragging him toward her.

"I said let me see!"

"You better do it. She really means it when she says it like that."

Almost sheepishly, Deacon surrendered his hand. She made a sympathetic noise at the sight of his mashed nail. "William, fetch me some water and some clean cloths."

"It's fine," Deacon persisted in a softer tone, because she was holding his hand between hers and he was wondering how she'd managed to get them so silky smooth when he remembered a coarser touch.

"It's no trouble," she answered automatically, her voice strained because she was absorbing the warmth and strength of his grip, wondering what had happened in the last five years to build such callused roughness on his palms.

And she was wondering how that burred friction would feel against her skin.

Deacon jerked back abruptly, denying the contact, denying the hurrying of his heartbeats even as he wished for the freedom to indulge them both. He lifted the lid of one of the nearby barrels and stuck his thumb inside, withdrawing it all slathered in axle grease.

"There," he announced stiffly. "That will take care of it."

"As if grease was the answer to all man's ills," she muttered, embarrassed and flustered and afraid he would notice both things. "It's still going to hurt like a b—like the devil tomorrow.

Thank you, William, but Mr. Sinclair has taken care of it himself."

As William trotted over to add the extra water to Ulysses' bowl, Garnet grew uncomfortably aware of the man before her. Here was no sleek aristocrat. His shirt was soiled, his bared forearms streaked with dirt and grime. His hair stood in an untidy disarray and he'd worked up a healthy sweat. And she was suddenly shivering.

Then she discovered what Deacon had seen that caused his fast retreat. The door jangled.

"Garnet, are you and the lad ready to go?"

She turned toward Monty with a quavering smile. "I didn't know you'd come to town." Aware of Deacon's slated stare, she went quickly to the spotlessly attired older man, stretching up to place a fond kiss on his cheek. His gaze settled on Deacon.

"Sinclair. Looks like you've been busy."

"We're going to open tomorrow, Monty. Isn't that exciting?" Garnet knew she was too animated not to wake his suspicions, but her nerves were shuddering and she couldn't get them under control.

"If you say so, my dear. I'll give you and the boy an escort home."

"Let me get my cloak." Without a look toward the object of her agitation, she rushed to the office to snatch up her wrap, eager to escape Monty's curiosity and Deacon's influence. "Come, William. Don't keep your father waiting."

But William dawdled. "Mama, what if Ulysses gets lonely?"

"He won't, darling. He'll have all those lovely little mice to play with."

"But I don't want to leave him here all alone. What if he misses me?"

"William . . . " Her head was aching with tension and she didn't need the extra stress of dealing with his stubbornness. Monty, as usual, hadn't a clue as to how to handle the boy's petulant moods. He was looking with longing toward the door.

"I'll stay awhile," Deacon offered, winning the boy's teary gratitude. "I'll make sure he's all settled in before I leave."

"Would you?"

"I'll let him know that this is his home now and that you'll be back tomorrow."

"Really?" Then the boy's eyes narrowed. "How will you do that? Cats can't understand people talk."

"They understand me." A lot better than people, he could have added. "Go on with your mother, now. She's worked hard and is tired. You don't want to make her cross with you."

"I'm not cross," Garnet argued, but her tone contradicted her message. She sighed and held out her hand. William slipped his inside it.

Deacon went tight all over watching her fingers curl about the boy's so possessively.

"Lock up, Mr. Sinclair."

He smiled wryly at the unnecessary reminder. "Yes, ma'am."

He didn't move as Prior squired his family outside and helped them up into the buggy. Then the trio left together, and that togetherness churned into a bitter aftertaste.

For God's sake, she was a married woman!

He'd forgotten that. He'd forgotten everything but the memory of her gentle care. And to feel those tender ministrations again, he would have disavowed another man's claim before both man and God. If William hadn't been there, he would have taken Garnet up against him to ravish her ripe mouth, to wake her to the pleasures they'd shared between them despite all else that had happened.

His wanting her was an ache to the soul.

And that soul would be even more damned if he gave before those wrongful desires.

Garnet was no longer his to covet. She belonged to another man and all the longing, all the returning sparks of need he'd seen in those short seconds, couldn't erase that fact. She was married. And he would not break yet another commandment.

So how was he going to work beside her, smelling her fragrant hair, hearing the swish of her petticoats without acting on what both of them were vulnerable to? She could deny it all she wanted, but he'd seen the answering passion in her frightened gaze.

"I'd like to hire Herschel Rosen to work in the store with me."

Garnet regarded him across the supper table with surprise. "We don't know that we can afford a second employee."

"I'd be willing to take a reduction in salary until you absorb the expense with our profits."

Now she was suspicious. "Why would you do that?"

"If you want to open tomorrow, you're going to need someone more knowledgeable than me to greet your customers. I know how to purchase a stamp but haven't the slightest idea of how to post one. I can't make heads or tails of Rosen's credit files. So if you want things to run smoothly, I suggest you hire the man on, at least until I know what I'm doing."

"And Mr. Rosen is agreeable to this?" Her wariness was far from eased.

"I spoke to him this evening. He's an old man with no family. That store was his whole life. He'd be willing to do just about anything to remain a part of it." How well he'd understood that bit of perverse humiliation. He wouldn't share how the man had gripped his hands and wept in gratitude. "Besides," he added reasonably, "the townsfolk are used to seeing him there and it would build their confidence in trading with us."

"Sounds logical, Garnet dear," Monty murmured. He was watching Deacon's expression for signs of what he suspected. He knew the man was still attracted to his niece and that the interest was mutual. The idea of a mediator at the store where he couldn't be present was a good thing. Now all he had to figure out was Sinclair's motive for suggesting it. He didn't believe the man was prompted by good business sense or humanitarian leanings. Despite all Garnet's talk to the contrary, she was still soft on Sinclair, so it was up to him to see to her safety where the slick Southerner was concerned. "I think you should hire the man on."

Garnet thought a moment, then nodded. "All right. If Mr. Rosen is willing, he can speak to me tomorrow morning."

"I'm sure he'll thank you for your generosity."

She waited a moment to see if the sentiment was attached to some sarcasm, but Deacon returned to his meal in silence, never answering her curiosity.

They weren't partners in business or in anything else, and it would be best for her to remember that. If only she could.

Chapter 13

ll day Prior's Mercantile was packed with the citizens of Pride. Drawn more by curiosity than necessity, they lined up to buy ribbons and fruit-jar rings, a handful of nails or a slate pencil just to get a look at the proud Deacon Sinclair working behind a counter.

By noontime, the circular space in the center of the store was crowded with old-timers perched on kegs of horseshoes and knife-scarred benches pulled up within easy spitting distance of the glowing stove. There, they sat, whittling, chewing, gossiping and mainly speculating on how long Deacon could maintain his rigidly correct demeanor, as if he were somehow above cutting chewing tobacco or matching threads from the walnut J. and P. Coats cabinet. The measure of a successful storekeeper was his ability to relate to those he served with understanding and a sense of humor. No one in Pride could accuse Deacon Sinclair of having either, so they approached him as something of a novelty, half intimidated, half bemused; many were smug over his reduced stature.

But the old gossips gave him credit: the man held tight to his dignity, even though he was aware of all the whispering and smirks aimed in his direction. And none would dare mock him to his face, once he'd fixed them with that bared-blade stare. Even those with questions approached with caution.

"There's something wrong with this sugar," a matron too old to fear a stony gaze claimed in a loud tone. Conversation hushed in the vicinity of the counter as Deacon glanced at the sack he'd measured out only that morning.

"Ma'am, it arrived fresh yesterday."

Refusing to back down from his quelling look, she pulled the bag open. "Then you taste it."

To humor her, he wet his finger and took a sample. His brow puckered. "It tastes like kerosene." Frowning, he strode to the back of the store where the barreled goods were stored; sugar, rice, salt . . . and kerosene. His mood darkened dangerously.

"What seems to be the trouble, young Sinclair?"

Deacon kept his voice low as he explained to Herschel Rosen. "Someone has contaminated our supply of sugar with kerosene. If I find out who did such a thing—" He broke off as the older man chuckled.

"Why, my boy, it is nature that played the prank on you. The oil, it just sneaks along the floor to spoil everything it touches. You must keep the other barrels up off the boards or they will be forever soaking up the flavor."

"So all this stock—"

Rosen shrugged. "A lesson you won't need to be taught again."

Calculating the loss grimly, he returned to the counter. "I apologize for your inconvenience, Mrs. Crawford. Let me refill your order from one of our counter bins . . . at no charge."

At the magic words "no charge," the widow ceased her grumbling and became all smiles. "What a gentleman you are, Mr. Sinclair."

He made no comment, but those at the stove had plenty to pass among themselves. Imagine, such generosity from a member of the gentry!

"*Mister* Sinclair!"

He headed to the bulk grocery section to see a humorless Margie Johnston pointing into the barrel of dried peas.

"Would you care to explain that, sir?"

There, afloat on the sea of tiny green pellets was an obvious contaminant. Deacon stared, determined not to show his dismay. He glanced about for the culprit and the reason, then relayed both calmly.

"What's to explain, Mrs. Johnston? A little boy's kitten, a closed cathole, and an open barrel. Nature, ma'am." A brief smile quirked his lips. "I'd be happy to dipper your peas from the bin up front."

"At no charge?" she prompted.

His smile never faltered. "At no charge."

He and the pleased woman returned to the counter on a tide of murmurings. The satisfied female left with her measure of unsoiled peas.

"Mr. Sinclair, my Manny came in with a note from me stating he was to get a good pair of trousers for fifty cents. When we checked our account from the previous owner, we found we were charged one dollar and fifty cents."

Deacon retained his sigh of aggravation. "Do you have the garment, Mrs. Wellington?"

"My Manny couldn't go without trousers to church, Mr. Sinclair."

Chuckles sounded from the stove area and were silenced by a look from Deacon.

"So the trousers are no longer new."

Not in the least bit chagrined, the farm wife stated, "Is it your policy to honor the mistakes made by your predecessor, sir, or would you cheat a poor family out of a hard-earned dollar?"

"It is my policy to satisfy my customers, Mrs. Wellington. I'll credit your account for the dollar and tell your Manny to wear the trousers in good health."

Her stiffness faded into a grateful smile. "Why, that's right neighborly of you, Mr. Sinclair. Who would have thought?"

Who, indeed? But by the end of the first working day, not a soul who passed near Prior's or walked the street of Pride hadn't heard about Deacon Sinclair's uncommon charity.

Deacon was loading supplies into the final wagon in front of the store when Garnet and

William arrived. Herschel was just hanging the "Closed" sign on the door and took a moment to doff his hat before starting down the walk toward his solitary dinner at Sadie's.

"How did our first day go, Mr. Sinclair?" Garnet called, as William ran to find Ulysses.

"Not quite enough in the till to retire on, but we're not broke yet." He held the door open for her in a moment of surprising chivalry.

Garnet stepped inside, then paused to close her eyes and breath deep, inhaling her entire inventory in one odoriferous accounting: the glaze on the calicoes, the starch in the checks, peppermint and wintergreen candies, leather polish on the shoes, neat's-foot oil and wax on saddles, tar on steel cotton ties, and naphtha soap. A wonderful scent of commerce. And the dusky smell of industry and warm man as Deacon moved past her.

"William, I need to discuss something with you and General Ulysses."

Alerted by the seriousness of his tone, William hugged the kitten to him. "Was he bad?"

Crooking his finger, Deacon led the way to the pea bin. Looking inside, William understood immediately.

"What is it?"

Keeping a sober face, Deacon told the boy's mother, "The kitten decided to relieve himself in the dried peas."

"Oh dear."

"William, did you cover the cathole?"

"I didn't want Ulysses to get cold." William's

features puckered in distress. "We're not going to get rid of Ulysses, are we? He didn't mean to be bad."

Deacon bent down to the boy's level. "No, he didn't. But if he's going to stay here, you're going to have to teach him manners. First, make sure all the bins are covered. Second, leave the cathole open so he can get outside to take care of his business."

William nodded. Then he looked back at the barrel of ruined goods. "Can you sell the peas now?"

"No."

"Who's going to pay for them?"

"Who do you think should pay for them?"

His eyes lowered. "Me?"

"Whose fault was it that they got ruined?"

"Mine."

Before Garnet could step in to voice the forgiveness written plainly on her face, Deacon said, "If your mother is in agreement, I think it would be permissible for you to work off the cost of the peas."

William thought a minute, then looked to his mother. "I'd like to work for Mr. Sinclair to pay off the peas, Mama."

Her eyes tearing up with pride, Garnet nodded.

Deacon glanced around. "I think sweeping out the store and polishing the counter fronts would just about cover it."

William squared up his shoulders and marched for the broom with Ulysses tangling about his feet. Only then did Deacon address Garnet.

"I know it's not my place to instruct your son, and all this inventory technically belongs to him—"

"It's a good lesson for him to learn," Garnet interrupted. "I want him to understand the value of things and the consequence of his actions."

Deacon actually smiled. "He's a fine boy. He'll make good choices. Prior has done a commendable job with him."

Garnet had to turn away, afraid somehow the truth would escape in her expression. She went to the receipt book and checked the figures there. It was far safer than studying the figure before her. As her mind rapidly calculated the totals, a frown formed.

"Why do we have more negatives than profits showing?"

"A couple of harsh lessons learned and some community goodwill," was Deacon's bland explanation.

"Would you mind elaborating?"

"I'd rather not."

Provoked by his flat refusal, she demanded, "I think you will. This is my store, after all."

"And you told me to run it. If I have to spend half my time explaining every decision I make, or running to you for approval each time some controversy arises—"

She waved him off with one hand while massaging her brow with the other. "Handle it as you see fit. William, it's time to go home."

"But Mama, I gots work to do for Mr. Sinclair."

"I'll bring him with me."

When she hesitated, Deacon drawled, "He'll be perfectly safe."

Surprised that he would think her worried, she replied, "Just see that he stays warm."

" 'Bye, Mama."

The sight of her son coming up to tuck his hand into Deacon's made all her reasonings falter. Was she doing the right thing in keeping the truth from them? She could see Deacon would make an excellent father figure for the boy, but what she didn't know was where she would fit into the equation. She'd spun a complicated web of deceit, and if she wasn't careful, she wouldn't be able to disentangle herself from it.

No matter how much father and son seemed to belong together, she couldn't forget that she and her father had belonged together, too. And Deacon Sinclair was directly responsible for tearing them apart. That pain supported her when her resolve weakened. And that truth gave her the starch to hold her head up and walk away without revealing anything.

There was something wrong in the amount of attention Montgomery Prior paid to Deacon's mother.

Deacon watched as they strolled the dilapidated gardens after dinner with an almost cozy

togetherness, heads bent, laughing like a courting couple. True, they were close in age, and his
mother had been alone for nearly five years.
But that didn't change the fact that Prior was
married. Or that he chose to conduct himself so
disgracefully right in front of his wife and
child.

If Garnet had been his bride, he wouldn't be
out walking with another woman.

And that was as far as he dared carry that
train of thought.

A knock at the front door distracted him from
his spying on the older couple. Garnet was
upstairs, putting William to bed, and the house
servants were busy with the remains of supper.
And the housekeeper was out flirting with the
master of the house.

Immediately ashamed of that thought, Deacon went to the door. His mother had never
given him reason to doubt her integrity, and it
was only his own frustration that allowed him
to cast them unfairly now. Disgusted at himself,
he yanked open the door to effect a hostile greeting for the stranger on the porch.

"What do you want?"

"I'm looking for the man of the house."

"I'm—" Deacon bit back the automatic reply,
then smiled with a wry bitterness. "He's occupied at the moment. What's your business here?"

"My business is with Mr. Prior. Fetch him for
me, if you'd be so kind."

Deacon gave the young man on the porch a

slow going over. He was a few years his junior, with longish red-gold hair and a thick mustache vainly tamed into curled ends. His smile exuded slick charm and easy confidence. And Deacon bristled, distrusting him on sight. He'd stayed alive a long time paying attention to instinct, and instinct was telling him this man with his cheery grin and unwavering black eyes was not bringing good fortune with him.

"Deacon, do we have company?"

He glanced over his shoulder to see his mother in Prior's escort coming up the hall behind him. Prior's greatcoat was draped about Hannah's shoulders. He blanked his features to the sense of disapproval rushing over him. "Someone to see Mr. Prior. I've yet to get the gentleman's name."

"Roscoe Skinner, at your service, ma'am. Might you be the lovely Mrs. Prior?"

Hannah blushed. "I am Mrs. Sinclair. You've been speaking to my son, Deacon."

"I do beg your pardon." His gaze touched briefly on Deacon, then fixed ingratiatingly upon Monty. "Then I must be here to see you, sir. Tyler Fairfax sent me."

If he needed another reason to dislike the man, that was it. Deacon stepped aside so the two men could shake hands. Monty's expression was mildly befuddled, as if he were trying to piece together the circumstances. Skinner was quick to fill in the whole.

"He sent me about the position you discussed. Someone to oversee the managing of your properties."

As Deacon stiffened in objection and alarm, another voice intruded.

"There must be some mistake."

Garnet swept down the hall to take charge of the discussion.

"This must be Mrs. Prior." Deacon wished he could knock the smarmy smile off the man's face. "A true pleasure to meet you."

But Garnet ignored him. Her attention was on her husband. "Why wasn't I told about this?"

Monty shifted uncomfortably like a repentant child being scolded. "You've been so busy, my dear, I didn't have time to discuss it with you."

"We shall discuss it now."

Monty took ahold of Roscoe's elbow to lead him toward the parlor. "Mr. Skinner has been kind enough to come out all this way, we can at least do him the courtesy of listening to his qualifications. Mrs. Sinclair, might you bring us some refreshment?"

Hannah bowed to his request and quickly headed for the kitchen. But Garnet wouldn't be so easily dismissed.

"Monty, I should like to talk to you in private first."

To Monty's relief, a crash from upstairs and a cry from William sent her hurrying to assess the damage. The moment she was out of sight, Monty gestured to the parlor.

"Mr. Skinner, after you." Then he placed himself purposefully in front of Deacon to block the way. "If you'll excuse us, Mr. Sinclair." The door closed behind him, shutting Deacon out in the hall and out of the conversation concerning the running of the Manor.

The instant Garnet returned after tending to Boone's latest disaster, Deacon demanded, "Why have you brought this stranger in to manage the Manor? No one knows these properties like I do. While I'm wasting my time pushing produce, you're letting some outsider take over what I was raised to control."

She put up a hand to shush him, looking no more pleased than he was by this new development as she reached for the door handle. It turned at almost the same instant and Monty met her with a jovial smile.

"Ah, my dear. Do come in and bid Mr. Skinner welcome. I've just hired him as our new manager."

And as the door closed once more, Deacon had one parting glimpse of a very smug Roscoe Skinner standing on the threshold of all that should have been his.

"How could you do this, Monty?" Garnet railed, as she paced the floor of their shared suite. "How could you bring in that man on Tyler Fairfax's say-so without consulting me first?"

"I did it for you, my dear."

"For me? Why?"

"It's unseemly for you to control the running of this estate. As my wife—"

"I'm not your wife!" She lowered her voice to repeat, "I am not your wife. You've no right to interfere in my plans."

"I have every right. The right of concerned family who does not want to see you get hurt."

"Hurt? You don't think it hurts me to have you going behind my back on something as important as this?"

He refused to be shamed. "My only thought is to protect you, my dear. I am not such a fool as not to see that you are in love with that bastard who betrayed and abandoned you. Don't try to deny it. I'm only distancing him from taking control of your future again. If you must toy with him, keep him involved in something that cannot harm you. Keep him behind his counter and leave the establishment of your place in Pride County to ones who aren't motivated by mistaken desire."

"You make me sound inconsistent and silly, Uncle Monty, as if I am incapable of controlling my emotions around the man who so cruelly manipulated them."

He arched a brow, not needing to say anything.

Garnet huffed in indignation. "You forget what I've endured at his duplicity. I won't be so easily fooled again."

"Of course not, my dear," came his placating words. "And in the meantime, Mr. Skinner will relieve you of the burden of worrying over these acres so you can take the time to socialize and build up a new life for yourself. The life you deserve, Garnet, not the one he left you to."

She said nothing for a time, considering his argument, loving him for his sentiments. Finally, she relented. "All right, Uncle. He can stay. But no more surprises."

He smiled disarmingly. "I'm only thinking of you, my lovely."

And what he was thinking had much to do with his talk with Skinner. After hearing of the man's sterling and unfortunate past, and seeing his handsome face, Monty formed another plan to coincide with his niece's. Let her have her revenge on Sinclair for treating her so shamefully, but let her also find happiness apart from the threat to her heart that he still represented. She needed a distraction in that area, someone new to stir her passions and get her thinking of something other than the Confederate spy who had stolen more than just her trust.

And he knew such a man had arrived when he saw Roscoe Skinner.

Now to convince Garnet. Their game wouldn't last forever, and he had laid his own plans without her knowledge. Skinner could fit in nicely to pick up the pieces after he'd gone.

His niece needed a real husband to find true happiness. But he couldn't bow out of that position until he had a replacement in hand. Yes, Roscoe Skinner could work out very nicely, indeed, and what man would be objecting to taking a beautiful young wife with a hefty bankroll?

As long as that man wasn't Sinclair.

Chapter 14

~ ∞ ~

Like her son, Hannah Sinclair moved about the parlor with a graceful ease that defied a station of servitude. In watching her, Garnet's awareness of what a fraud she herself was intensified to a hurtful degree.

She'd had a rushed course on social practices from Monty. She knew the outward dos and don'ts—all from a man's point of view. He'd helped refine her speech. He'd sent her to the best clothiers to drape her in finery. But beneath the trappings of success resided the same uncertain country girl.

What on earth had made her think she could fit in here among these people who were bred to elegance and plenty?

"Good morning, Mrs. Prior."

Caught before she could make a discreet exit, she returned the older woman's smile somewhat wanly. "Good morning, Mrs. Sinclair."

"Was there something you needed?"

"No. You've taken care of everything before it

even comes to mind." Because that sounded a trifle petulant, she added, "And if I haven't thanked you, let me do so now."

"There's no need, ma'am. It's my pleasure . . . and my job."

That was the mark of true breeding: slipping in a barb of censure so gently, one never felt the stab of it. Deserving the prick of conscience, Garnet gave before a battering of guilt, something she'd never anticipated when laying out her plans. She hadn't expected to suffer such empathy for the losses of her enemies. But they didn't feel like enemies, now that she knew them. She only felt more isolated and ashamed.

"I would like to thank you . . . and apologize."

Putting down her feather duster, Hannah gave her full attention to the new mistress of the house. "Apologize? For what, dear?"

Garnet blinked back the sudden burn of regret. "For taking your home. You've been so gracious in your treatment of me and my family, and we've done you the most grievous harm."

Hannah came to place a supporting hand upon Garnet's shoulder. Her tone was gentle, without a hint of reproof. "Dear girl, you weren't responsible for our circumstance. If you hadn't bought our mortgage, someone else would have. Someone who might not have been so kind as to let us remain among the things we love. So there is no need for you to apologize. We are far better off than many of our friends.

There are worse things to lose than pride and property."

Garnet nodded. How well she understood that sentiment. Losing a loved one, losing one's history and identity—those were much worse. Allowing a bruised heart to encourage a fit of retribution, could that be any better?

"My dear, are you all right?" Hannah coaxed, with a concern that only deepened her despair. "You seem so low of spirits this morning."

"This isn't how I expected it to be, is all," she admitted with complete honesty. "I fit like a square peg in a rounded hole."

"It's not apparent to anyone but you." When she saw that claim had failed to lessen the younger woman's woeful look, she added, "What can I do to help?"

Her sincerity overwhelmed Garnet to the point of weeping. But she held on to that last scrap of dignity to confess, "I don't believe anyone can perform the miracle of transforming a Cumberland country girl into bluegrass belle. I've put on the outside affectations, but I've no knowledge of what's required. Monty wants me to give a grand party." Her laugh was fragile with inadequacy. "I've never entertained more than one person at a time and fear I'll shame him and this house most disgracefully."

Hannah's arm banded her easily. "Is that all that has you bothered? I can help with that, if you'd like me to. I've prepared a daughter for society, and there's no great mystery there. It's all a bluff, you see, learning to hide your true feelings behind a smile and a show of manners."

"Really?" Garnet's tone quivered with hope. "You'd help me?"

"Of course, my dear. Sinclair Manor is known for its hospitality, and you will do it proud."

Measuring out lengths of bird's-eye for diapers, toting strong-smelling onion starts to the back of one-horse carts, and dipping green coffee beans a pound at a time out of the Brazilian jute bags wasn't the future Deacon had envisioned for himself.

It wasn't so much the embarrassment of his lowered situation. Not one of his customers treated him with a fraction less respect than he'd known as the master of his estate because he refused to act any less the man. No citizen of Pride was going to see him humbled in word or spirit. He had too much breeding for that. And he had too much intensified training to be selling plows to cut the land rather than directing where those cuts should be made upon acres of his own.

He was a Sinclair, carrying the expectations of all those long dead and buried Sinclairs, men who'd forged their own way and controlled their own destinies. Not men who sold turpentine to combat rheumatism. It was the disappointment of all those generations that weighed heavily upon him. Behind it, he could hear his father's firm dictates: "You were made for better things than this, Deacon. Don't disgrace me."

What had he done all his life but try to escape that claim?

And now some sly-eyed stranger on Tyler Fairfax's say-so was making it impossible.

He thanked the dressmaker, Myrna Bishop, for the small sackful of sewing notions she'd purchased and nodded that he'd relay her best wishes to his mother and sister. As he put her coin in the till, he studied the scant pieces of change wryly. At this rate, his commission on sales would earn him a handful of Sinclair dirt every six months.

"A sad state of affairs, eh, Mr. Sinclair?"

He sighed as Herschel added two pennies. "There must be a way to increase our profits."

"There's the space overhead dat sits empty. If you could find someone to let the upstairs—"

"Excuse me." Myrna Bishop returned to the counter. Deacon hoped it wasn't to get her money back. "Did I hear you say you had space for rent?"

"The whole second floor. Do you know anyone who might be interested, Mrs. Bishop?" He refused to give his optimism a free hand until he had rent money in it.

"My niece from Mobile is coming to stay with me. She lost her husband and is planning to start a millinery business. She'd talked of moving on to Louisville, but there's no reason she couldn't set up right here, with family close by."

"When she arrives, have her come talk to me.

I'm sure we can make some mutually beneficial arrangement."

Myrna gave Deacon an appreciative once-over, seeing him in a new light, then smiled. "Perhaps you could, at that."

It didn't take Roscoe Skinner long to make his authority clear in Pride. By afternoon, he was in the store with several of the Manor's new share-croppers, working out appalling terms of inter-est for liens against their crops to come. Once they'd determined the profit to be made off the square plots of land and figured a weighty amount to be taken off the top, the paltry remains were divided down into monthly allot-ments of credit redeemable at the mercantile for all the necessities of their meager lives.

New to these dealings, Deacon stood back and watched Herschel hammer out a tough but fair arrangement on behalf of the store. It was Skinner who tightened the financial noose almost to strangling those who would work the land. They cast woebegone looks up at Deacon, as if pleading with him to intercede. They must have known he was powerless, but those looks haunted him just the same. Had it been his land, he would never have drained them beyond the point of living comfortably to the mere grimness of existing. That was no way for a man to stand with pride in front of his family.

Skinner, with his broad, blameless smile and

his ruthless manipulating of unfortunate circumstance, was the perfect negotiator. He'd leave the tenants frustrated with their lot, pinning their dissatisfaction erroneously upon the store or the Priors. Unless the Priors had set the terms of his dealings.

Which was another thing altogether.

Garnet herself arrived close to closing, just as Skinner wrung the final juice of independence from the last sharecropper of the day. He greeted her with an ingratiating bow and the presentation of his ledger.

"Feast your eyes on them figures, Mrs. Prior, and tell me I ain't done a good day's work."

While she was tallying up his mathematics, he was admiring another sort of figure: the one sweetly encased in turquoise satin.

Deacon busied himself counting up the day's receipts, his jaw locked, his fierce glare cast downward. Where had Fairfax found this particular polecat? Or had they just naturally scented one another out under the same dark porch?

"My," Garnet murmured. "This speaks of an impressive profit. The farmers were agreeable to the terms?"

"Oh, yes, ma'am."

Agree or starve. Deacon started counting over again, trying to concentrate on what he was doing instead of what Skinner was doing with his roving gaze.

"And this is legal?"

"Yes, ma'am. Set up by our government, ma'am, to get the farmers back on their feet."

Knock the feet out from under them, was more like it.

"I'm ready to close up, Mrs. Prior," Deacon announced, slamming the cash drawer to punctuate his claim.

"If you'd wait just a moment, Mr. Sinclair, I'd like a word with you. Have Mr. Rosen file these documents, Mr. Skinner. And yes," she added almost reluctantly, "you've done a good day's work."

"Thank you, ma'am. Kind of you to say so." With a bobbing bow, he was quick to rejoin Herschel in the back room to finalize the terms in the store's bookkeeping records.

When they were alone, Garnet demanded, "You have been glowering like a lion ever since I arrived. Is there a problem, Mr. Sinclair?"

"You know the problem. We've already discussed it, remember?"

"Refresh my memory."

"Fairfax is behind that man's employment. Whom do you think he's loyal to?"

"Doesn't loyalty go to the highest bidder, to your best experience? Skinner looks to make a tidy fortune off his dealings."

"His thievery, you mean."

"What he's doing isn't legal?" Concern puckered her brow.

"Legal but immoral."

Relieved, she countered, "An odd judgment for you to be making, sir."

"He doesn't care about those poor people scratching a living out of the dirt. The terms he's forced them to take will swallow them whole."

"And that bothers you, does it?" Her black eyes snapped in angry challenge. "Since when does the welfare of some farmer concern the mighty Deacon Sinclair? Why do you care what they suffer, as long as you receive your cut of the proceeds? Your concern is as false as your warnings, sir. Keep them to yourself in the future. Good day."

As she stormed out, Deacon ground his teeth on a particularly odd truth.

He did care.

He did care what happened to the people of Pride. A new revelation for someone raised to contain his interests to within his own property lines.

"How goes it, Mr. Skinner? Are they treating you well out at the Manor?"

Roscoe joined Tyler Fairfax on the porch of his family's home. For all their wealth, the property was in a shabby state of disrepair. Rather like Tyler himself. He was draped in one of the dusty iron chairs, as rumpled as an old bedsheet and reeking of his family's product. A large tumbler dangled from one hand with a single swallow remaining. Despite his negligent appearance, the sharpness of his gaze contrasted with his obvious drunkenness.

Roscoe eased himself down on the top step and allowed a pleased smile to spread. "Took me in like family and opened their ledgers wide."

Tyler laughed and sucked up the last of his bourbon. "Told you, didn't I? You keep your eyes and your ears open and you let me know what our dear friends at the Manor are up to. It's important that they trust you."

"I don't see a problem with the old man, but Sinclair—he's another matter."

For an instant, Tyler's amiable expression changed, twisting into something dangerous. "Sinclair has always been another matter. Don't you underestimate him. The man is as deadly as a rattler, and he'll strike if you force him into a coil."

"I ain't afraid of him."

"Then you're a fool."

Roscoe let his own mask slip for a moment. His black eyes glittered with lethal purpose. "Don't call me that, or you'll find out that Sinclair ain't the only dangerous man around here."

Their stares locked for a long minute, then Tyler turned back to his empty glass with a chuckle. "Maybe you are his match. That's why I sent for you. You had no problem playing both sides for your own benefit during the war and we both reaped handsome rewards due to your lack of . . . conscience. There's money to be made here, Roscoe. And it might as well be ours."

Skinner smiled and the oily sheen disappeared from his gaze. "I couldn't agree with you more."

"Get the old goat to lean on you for advice, then I'll tell you what to whisper in his ear."

"What you got in mind, Fairfax?"

Tyler grinned. "Don't trouble yourself with my plans, Roscoe. You do what I tell you and you'll be a rich man."

Roscoe shrugged and gained his feet. He wasn't all that interested in Tyler's goals, anyway.

He'd pretend to work for Fairfax just as he pretended to work for Prior. He'd collect double pay, which he didn't mind doing, and he'd play both sides with equal indifference. It wasn't the money that mattered, nor did he care about the small-town politics in Pride. He had his own agenda concerning Deacon Sinclair. And to that end, he would act out the expected roles. After all, that was what he and Deacon had been taught to do during the war. And it was time Sinclair learned that he was just a little bit better at it.

"I'll keep you posted, Fairfax."

"You do that, Roscoe. You do that."

Tyler leaned back and watched the man climb aboard his blooded stallion and rein it away. Roscoe Skinner wasn't the type you trusted with your secrets or your intentions, but Tyler knew he'd get his money's worth. Skinner would finish what he'd started, but it was wise to remember that he always had more than one iron glowing in the fire. Having been burned once by impulsive behavior, Tyler had no desire to feel the flame again. He was studying the disfiguring scars on his hands for a long brooding moment, then yelled, "Tilly, fetch me another bottle."

The movement at the door brought his head around in a leisurely loll, but it wasn't his family's maid Matilda. His insides seized up, the liquor roiling in an uneasy tide.

"Daddy, you shouldn't be up."

Knowing his son's concern was as false as his smile, Cole Fairfax ignored both to wheeze, "What scheme you got cookin', boy?"

"Nothin', Daddy."

Cole's cane struck the doorjamb. At the sound, Tyler leapt from his indolent slouch in the chair to a defensive stance.

"Don't lie to me, boy. I can always tell when you're lying, you little cur. Now what mischief are you makin'?"

"Just playin' at politics, Daddy. Seein' to our best interests, as always."

Cole made a disgusted sound. "You gotta have some kind of character and seriousness to politic, boy, and you got neither. You'd best tend our business here and leave the rest to them that are suited 'fore you go doing something stupid that'll cost us money."

"I'm not risking anything of ours, Daddy."

"Everything with you is a bad risk, whelp. You quit your playin' and get down to some hard facts. I'm dying, boy."

Tyler's expression never altered from its fixed glaze of caution. But in the flicker of his eyes was the question *"When?"*

Cole leaned against his cane, struggling for air and with his loathing for the one he depended upon. "This will all be yours, boy, and you'd better start takin' that serious or I'll leave it all to charity and you'll have to learn how to make a livin' off your own misbegotten talents."

"I'm takin' care of things just fine, Daddy. You can trust me—"

"Trust you?" That bellow cost him long minutes of painful coughing. Finally, he concluded with a raspy chuckle. "I'd sooner put a serpent to my breast. I got my eye on you, boy, and you won't betray me like your faithless mother did, you hear?"

Tyler waited for the sound of his father's halting steps to carry the wasted figure back into his parlor lair, for the scent of sickness and the shivery sense of fear to abate before he took a deep, cleansing breath.

"You old bastard, you got no idea what I'm capable of. But you'll find out," he promised. "And won't you be surprised. You'll all be surprised."

Chapter 15

⁓◦◦⁓

Within the week, replies to the Priors' evening party began streaming in. Staring at the stack of affirmatives, Garnet felt panic press upon her. This would be her proving ground, and these people her judges. They were attending not out of friendship or respect, but because of curiosity.

They all wanted to see who had ousted Pride's premier family. And all hoped to watch fireworks as they appeared under the same roof.

She would be scrutinized, categorized, and picked apart. Would any of them be fooled by the bluff she was learning to play under Hannah's tutelage? Or would they all see exactly what she was—a backwoods girl who was buying her way into their circles with money she hadn't earned?

Now she understood Deacon a little better. This was the playacting he had been called to do in the service of the South. Only he was a smooth professional, and she an amateur.

Beneath her determination to succeed was the

remembered truth that Deacon had surrendered up his first love because his family and peers found her unacceptable. If she wanted to be a part of his life, either directly or on the periphery, she would have to win over not just the tender-hearted Hannah, but his suspicious sister and the town's elite. Once that task was accomplished, her only hurdle was Deacon himself.

Monty was right: she did love him. He continually impressed her with glimmers of humanity that seemed to surprise him as much as those around him. He was maturing from isolated aristocrat to a caring member of a community. And as uncomfortable as he was with the progression, he wore it well. A decent man lurked beneath his surface indifference. That was the man she'd fallen in love with and she was beginning to suspect that he was more that man than the coldly motivated spy who chose duty over emotional involvement.

Clutching at all she'd learned to steady her quaking knees and welcoming smile, Garnet stood in the parlor at nine o'clock to receive her guests, and for the next hour, bowed and smiled and struggled to remember the faces and names of the endless parade of Pride citizens come to shine in their dressy best. In a show of support that puzzled and invited whispering, Hannah Sinclair was often at her side, her hand lightly on Garnet's elbow in a show of silent approval—almost as if she were bringing the young woman out into Pride society under her wing.

And the most puzzled of all was her son.

Deacon stood apart from the guests out of habit, and from that separate stand was able to observe the happenings dispassionately. He tried not to think about the last elaborate affair under the Manor's roof. His mother and father had been the ones to receive the guests. His father, in a full dress uniform that had yet to see the wear of battle, was a handsome sentinel at his mother's side.

Patrice had been a vivacious girl with the county's blades hovering around her. That night, she'd announced her engagement to Jonah Glendower, Reeve Garrett's half-brother. It was his father's triumphant moment: his daughter set to wed in what he considered a prime match between the area's most powerful families. He'd been proud and content. After the guests had gone he drew Deacon aside to pour modest glasses of bourbon and toast the future of the Sinclair name. Then he'd taken Deacon's vow that his son would carry on in the family tradition if he didn't return from the supposedly brief confrontation with the North. Deacon gave his oath with the same solemnness with which his father had surrendered his life.

Thank God his father had never seen him break it.

"A lot's changed since then."

The sound of his sister's voice and the gentle touch of her hand on his arm startled Deacon from his ruminations.

"Everything's changed," he amended, before

looking down at her. Heavy with Reeve's child, she was no longer that flighty girl who'd bedeviled him when they were children. He liked the sensible woman his sister had become, and begrudgingly he admired her husband for his ability to protect her and make her happy.

She put a hand to the small of her back, reminding Deacon of her condition. His arm banded her in immediate support.

"Would you like to sit down?"

"No. I'd like to have this baby so folks would quit fussing so much. I thought Mama would have a conniption when I showed up, but Mrs. Prior insisted that I be here, fat with child and all. But for Mama's sake, I'll keep a low profile."

Deacon glanced at her big belly. "That'll be kinda hard to do."

She poked his ribs with her elbow, then grew serious.

"She's quite the hostess, your Mrs. Prior."

Deacon's features hardened, the light leaving his eyes. "She's not *my* anything."

Patrice didn't bother arguing, which bothered him plenty.

"She's very lovely. No wonder you fell in love with her."

Squirming under his sister's observations, Deacon switched his to the woman in question. Yes, she was lovely. Lovely and poised and looking every inch the society matron. As hostess, she was dressed for tactful understatement, not wishing to outshine any of her guests. He could see his mother's touch there. But why Hannah Sinclair would school her in etiquette the way she would a daughter was a mystery to him.

Garnet *was* every inch the lady. In her modest gown of pale blue moiré with a pattern of raised velvet flowers of the same subdued hue imprinted upon the full sweeping hem, she was every man's dream of a hostess for his home: tasteful, refined, and yet simmering with an innate sensuality that all the manners in the world couldn't contain. She was the kind of woman a man would show off on his arm with pride while dreaming of the night to come when propriety could be cast off along with elegant clothing. His stare cut to Montgomery Prior, who was chuckling over some story with Judge Banning. Is that what he was dreaming when his gaze touched fondly upon his bride?

Jealousy burned like a brand in Deacon's heart.

"Deacon, I would like to sit down."

Patrice's quiet request called him back from his envious musings. With a solicitous hand upon her elbow, he guided her to the fringe of the company, holding her steady as she lowered into a chair like a freight wagon dropping a load of bricks. Reeve was instantly there to attend her, nodding to dismiss Deacon, then fussing until Patrice slapped at his hands.

"I'm fine," she insisted testily.

But in studying her drawn expression, Reeve could see that wasn't true.

"What's wrong, 'Trice?"

"Nothing that can be easily mended, I'm afraid." Suddenly, her mood shifted. "Reeve, would you be good enough to fetch me a glass of lemonade? I find myself positively parched."

She'd spotted Tyler Fairfax arriving with his sister, her best friend, Starla Dodge, and her husband, the town's banker. The unlikely trio made her arch a brow, but she was quick to call Tyler over with a beckoning smile. He took up her hand in his gloved one and held it gently. His jaded stare softened with an affection reserved for her and Starla.

"I hope you don't mind me sayin' so, but darlin', you sure look beautiful this evening."

"I look like one of your bourbon barrels," she complained, flattered nonetheless. She nodded toward Dodge. "It seems you've mended your fences with your brother-in-law."

"The Yank?" Tyler shrugged. "He ain't so bad. Star's crazy for him, so what can I do?" His voice lowered a notch. "It would be bad form to kill him, now that he's making me an uncle."

Patrice's gaze leapt to the always glamorous Starla, then back to her proudly grinning brother. "Starla and Dodge?" At his nod, she pouted. "Why didn't she say something to me?"

"She wants to keep it quiet until she's sure things will go well, after her losing the baby last time and all." He looked away, uncomfortable with the topic and the painful memories that clung there. "The Yank, he spoils her something fierce, and she swears she's healthy as a hog, so I guess it's all right to let you know."

"I'll scold her about it later. Sit down with me for a minute. We haven't talked for ages."

Tyler's expression lost all its sharp edges, his look so needy, so anxious, it caused Patrice a moment of distress. The ill-will between them over the actions he'd taken against Reeve before their marriage put a damper on the friendship they'd once shared and suddenly, she realized that she'd missed it and him, the unrepentant scapegrace. She tugged at his hand, encouraging him to sit. His obvious pleasure twisted poignantly about her heart, but she blocked it in deference to her purpose.

"Tyler, what do you know about the Priors?"

The guarded look returned in a blink. "Why do you ask, darlin'?"

"I was just curious about how you came to sell the Manor to them."

His caution intensified. "Patrice, I don't want to get into no argument with you about your brother selling off the mortgage to me."

She pressed his hand gently, as if she no longer felt any bitterness over that situation. "I don't want to argue either."

He regarded her warily for a moment, then fixed his attention on the comely Mrs. Prior. "She sought me out, wanting to buy the place. Real insistent, she was."

"Wanting to buy any plantation?"

He shook his head. "No. Just this one."

She followed his stare. "Why?"

"I don't know, darlin'. You might want to ask your saintly brother what he done to make her want to pay three times what this place is worth just to stand there in that doorway, smiling at all the neighbors."

The idea of getting her stoic brother to spill his guts concerning a lost love affair was as far-fetched as it was unlikely. So that left one alternative.

"Maybe I'll just have to get to know Garnet Prior better."

For the first half of the evening, Garnet concentrated on Hannah's lessons. It was during this critical time that she would pass or lose her laurels. She circulated in an unobtrusive manner, speaking in a gently modulated voice, trying to commit the names of her guests to memory so as not to embarrass herself or them upon their next meeting.

As hostess, she was excused from dancing in the quadrilles. There were enough ladies to fill the sets, while Monty attended those who didn't dance with a courtly charm that had them blushing. She noticed he paid particular attention to Hannah Sinclair, and if she noticed, so would others. Making note to speak to him about it, she had no time as the first half of the dance programme ended and guests were excused to a separate room for supper. Monty had offered his arm to the widow Sinclair, leav-

ing her adrift in a sea of unfamiliar faces. To her
dismay, she saw Roscoe Skinner approaching.
He was groomed and sleek and grinning like a
fox. Something about the man made her inex-
plicably uncomfortable. Perhaps the directness
of his stare that seemed to peel away her outer
defenses to get at inner thoughts she'd prefer to
keep private. Or the way Monty kept pushing
them together.

"Might I escort you to supper, Mrs. Prior?"

She glanced up in surprise, staring at the elbow
Deacon offered as if she'd never been extended
such a courtesy before. In truth, it wasn't one
she'd expected from him. Then she saw his attention wasn't focused on her, but rather on Roscoe.
Her moment of tender anticipation faded. His
gallantry was meant to thwart the new overseer,
not to please her. Skinner drew up short, eyes
narrowing at the interception of his plans, but he
bowed as if there were no hard feelings. The glitter in his stare said there were plenty.

Glumly, her features set in lines as somber as
his own, Garnet placed her fingertips upon Deacon's sleeve so he could lead her, as hostess, into
the dining room first. Monty brought up the rear
as guests were seated agreeably, the host at one
end, the hostess at the other. As her escort, Deacon wordlessly assumed a position at her side.
After the salmon and fried smelt were trowled
out to each guest, she was relieved when he
offered her a glass of wine. She needed the forti-
fier with him so close at hand. Raising the first

glass, Deacon bowed to her as lady of the house, the other gentlemen following suit.

"I trust you are having an enjoyable evening," Deacon murmured, never looking directly at her. "From all indications, you are a success."

"Thank you." *Thank you, Hannah.* "You are too kind."

"No, I'm not. You know me better than that."

Waiting for the servants to finish dishing up the meal, she was relieved from the obligation of answering. But yes, she did know better.

She did know that he could be kind, though he chose not to be. She noticed that the party guests went out of their way to give him plenty of space, addressing him only with polite nods of acknowledgment, as if afraid to confront him directly. She didn't see him as an intimating figure, but rather as a lonely one. But before she could engage him in inclusive conversation, she caught a blur of movement darting in from the hallway under the table. Ulysses had somehow come to visit.

Oh no!

She was halfway out of her seat, gesturing frantically for the nearest waiter, when Boone burst into the dining room like a wildly galloping horse. He made a beeline for the table, too intent upon the chase to realize what Garnet saw at once: that he couldn't easily fit between the guests or under the edge. He lunged, knocking the guests on either side from their seats as he disappeared beneath the table. Unfortunately, he tangled in the scalloped lace hem of the linen cloth, dragging it under with him.

And all the place settings, wineglasses, and silver followed, avalanching into the laps of all those on that side of the table.

In that instant, Garnet saw her social doom.

When the last apology was made and the final guest on his away, Garnet left the servants to the disaster in the dining room, and, with the mournful sound of Boone howling on his rope outside, she slowly climbed the stairs. Hannah already occupied her spot on the edge of William's bed, assuring the little boy that neither he nor the kitten he hugged to his chest would be cast out in disgrace. She watched the older woman tuck the boy in with gentle words, missing her own mother, thinking how lucky Deacon was to have enjoyed the tender care of this woman all his life. She would have entered the room to add her own reassurances, but William snuggled in and was immediately asleep with the purring puff of fur balled up on his chest.

Feeling unneeded, she wandered to her room, having just closed the door when she heard Monty's low voice mixing with Hannah's dulcet tones. After they moved along the hall together, a sense of failure and isolation crept in through her downed defenses. She caught a glimpse of herself in the mirror—the fine lady of the house in wine-stained satin, her features lined with anxiety and despair. A fraud in her own heart, and now, in everyone else's mind.

He almost missed her. Her shadow skimmed along the dark tracery of the leafless bushes—a figure in men's trousers with a most provocative walk. There was such solitude in her lonely travels, but respecting her private thoughts and her need to work through them, Deacon sat on the back porch rail, allowing her the peaceful embrace of the night and himself the pleasure of simply watching her.

He wasn't alarmed when she disappeared into the darkness, knowing she'd eventually return. Whatever preyed upon her mind, and he had a fairly good idea of what that was, she kept to the moonlight for over an hour before approaching the house with shoulders slumped and spirits dragging.

"Nice night for a walk."

His voice startled her into drawing up short. For a long beat, she remained safely in the shadows, then finally came to the stairs.

"If you say something cuttingly clever about not making silk purses from sow's ears, I'll be forced to shoot you, and I really don't need the extra burden tonight."

Because her retort smacked of the impertinent young woman living within hewn wood walls and not the sophisticate he'd seen of late, Deacon allowed a lopsided smile. "I wouldn't want to be responsible for any more of your burdens."

She stared up at him as if doubting that was true. In the muted light, in her mannish garb, with her heavy hair concealed beneath a flat crowned hat, he was looking once again into the face of innocence that had captured him five long years ago. And as tears made silvery traces down stubbornly held features, that endearing contrast made him lose his heart all over again.

She stiffened at the soft sound of his laughter.

"I shouldn't be surprised that you'd find my misfortune funny."

"It's not that," he chuckled. "I was just remembering the look on Skinner's face when that bowl of gravy landed in his lap."

Garnet drew a pained breath. He could see her shoulders tremble. Feeling poorly about taking amusement from her distress, he was about to apologize when she said in a slightly strangled voice, "Or Tyler Fairfax covered in buttered yams."

His grin flashed bright and they shared a moment of quiet laughter at the ridiculousness in her social tragedy. Slowly, she came up onto the porch and he stepped aside, expecting her to pass. Instead, she stopped beside him, still chuckling helplessly even as more tears glimmered upon her cheeks. Unable to help himself, he brushed one trail away with the leisurely swipe of his thumb.

"You'll survive it, Garnet. At least you'll be the talk of the town tomorrow. Isn't that a hostess's fondest wish?"

"As a topic of envy, yes, of sport, no." Beneath the wry observation lurked a quiver of vulnerability that acted upon a part of Deacon's soul that he thought he'd lost.

"No one will make sport of you," he promised, following that claim with a rumbling, "At least, not in my presence."

She stared up at him, puzzled by his compassion, by his intensity.

Then all curiosities fell away as he bent and kissed her.

Too surprised at first to do more than instinctively part her lips, Garnet let the sweet sensations overcome her staunch defenses. After all, wasn't this magical taste of heaven what she'd yearned for every night since he'd ridden out of her front yard? A soft sound of confusion escaped as a sigh.

Deacon . . . don't . . . don't stop.

When his hands fit with a possessive familiarity upon the slope of her shoulders, she swayed into him, surrendering to her need to know again the passionate response only this man woke in her. Heat roared to places too long ignored. Her breasts ached. The juncture of her thighs throbbed in tight little pulses, demanding more than just his kiss to heal the miseries of this night, to bridge the loneliness of the years.

Hands fisting at the collar of his coat, she met the reacquainting movement of his mouth, slant for hungry slant, feasting on the pleasures with a starved urgency. Letting the tide of remembered emotions catch her in its delicious rip and ebb. Gasping for breath and for some smidgeon of control, she lay her head against his chest, her arms circling his neck in a desperate attempt to remain standing on suddenly unreliable legs. Her body was taut and trembling, the same tension straining her voice as she said his name in a torment of want.

"Deacon . . . "

He responded, but not in the way she'd hoped. She felt him withdraw before he ever moved an inch. His muscles took on a denying stiffness. His ragged breathing slowed and grew regular upon one lengthy inhalation. And hands that had pulled her to him with such claiming forcefulness, now pushed her away with firm purpose.

She didn't want to look up to read what was in his expression, but she had to know, and forced her gaze to lift in search of his. His slated stare was impenetrable, keeping her away, just as his kisses had called her closer an instant earlier. The change in signals deepened her confusion and left her vulnerable to his next painfully proper statement.

"I shouldn't have done that. I had no right. I've insulted you and your husband, and for that I apologize."

He stepped back, setting the distance between them once more, a distance that seemed all the more impossible to breach, considering his shattering aloofness. As if their passion was a fleeting mistake that could be quickly forgiven and forgotten and not a long, smoldering remnant of their first encounter.

His remoteness gave her the courage to adopt a like attitude. "No apology necessary," she assured him with a thready conviction. Then she let him walk away while every fiber of her emotional being cried out for her to reach out, to grab on, to not let go of what he'd betrayed with that kiss.

The desire was still there.

But if love lingered along with it, would it be so easy for him to extinguish the same feelings shivering through her with a feverish weakening of heart and mind?

She sank down upon the porch steps, her fragile mood allowing sobs to escape her in silent shudders.

What had she done? Had she outsmarted herself by creating a convenient marriage that was meant to protect her and that now, it would seem, prevented her from achieving the happiness she sought?

How could she ever unravel the web she'd spun, now that she was trapped within its sticky lies?

Chapter 16

To Garnet's surprise, a tray full of calling cards awaited her when she finally managed to shake off the effects of a near sleepless night to brave the new day. She was still staring at the sight incomprehensibly over her morning coffee when Patrice Garrett was announced.

Patrice summed up the significance of the cards with a smile. "Goodness, you *are* a success, Mrs. Prior."

While waiting for her voluminous guest to make herself comfortable on one of the parlor sofas, Garnet said, "Please, call me Garnet. And why do you say that?"

"The speed in which your hospitality is repaid with cards or visits determines how desirable you are to our fickle society. I would say you are a much sought-after commodity. Congratulations."

With a confused sigh, Garnet sank into an adjacent chair. "After the disastrous, not to mention messy, evening I gave them? I don't understand. I'd think I'd be avoided like some plague."

"Ah, but you see, you provided unequaled entertainment and handled your embarrassment with proper dignity. That's what your guests are applauding. They admire nothing more than courage under fire, and you, my dear Garnet, sustained a direct hit without flinching."

After turning down an offer of refreshments, Patrice got to the point of her visit with another unerring volley. "How do you know my brother? I understand from him that you met during the war."

Instantly on guard, Garnet found that her curiosity was nonetheless sparked. "He spoke of me?" She phrased the question with infinite care, aware that Patrice would pick up any nuance in her voice. It was one thing to fool a man and quite another to deceive another woman.

"Not by name, but you obviously made a considerable impression on him." Revealing that tantalizing tidbit, Patrice fussed with the folds of her skirt, pretending not to be shrewdly watching for a reaction to her words. Garnet understood the purpose of the exchange. In order to learn a little, she would have to give a little. She sensed that Deacon's sister was a cunning barterer. So she would tempt with a sliver of information, too.

"He arrived at my door early in the war. I treated him for a bullet wound from some deserters looking to steal his horse." She said that smoothly, as if she didn't know now that nothing about his arrival was coincidental. "He was on his way here to tell you your father had died." Patrice looked so perplexed, Garnet paused. Had he lied about that, too?

"Deacon never came home with that news."

"Your father didn't die in battle?"

"He did, only Deacon didn't bring us the news in person. It was more than two years before we saw him, just briefly, and then not again until after the war was over. I wasn't aware that he'd been wounded. My family owes you its thanks, then."

"Just doing my Christian duty." As Deacon had been doing his Confederate duty. He hadn't taken the news of his father's death home because he'd been busy betraying her. Some of her anger must have shown in her expression, for Patrice pounced like an expectant cat.

"And what duty prompted you to come here to pull his future out from under him? What did he do to make you hate him so very much?"

Garnet looked her squarely in the eye. "He used information that he got from me to put my father wrongfully in prison. Where he died."

No shock, no denial appeared on Patrice's face, just sadness. "I'm sorry for your loss, Garnet. I can't pretend that I know exactly what my brother did for the Confederacy. My guess is that they were unpleasant things, things that had him risking his life and telling lies to protect it."

Garnet came up out of her chair to pace in short, fierce strides. "I didn't have your brother at gunpoint, Mrs. Garrett. He came to me with deliberate lies and used them to destroy my family and my trust."

"It was war."

She cast off Patrice's excuse with a flick of her hand. "It was unfair. And it was unconscionable. He didn't have to do his job so . . . well." She clamped her lips together to seal in the rest of her disgrace and disillusionment. But she could see from the softening of the other woman's expression that she'd guessed more than Garnet had intended.

"Then I apologize for my brother, because he won't, no matter how much he might regret what he did. He wasn't raised to say that he was wrong or that he was sorry. A prideful failing in my family, I'm afraid."

"My father is dead. My home was lost, burned to the ground. I don't want an apology or excuses."

"Then what do you want?"

Garnet hesitated at that gently asked question. Then she knew, with a crystal clarity. She wanted to hear that it hadn't all been a lie. She wanted to know that her trust and her love hadn't been wrongly given. She needed to learn that the father of her child was not a cold, emotionless monster. But that was not what she told Patrice.

"Who was Jassy?"

She could see by Patrice's sudden blankness that she'd fired a well-placed shot.

"Jassy? She was my childhood playmate, my best friend. Deacon told you about her?"

"He said she was a servant here." And that he'd been in love with her. "Where is she now?"

"She was sold."

"Sold?"

"She was a slave. She was sold South when she and I were thirteen and Deacon sixteen."

Reeling with that information, Garnet resumed her seat in a daze. He'd been in love with a slave girl. And his family had sold her to save themselves from the disgrace. Dear God . . . poor Deacon.

"Mama, can Boone come back inside now? Mr. Sinclair took Ulysses back to the store with him, so there won't be no more chasing."

William skidded to a halt when he saw his mother wasn't alone.

"Darling, I have company. We'll talk about this later."

"But Mama, Boone's been out all night—"

"William, you know Mrs. Garrett, Mr. Sinclair's sister."

William bobbed a quick acknowledgment, then returned to his petition. "It weren't Boone's fault, Mama. It was mine. Maybe I should be tied up in the yard instead a him."

Garnet's stern look dissolved into a tolerant smile. "You may let him inside, but make sure his feet are clean."

"I will," he vowed cheerily, darting for the

door. He pulled up short, remembering his manners. Turning toward Patrice, he assumed a stiff posture and bowed. " 'Scuse me, Mrs. Garrett."

Patrice began to smile, then the gesture froze before full completion.

"Patrice, are you all right?"

She blinked when the boy disappeared down the hall, seeming to come out of her sudden trance. "I'm sorry, it's just that he looked so much like—"

Deacon.

She didn't have to finish. Garnet knew with a sick certainty that Patrice had recognized her brother in the boy.

Patrice fixed her with a penetrating stare. "You have to tell him. He has a right to know."

"No," Garnet argued with a fearful ferocity. "He has no rights where I'm concerned."

Patrice struggled to lift off the sofa. "If you won't tell him, I will."

"No! You can't." Garnet had started toward her when Patrice suddenly fell back, one hand at the small of her back, the other pressed to her huge middle. A look of surprise was rapidly replaced by one of distress.

"Patrice—?"

"I thought it was just a backache," she panted.

"How long have you been having pains?"

"Since yesterday."

She gasped as the floor about her feet grew wet with birthing water . . . and blood. Staring at it, her features tightened with a new source of dismay.

"The baby . . . "

Alarmed, Garnet fought for calm as she called for one of the house servants, then spoke reassuringly to the pregnant woman. "Don't worry. I'm sure everything's fine."

But abrupt wrenching pangs added to Patrice's anxiety. She gripped Garnet's hands frantically to plead, "Where's my mama?"

One of the maids peeked in at that moment and went wide-eyed with fear.

"Where's Mrs. Sinclair?"

She shook her head at Garnet's terse demand. "She went into town with Mr. Deacon this morning."

"Reeve," Patrice groaned. "I want Reeve."

"Bitsy, wake Mr. Prior and tell him what's happened. Get Mrs. Harkness from the kitchen and have her take Mrs. Garrett to my room upstairs. Have a horse saddled. I'm riding for the doctor."

"And Reeve."

"And for Mr. Garrett." Garnet patted Patrice's clutching hands. "You just relax as best you can, Patrice. I'll take care of everything."

Time wasn't a luxury she could afford. Garnet raced upstairs, tearing off her fancy morning gown, replacing it with britches and one of Monty's white shirts. She hurried down the steps, coming face to pallid face with Patrice as she was being helped from the parlor by two of the servants. A blotchy trail of crimson followed behind her, adding to Garnet's haste. She didn't pause. Patrice was in good hands. Their cook had birthed eight healthy children on her own and would see to the frightened young woman's care. The only thing she could do for Patrice was ride hard and fast into Pride to bring her the help and comfort she needed.

Cold morning air cut through the thin shirt fabric as Garnet sent her mount galloping across the Manor's fallow acres. Taking the roadways would only slow her down, and minutes counted. She couldn't block out the sight of that blood pooling on her floorboards. The only birth she'd ever witnessed was her own son's, which was long but blessedly uneventful, but she knew that at any birth the mother and child could be in serious peril. Dismissing her own risks, she goaded her horse to greater speed across the dangerously rutted ground.

She couldn't let Deacon's sister die.

Mindless of the odd looks she drew from those on the streets of Pride, she urged her lathered animal up to the front of the store. Swinging down onto wobbly legs, she scrambled inside, past properly garbed matrons who gasped in shock and shielded their daughter's tender vision, past loitering gentlemen who unashamedly gawked.

Alerted by the sudden murmuring of his customers, Deacon turned to follow the commotion as he measured the final scoop of rice into Carolyn Breedlaw's bag. Grains scattered across the counter and rained down to the floor as he registered the tense purpose in the mannishly clad Garnet's face. She wasted no words.

"Deacon, where's Reeve Garrett?"

His voice nearly failed him. "Patrice—"

"Do you know where he is?"

He turned to a boy who stood gazing dreamily at the jars of striped candy sticks. "Herman, run down to the livery and fetch Mr. Garrett."

"And the doctor," Garnet added breathlessly. Chilled to the point of numbness, she struggled to draw in air. She could only nod gratefully when Deacon draped a heavy coat about her shoulders. She pulled it tight with trembling fingers. Deacon's hands clamped onto her shoulders.

"Garnet, my sister . . . is she all right?"

"The baby's coming," she managed between chattering teeth.

He leaned in closer, his voice low, commanding, cutting through her exhaustion. "It's more than that."

She didn't want to meet his stare, knowing he'd read her anxiousness and see the truth. Instead, she nodded. The bite of his fingertips drew her gaze upward. His eyes were closed, his features absolutely still.

"Patrice, where is she?" Reeve shouted, as he ducked into the store.

"At the Manor" was all Garnet had time to say before he was gone.

"Mama," Deacon murmured faintly. "Mama's

at Mrs. Bishop's dress shop. We came into town together in the carriage."

"If you want to take my horse, I'll see your mother home."

Torn between his worry over his sister and his obligation to his mother and the shivering woman before him, Deacon considered for a moment, then said, "I'll drive both of you back. From the looks of you, your horse is all in anyway. Herschel, mind the store for me."

Garnet huddled in the backseat next to a weeping Hannah Sinclair as the carriage sped toward the Manor. She knew Deacon was sparing the whip on their account, but they still made good time, arriving just after the town doctor. Impatiently, Deacon handed the two of them down before rushing up the front steps. Reeve stood in the hallway, expression stark. His grimness brought Deacon up short.

"She's not dead," he stated, as if claim could make fact.

"No," Reeve told him, then gripped his arm as he started for the stairs. "The doc's with her. She's lost a lot of blood. Mama, he said you could go up."

Hannah raced passed him in a swirl of rustling taffeta.

And they began to wait.

With her room occupied by doctor and patient, Garnet remained in her clinging garments while her house rapidly filled up with friends of Patrice Garrett. She was surprised to see a distraught and sober Tyler Fairfax on the doorstep. After she conveyed what little she knew, Tyler strode into the parlor to where Reeve wore a restless path in front of the hearth. Saying nothing, he crossed to him, yanking him up in a fierce embrace, hanging on tight when Reeve's strength briefly buckled.

And then the breathtaking Starla Dodge arrived with her Yankee banker husband. She, too, had hugs for Reeve, then fell into weeping against her brother's shoulder. The horror of her own miscarriage was still too recent for her to find optimistic words. Dodge braced his friend with a tall tumbler of whiskey and a solid arm of support. Drawn up in the close camaraderie of their shared past, they didn't notice Garnet as they gave and took comfort from one another. Nor did they include Deacon in their inner circle.

Deacon stood apart from them, as silent and still as a piece of statuary. And was treated with the same compassion. No one approached him with meaningful hugs or words of reassurance. As if he didn't need them. As if he were somehow immune to the gamut of emotions from which the others suffered.

It wasn't true.

And it wasn't fair.

Garnet started toward him, her heart swelling with sympathy. Then Monty stepped into the room, cutting her off with his cheery announcement.

"Mr. Garrett, may I be the first to congratulate you on your son."

Reeve accepted the kisses and back slappings, then asked in a quiet dread, "And my wife?"

"She is resting comfortably. The doctor said you could go up now."

In the next few minutes of chaotic relief, Deacon Sinclair slipped out of the room without notice.

By anyone but Garnet.

Drained by the rip and ebb of emotions, Garnet sought out her own son, miracle that he was, to make sure he hadn't been frightened by the upheaval in their home. She found him outside, romping with Boone, sweetly oblivious to the adult happenings around him. Bitsy gave her a wave, her fondness for the child making her a loyal watchdog in his mother's absence.

Not wishing to encounter any of their unplanned guests, Garnet took the back stairs, pausing at the top landing when she saw movement through the door opening out onto one of the back balconies. Her breath caught when she recognized the straight-backed posture and oh-so-solitary figure of Deacon Sinclair.

She should have kept walking. She was too vulnerable to his circumstance to remain objective, and that wouldn't serve her cause. If she weakened to him, her indifferent leverage was lost, and there was precious little else she had to cling to where he was concerned.

But she couldn't forget how alone he'd been

in the parlor below while surrounded by his
family's friends.

He knew at once that she was near. The
moment she joined him in the crisp morning air,
his shoulders set with an even greater stiffness.
He didn't turn and she suffered an instant of
misgiving. This wasn't a man who needed or
wanted comforting, especially from a woman
still seen as an enemy. Surely his friends below
knew him better than she, and knew enough to
give him the space he desired. She was wrong to
think him vulnerable. Until she saw how desperately his fisted hands worked at his sides.

He was far from fine.

"She's going to be all right." She restated the
fact, just in case he hadn't fully absorbed it yet.
After a long second, he nodded. "Deacon, both
your sister and the baby are all right."

Again, the nod, this time accompanied by a
jerkily drawn breath.

Garnet approached slowly. She had to touch
him, to make the contact that would let him
know he was not alone. When her palms fit to his
lower back, he gave a violent start, of objection
or surprise, she didn't know, but she didn't withdraw. She moved her hands in a spreading circle,
trying to soothe the tension from his stance. It
was like trying to soften the brick of the building
behind her. Disheartened, she said, "Perhaps you
should go below and be with your friends."

"They're not my friends. If I were lying in
there close to dying, there'd be no one standing

in that parlor. They're here for Patrice. Everyone
loves Patrice."

It wasn't envy or bitterness coloring his voice.
It was something different, something deeper.
She encouraged him to go on, with her silence
and her continued touch.

"I don't know what to say to them. I don't
know how to let them know that I treat them
with such coldness not because I dislike them or
think myself better, but because I was raised to
believe openness and weakness were the same
thing. I don't know how to change that."

He took a fractured breath and Garnet's arms
slipped about his middle. She leaned against his
back, listening to the unexpectedly fast pace of
his heartbeats, not letting him discourage her
with his unyielding posture.

"I've treated my sister badly, letting her
believe I thought her silly and frivolous, pretending I held her in contempt for her passionate nature. I've done things I'm ashamed to
admit to, things that should have made her
curse me, but still she gave me forgiveness and
love. I never told her how much that meant to
me, how much she meant to me. And if I'd lost
her before I had the chance . . . "

His hands fit over Garnet's, clutching fiercely.

"I don't know how to say the words."

"It's not difficult," she told him tenderly. "Just
three words. I love you."

She hadn't meant to put so much of her own
feelings into those words. He went completely

still, breath suspended, the restless kneading of his hands stopping. She waited for him to speak. When he didn't, she prompted, "You've never told anyone that you loved them?"

He answered with silence.

Fighting down a prickle of envy, she asked, "Not even your Jassy? You must have said those words to scare your family into selling her."

"Who told you that?"

Refusing to be intimidated by the sudden frostiness of his tone, she replied, "Patrice did."

He let go of her hands, his body language denying her as much as his words. "Patrice doesn't know anything about that. She had no right to tell you any such thing."

"Then you tell me, Deacon."

He was motionless for so long, she didn't think he would answer. But when he did, it was with an unusual degree of candor brought on by his susceptible mood.

"You don't understand, Garnet. How could you? You don't know what it means to have the weight of our traditions rest upon your shoulders. I was my family's future, and it was a duty I wasn't allowed to treat lightly. I've been living for my family's past and future generations since I was five years old. My thoughts, my decisions, my ambitions, they were never my own. When I was five, my father took me to the fields where one of the hands was being disciplined for trying to run away. When the overseer started whipping him, I didn't see a piece of property, I saw another human being. I asked my father to put a stop to it, and when he wouldn't, I started to cry and ran back to the house. Of course, that humiliated him and he wasn't a man to take disgrace lightly. That night he asked me which end of that whip I'd prefer to be on, that I had to choose the direction my life would take, right then at that moment. Did I want to bear the responsibility that went with all I would inherit, or would I be on the receiving end of those decisions? I didn't understand. I couldn't answer him. So he beat me with his riding crop and he asked again. By then, I knew which end of the whip I wanted to be on and said so. Then my father told me that he loved me and because he loved me it was his responsibility to see those lessons were learned."

The horror of it left Garnet momentarily speechless. She pictured him at that tender age, the image of William, subjected to such brutality. Finally, she whispered, "But you were just a baby."

"No. I was a Sinclair. And I never forgot any of my father's lessons. He used to say that to control the destiny of many, one had to put aside one's own needs and wants, that the sign of a man was in how well he could divorce himself from his true emotions."

Men don't cry. Not ever.

She could hear his father talking through those words he'd passed down to her son and she knew a sudden, all-consuming fear. If Patrice told him that William was his child, what kind of man would Deacon make him into? The kind of Sinclair that tradition demanded?

No.

No one was going to do that to her child in the erroneous name of love.

"Didn't you ever question if he was right?"

Deacon revolved slowly to stare at her as if she'd suggested something totally foreign. "What?"

"Didn't you ever wonder if he was wrong?"

He hesitated, reluctant to speak so traitorous an admission. "Only twice."

She waited for him to go on.

Having gone so far in his confessions, it was more difficult to stop than it was to continue. So he continued.

"She was more than just a servant." He was speaking of Jassy, of course. Garnet stiffened slightly, unable to repress her jealousy of this long-ago lover who still had the power to soften his steely gaze. "She was smart and sweet and spirited, and she wanted so much more than circumstances would allow her. I wanted to give her those things because she deserved them. She was a friend to Patrice and to me. We taught her and her brother Jericho to read and write, and they both were so eager to learn. Maybe it was wrong of us to give them that knowledge. The law forbade it and so did my father, but it seemed so unfair to 'Trice and me. What did we know? We were children. And I was a fool.

"Jassy was beautiful. She made you feel special when she smiled at you. I was fifteen, sixteen, her master's son. I made promises to her to win those smiles, and she boasted of them to others. Word got back to my father, and he called me into his study to tell me how things had to be. I could have Jassy for a mistress, but I couldn't care for her. I could take her body, but I couldn't give anything in return. That's what my position demanded. It would have meant stripping her of her pride, her value, in front of those she cared about and respected. It would have been an unforgivable insult after all the kindnesses she'd offered. But that's all my father would allow me to give. And he left me with the choice."

His expression was absent of any clue, so Garnet prompted, "What did you do?"

"I sold her, away from her family, away from her friends, away from me. Because I loved her too much to let her mean so little to me." His mouth twisted up on one side into a cynical half smile. "So you can see why I'm not in such a hurry to claim love for another."

"You said twice. When was the other time?"

"When I went back for you."

Chapter 17

Stunned by his unexpected admission, Garnet was slow to respond with the sudden barrage of questions sweeping over her. She couldn't have spoken past the huge knot of emotion wedged up into her throat had she had the chance.

"You're shivering."

His comment fell short of describing the devastating tremors that had taken control of her system.

"You should get those damp things away from your skin before you catch a chill."

If his intention was to distract her from his earlier statement, the lowering of his voice to a smoky register more than succeeded. The intensity of his stare mesmerized her. As he reached out to unfasten the first button of her shirt, her heart began to beat like a long-caged wild thing at the prospect of being freed.

Slowly, he worked his way down the front placket, the movement of his fingers a purposeful enticement. With a shrug of her shoulders, the heavy coat he'd draped about her at the store became a circling of dark wool about her ankles. His gaze keeping hers a willing hostage, he gripped the hem of the shirt and lifted it over her head. Beneath it, she wore only a chemise. While her arms were yet raised, his hands stroked down them with a soul-shaking leisure, warm palms over chilled flesh, from wrists to shoulder caps. At the same time, he bent, inviting her arms to encircle his neck, her hands to clutch at his head as his mouth touched hot and moist to the jut of her collarbone.

The breath left her lungs in a forceful exhalation.

Shocks of excitation followed the gradual trail his lips made along the edge of delicate lace, over one ample hill to the deep valley created by the snug pull of batiste. As the tip of his tongue dipped down to taste that shadowed crevice, her nipples beaded, tightening into achy pulses of need. She couldn't breathe as his hands eased down and around the curve of her ribs to claim the full underside of each breast. The first rub of his thumbs across those tender peaks drew a shaky moan, so wanton, so raw, she couldn't believe the sound had come from her.

There was no point in her pretending that this wasn't what she wanted, or that he wasn't who she wanted it from. The scorch of his breaths against uncovered skin woke her entire body to remembered pleasures, making her yearn for them all over again as she tipped her torso toward him in blatant offering. The fact that she was in partial undress out on an open balcony being made love to by a man who wasn't her husband fled to a far corner of her brain as he suckled through the thin barrier of her chemise.

Just as her legs threatened to fold, Deacon sank down onto his knees, lowering hers to rest atop his thighs. His mouth continued to provoke riotous responses while one hand raised similar havoc at her other breast. His free hand caressed along the indentation of her waist, over the swell of her hip to finally fit to the widespread inner seam of her man's trousers. His palm cupped the soft mound of her femininity, pressing, revolving slowly until her sweetly curved bottom picked up the rhythm, a tempo echoed by her suddenly altered breathing as it gusted in rapid snatches.

Her hands fisted in his hair as her head fell back, her eyes closing, back arching so that her breast flattened against his face. He sucked harder, pulling hot licks of urgency toward a desperate end.

With the heel of his hand riding her in an ever-increasing hurry, Garnet surrendered the passion roaring through her blood. Shattering waves of sensation broke at last, sweeping her out beyond the limits of self and sensibility, to a point where heart and soul were controlled by a hot, pulsing paradise. She drifted back in a dreamy languor, vaguely aware that Deacon's kisses moved from her throbbing breast to the taut bow of her throat, from there, in a gliding sweep along her left arm, to where he held her hand in his. Pausing at the heavy gold band she wore. Then he shocked her back from her sated lethargy with one soft-spoken truth.

"I came back for you, Garnet, but you had already moved on to another."

She slid from his lap as he gained his feet to look down upon her through eyes absent of any identifiable emotion. Slowly, he bent to pull the coat around her bared shoulders, closing it over the dampened bodice and the loose spraddle of her thighs. Without another word, he went inside, leaving her in a confusion of bliss and bereavement.

Unaware that they had been observed.

Drained by her ordeal, yet dozing upon a balm of satisfaction as she listened to the sounds of her new baby snuffling at her side, Patrice Garrett was too weary to open her eyes when she heard someone moving at her bedside. A light touch brushed wayward strands of hair from her brow for the placement of an equally gentle kiss. Reeve? As she struggled for the strength to smile, she heard words spoken in low reverence.

"I love you, Patrice."

Not Reeve. Impossibly, it sounded like . . .

"Deacon?" She whispered his name as her eyes fluttered open with a frail awareness.

But he'd already gone, letting her slip back to

sleep with his cherished claim held close to her heart.

By early evening, the doctor pronounced Patrice and her as yet unnamed son fit enough to travel home. Bundled up snugly, they were driven to the Glade by a proudly beaming Reeve. Hannah followed in a gallant Montgomery Prior's escort. And Garnet took advantage of the silence in her home to have a hot bath drawn.

But even the steaming water couldn't soothe away the feel of Deacon's touch, nor the betraying way her body had responded. Nor could an intemperately large glass of wine soothe her troubled mind as she huddled beneath the covers of his big bed.

He'd come back for her.

What exactly did that mean? Without a declaration of love to preface it, perhaps it meant nothing at all, beyond a way to manipulate her emotions. And those feelings were being snapped about like a bedsheet on a clothesline in a battering March wind. Having displayed her vulnerability, what was the next step in her rapidly disintegrating plan? The very lie she'd concocted to keep Deacon at bay was also keeping him from admitting the one thing that she longed for—that he loved her. She had to think calmly, logically, of what to do now—not all that easy when her body still hummed from his expert handling.

In her naïveté, she'd underestimated how

complex Deacon Sinclair was. He wasn't a man who showed his emotions. She understood that, now that she knew a little of his past. But could that heart be touched by a deceitful woman who'd done her best to strip a proud man of his dignity in the name of retribution? A woman who quickly gave way to the very sentiments she pretended to abhor?

Now, how to resurrect her dreams? Did she admit to the true parentage of her son? Could she ever hope to gain Deacon's love and trust, as long as she played his past betrayal against her current lies? As long as she lived under the roof that bore the traditions of all the Sinclairs before him, denying him his rightful place among them, how could she expect him to admit to any love for her?

With her world gone up in flames, reeling with the knowledge of her father's false imprisonment, she headed north in a panic, to the one safe harbor she knew. Her mother's brother, Monty, had sent her a letter upon hearing of his sister's death years before. In it, he said anything she needed, any time, he'd see was hers. He'd been surprised to see her on his doorstep, but he'd made good on his promise.

When she'd discovered her pregnancy, her uncle wanted to take her back to England with him, a home he hadn't seen for nearly twenty years. He'd begged her to give up her quest for justice, citing her mother's own end. Julia Prior had fallen deeply, and, according to her family, unwisely in love with William Davis. Against their wishes, in spite of their threats, she'd married the poor farmer and without a moment of regret, she'd left behind her comfortable life. Garnet thought the story wildly romantic, the Prior family less so. They'd tried to control their daughter by cutting off her funds. To their dismay, the money made no difference to a young woman lost to love. Both sides had been too proud to make the first step toward reconciliation, and now the only family Garnet had after her father's untimely and unfair demise was a foreign-accented stranger with a grandfatherly manner and an unbreakable vow to see her happy.

But happiness eluded her.

Like her mother, the money didn't matter to Garnet. It wasn't this big house, the closet full of fine clothes, it was family. She had wanted a home for William. But this wasn't their home. The cool elegance of its halls and the cold embrace of this big, lonely bed held no welcome, and each day spent within them only reminded her of that exclusion. Tradition wasn't something she could buy. Just as love wasn't something she could pull from a heart that had hardened itself to the surrounding world.

There would be no happiness for her within this house unless she bore the name Sinclair. And that wouldn't happen as long as she was Mrs. Prior.

And that left one question. The only question.

Could she risk everything on the hope that Deacon Sinclair loved her?

Or that he could ever forgive her?

The best atmosphere for conducting business was over the green felt of a card table and a full glass of bourbon.

Montgomery Prior enjoyed both, but not as much as he liked working a deal.

After leaving Hannah at her daughter's grand horse farm, he traveled into town, where a not-so-chance meeting with Judge Banning became a lucrative opportunity with some of the county's most influential and unscrupled gentlemen. For the first few hours, Monty played the good sport, losing more than he won and listening more than he talked. As the liquor loosened tongues, opinions overcame popular sentiment, and he was able to get a true reading on his neighbors and the one thing they worried over most.

"Roads," Alf Dermont growled. He might not have been the most prestigious of their number, but he spoke for all of them. "Choke you with dust all summer and drown you in mud in the winter. Why, hell, they ain't nearly wide enough for two wagons to pass in most places, and whilst we're out there buried to the axles, some fancy official is making promises from the town's porches—promises he ain't never gonna keep."

"Internal improvements," Judge Banning agreed. "Now, there's a topic no local politician can brace without sinking in the mire himself."

"And why is that, Judge?"

Banning gave the Englishman a condescending smile. " 'Cause neighborhoods build their own roads, then the landowners have to get permission from the county board to fence their fields and put up their gates to keep livestock from wandering. Governments are particularly keen on ignoring problems that they don't have to trip over every day."

Monty casually studied his cards, then declared himself out of play, allowing a grinning Tyler Fairfax to scoop up the pot. "So the man or men who managed to achieve these improvements would be deemed heroes by the local populace."

Tyler regarded him shrewdly from across the table. "What are you gettin' at, Prior?"

"You said this particular circle has an interest in politics. If a man wanted to be county supervisor, that would be a position of considerable power. If he hand-picked the county board members to share in his good fortune, then approved lucrative requests for, shall we say, favors, I'd think a man could profit quite nicely."

"And your interest in this would be—?"

Monty smiled in the face of Tyler's suspicions. "Why, as a citizen of Pride, I want only the best for her . . . and for me. In fact, I would be willing to organize a local bond issue through my contacts in the North to get improvements on the roads, and I'll start by contributing generously, and by negotiating an extremely high rate of return for those farsighted enough to invest in the future of their community." He laid his cards facedown on the table with a sigh. "This is not my night for gambling. If you gentlemen will excuse me, I'm going to take a moment of air."

And in doing so, give them an opportunity to discuss the proposition he'd laid on the table next to his hand.

He'd stood on the Bannings' front porch for all of thirty seconds before the judge joined him.

"I like your vision, Prior. And I'd like to discuss this idea of an improvement bond. It would take a certain amount of influence away from our local banker, and that would please me."

Monty smiled. "And do you have any choice in mind for supervisor, Judge?"

"Oh, I think that's a hat I might like to wear."

"And you'd wear it well, sir."

After Banning returned to see to his other guests, Tyler Fairfax came to stand next to Monty. The Englishman wasn't misled by the younger's obvious intoxication. There was an edge to Fairfax that all his daddy's bourbon couldn't dull.

"I don't know how things work where you come from, Prior, but 'round here, we wash each other's backs."

Monty blinked. "I'm afraid I don't understand."

"If you want me to invest in your scheme, you help me in one of mine."

"Ah! Reciprocal interests, so to speak."

"Whatever."

"And what is it that I can do for you to guarantee your support?"

Tyler let loose of a wide grin. "You can place a certain order for me through your store. You see, I'm into community improvements, too."

Deacon stared down at the order form and then up into Tyler's smugly smiling face.

"Is there something wrong with the order, Reverend? It seems pretty black and white to me."

"Wrong? You were wrong in thinking I'd fill this for you and your hooded friends." He let the offensive form flutter, discarded, to the counter top. Tyler picked it up and gave the writing on it another look.

"Why, if my eyes don't deceive me, the signature on the bottom of this order is Montgomery Prior's. Isn't he your boss man? Are you sayin' he don't have the authority to choose merchandise for his store?" Green eyes slitted. "Or that you have the authority to defy him?"

Tyler's casual claim drew attention from those lingering by the stove. And from another source.

"What's going on here, gentlemen?"

Garnet slipped up to the counter with her best diplomatic smile. She looked between the two men who held each other's glares with the intensity of wolves guarding territory. Tyler was the first to break free, turning to Garnet with his most charming manners.

"Why, I just don't understand it, Miz Prior. Your clerk here is refusing to fill an order for me that's been authorized already by your husband. Is there some problem?"

Garnet glanced at the list. Winchesters and Henry rifles with 45-70-caliber bullets. She schooled her features to reveal none of her alarm. "Are you planning to wage your own war, Mr. Fairfax?"

Tyler laughed. "Oh, no, ma'am. Nothin' like that a'tall. I'm a member of a shooting club."

"Tell her what you shoot at."

Garnet ignored Deacon's fierce challenge to say calmly, "It's none of our business, as long as it's legal."

"Legal, my a—"

"Mr. Sinclair, please take care of this order."

Deacon met her demand with an equally terse, "No."

After a moment of tense exchange, Garnet called, "Mr. Rosen, please take care of Mr. Fairfax and see his order is filled to his satisfaction."

Herschel approached cautiously, but nodded. "Yes, Mrs. Prior."

Garnet leveled a look at Deacon. "I'd like to speak to you for a moment, Mr. Sinclair."

She led the way to the feed room. When he closed the door behind them, she turned on him in a cold rage.

"How *dare* you question my husband's orders?"

"Do you have any idea what he wants those guns for?"

"I don't care."

"You don't care? They put a bullet in our banker because they didn't like his politics, and you don't care? They try to hang my sister's husband and burn his roof over his head, and you don't care?"

She sighed fiercely. "Of course I care. I just can't allow you to make a forum of it in front of half the town."

"What better place to make a stand for what's right?"

"We're here to do business, not make judgments."

"You're wrong."

She drew a breath, frustrated by his stubbornness, by his correctness. It was no longer the issue that fueled her anger with him. It was the sleepless night she'd spent, fighting the desire to seek him out, hating the fact that she was still no closer to understanding his motives than she was while watching her home burn to the ground at his command.

"And who are *you* to be the moral conscience of this community?"

The slight flicker behind his eyes before he assumed his impassive face told her she'd hit the mark. She pressed on ruthlessly.

"You condemn them for doing with guns what you did with words and false charm."

"I was fighting my country's war. They're creating their own."

But she could read him well enough to see he didn't completely believe his own argument.

"What war, Deacon? A war against a decent farmer who only wanted to make a difference for a cause he was devoted to? A war against an unworldly backwoods girl who was foolish enough to believe every word you told her? And you argue the moral rightness of what my husband does? How dare you? What makes you any better or any different than they are? They hide under sheets, and you hid behind lies. You both prey upon the weak to get what you want, and you do so without the slightest degree of remorse."

She wanted him to argue that it wasn't true, that he was better, different, more noble in his ideals. But he said nothing in his defense.

And that made her all the angrier, because if he was guilty of everything she said, she was a fool for loving him.

When he finally spoke, his words were no comfort.

"I've had to live with the consequences of the choices I've made. If you deal with Fairfax, be prepared to do the same . . . Mrs. Prior. Just be sure you know why you're willing to sacrifice your conscience. That'll make all the difference in how well you sleep at night."

He started past her to the door. Her question made him pause.

"And how well do *you* sleep, Deacon?"

He turned slowly, fixing her with a steady stare. His voice held no inflection.

"The last time I rested well was the night I slept with you."

Riotous emotion brought tears to her eyes

and a shiver of fury to her tone. "Damn you, Deacon."

His half smile mocked himself, not her, as he opened the door. Sound from the store rushed in but couldn't drown out his quiet reply.

"I'm sure you're right about that."

"Mr. Sinclair!"

Assuming a tolerant smile, Deacon went to join Myrna Bishop. He glanced curiously at her companion, a slender blond woman with an unnervingly direct stare.

"Mr. Sinclair, may I present my cousin, Constance Collier? She's the one I spoke to you about."

"The hatmaker."

"Actually, I'm a teacher by trade," the woman corrected, as she extended her hand in a forthright manner. Her accent was decidedly Northern. Deacon took her hand, slightly surprised when she gave it a vigorous shake. "But dear Myrna has convinced me that millinery work is the safer profession."

Myrna shot her a disapproving glare, then turned her charm back to Deacon. "Constance is interested in your upstairs rooms."

"There are no living accommodations, Miss Collier."

"It's Mrs.," she amended again in her pleasantly low voice. "And that's quite all right. Myrna has convinced me to stay with her for the time being. At least until I can get my feet under me again."

He felt Garnet beside him before he actually saw her. "Mrs. Prior, this is Mrs. Collier. She'd like to discuss leasing the upstairs for her millinery shop."

Garnet smiled. "How nice. We'd hoped to put the space to good use. How soon would you like to occupy it?"

"As soon as we can come to financial terms."

Garnet glanced about. "Is Mr. Collier with you?"

"I'm a widow, Mrs. Prior." Her attention slipped casually to Deacon. "I've been handling my own affairs for some time now."

Garnet's smile stiffened. A widow. She reassessed the other female, who had suddenly gone from safely married to dangerously unattached and openly flirting with Deacon Sinclair. She was of good height, though lithely built, attractive in a rather angular way. There was a quick intelligence to her gaze and a simmering sensuality to her bowed smile. And Garnet felt the threat to her territory, though it wasn't truly hers to protect. She was supposedly wed, and Deacon and the slyly smiling widow were free of any entanglements.

At that moment, she would rather have leased her upstairs rooms for Klan meetings than to one available milliner.

"I'm not a wealthy woman, Mrs. Prior, but I would be agreeable to any fair amount. I'm looking forward to establishing myself in Pride as soon as possible."

And staking her claim on its unattached men. Garnet bristled. Forcing herself to remember that she had no apparent cause to reject the woman's offer, she gestured toward the store's office. "Let's talk, Mrs. Collier."

The bold blonde paused to bestow another come-hither look at Deacon. "It's a pleasure to meet you, Mr. Sinclair. I'll enjoy being above you."

That was one image that would keep Garnet from finding a decent night's rest.

Chapter 18

The first sound to greet her as she entered her front door was that of delighted female laughter. Her already testy mood darkening, Garnet passed her cloak to a waiting servant and went to find the source.

It was a cozy sight, Hannah Sinclair and her supposed husband seated side by side on the parlor sofa. Almost like a courting couple. It would seem every female in Pride was actively in pursuit of romance, with herself the one obvious exception. The moment Hannah saw her frowning in the doorway, she jumped up as if caught by a displeased chaperone. Murmuring that she had to check on the kitchen, she excused herself from the room.

"Rather inappropriate of you to be entertaining our housekeeper in my absence, wouldn't you say?"

Undaunted by her tart assessment, Monty quirked an eyebrow. "My, we are on edge this evening. Anything you'd care to discuss, my dear?"

No, she didn't care to go into what weighed upon her heart, so she vented what was on her mind.

"You and Mrs. Sinclair have become very close."

"She is a charming woman. I enjoy her company." His mild smile said he missed the point.

"And if others suspect you enjoy more than that?"

There was no mistaking her meaning, and clouds gathered upon Monty's brow.

"Mrs. Sinclair is a lady. Who has suggested otherwise?"

"No one . . . yet. But if you continue to seek her company as if—" she checked the hallway, then continued, "you were not already married, people will talk."

"People will always find something to talk about, whether it's the truth or not. Come, child, what's really bothering you this evening?"

She could hardly say she was chafing over the possible attraction between Deacon and their new tenant. Instead, she picked a safer yet no less volatile topic. "Why did you agree to sell Tyler Fairfax guns?"

His brows soared, but he refused to look guilty of anything. "I thought our business was to sell things. Is that a crime?"

"It could be the cause of many."

"My dear, you yourself encouraged dealings with Mr. Fairfax, and I believe it was also you who wanted me to belong in the community. I've done both those things, and yet you fault me for them now."

She scowled at him, not quite taken in by his expression of innocence. "Lately, I've heard unsavory things about your new friends."

"From what source? Your Mr. Sinclair? I would hardly expect him to be approving. Are you now accepting his judgment over mine?"

"Perhaps he knows these people better than you or I."

"If he was such a good judge of character, why did he lose his home? And why did he let you go?"

She winced at that rapier-sharp question. "Perhaps he's learned from his mistakes."

All traces of the befuddlement fell away as Monty demanded shrewdly, "Is that what you think has happened where you're concerned?"

"Is that so hard to believe?" Pride starched up her posture, but it was hope quavering in her voice. A fragile hope that what she and Deacon had had was strong enough to prevent him from turning to another woman—even if he had every right to, and she none to protest. Monty's attitude softened with care.

"That a man would call himself ten times the fool for missing the chance to marry you? No, darling, that's not so far-fetched. But this particular man—?" He shrugged eloquently. "Perhaps he does regret it now that you hold all that once was his." As a startled pain crossed her features, he added gently, "That may sound cruel but it is also true." He embraced her gently. "Now, my dearling, think on that while I'm away this evening and guard your heart from foolish wishes."

To distract herself from the ache his words woke inside more than from real interest, Garnet asked, "Where are you off to?"

"I'm going into town to play a few hands with my new friends. Now, now, dear, do not look so disapproving. I am nobody's mark when it comes to scheming. I'm not above a plot or two myself when it comes to seeing your future secured. The day will come when you'll want a real husband instead of an uncle to act the part. I'm looking to that end, my dear, and I'm not looking in Sinclair's direction."

Had she been less wrapped up in her own misery, she would have latched on to that odd claim with a demand to know what he was up to. She accepted his quick kiss to her brow and didn't question his hasty escape. Only one thought plagued her turmoiled mind.

Was she being manipulated once again by the coldly cunning Deacon Sinclair?

And Hannah Sinclair, who'd been about to enter the room with a warm toddy for her distraught mistress, paused as if struck by lightening as she heard what passed between the supposed man and wife.

Of course. Now it all made perfect sense.

Slowly, she smiled to herself, then carried the soothing mix into Garnet, keeping the newfound knowledge to herself as a comforting secret.

Patrice Garrett greeted her brother with a smile and a shushing gesture. The babe in her arms had finally drifted off to sleep, freeing her for the moment. Instead of waiting for her in the parlor, he followed her upstairs, into the room made up for the child's nursery. He lingered beside the bassinet as she gently placed the boy upon his back, pausing for a tender moment as the little miracle she'd created whimpered, then took comfort sucking on his own tiny fist. In a matter of seconds, he was as limp as one of the rag dolls she'd played with when only a child herself.

To Deacon, it didn't seem like so very long ago.

Patrice motioned for him to come with her. He hesitated, staring down at the child for another moment at a loss with his silence.

"I'm exhausted and still plump as a Christmas goose, but I'm happy, Deacon. I've never been so happy."

He smiled thinly, glad for her, yet never so aware of his own empty existence. "Where's your husband?"

"Reeve's out in the stables. We've a mare about to foal, and he's concerned about her."

"Things are going well for you, then?"

"Everything is wonderful."

He nodded. "Good." A pause, then another, more distant, "Good."

"We've decided to name him Jonah. Jonah Garrett Glendower."

Again, Deacon nodded, noting the significance with a deepening isolation. Jonah, after Reeve's half-brother and his sister's first fiancé. The man who'd stepped in front of a firing squad in his place, altering the future of everyone around him with that martyred act. Vaguely, he asked, "Glendower?"

"A promise Reeve made to his father that our children would carry on his family name. A shame he couldn't be alive to see his heir. He would have been so proud, I think." Momentary sadness etched her features.

"So would our father, Patrice. It might not have been the man he wanted for you, but it was the match."

"Yes, a great joining of the Manor and the Glade."

"Or it would have been, had I handled things better."

"Stop it."

The sharpness of her tone cut through his melancholy. His manner immediately toughened. "Stop what? Beating myself with the truth—that you, his wayward daughter, found favor, while I, his chosen, failed him?"

"Stop living in his shadow. He's dead, Deacon."

He flinched, but his reply was icy. "I know. And I've allowed all his dreams to die with him."

"His dreams, Deacon. *His* dreams. What about *yours?*"

He regarded her so blankly she wanted to slap him just to knock a bit of sense into his thick head. With a sigh, Patrice changed her tactics. Confrontation would only force her brother to retreat further behind his armored shell. That wasn't how to reach him. She knew little of the mechanics of the great war that had taken so much from her family, but she understood how a flanking maneuver worked. And if she was successful, Deacon would never know what had hit him.

"When I was a child, winning Father's approval was all that mattered to me," she began, laying a careful groundwork. "I was so focused on what would please him, I never gave a thought as to what might please me. After he died, I put you in that same position. I needed to make you proud of me by making the choices you wanted me to make. I was a child who was afraid to recognize what *I* wanted, what *I* needed. You yourself were the one who told me to grow up, to think for myself." She smiled faintly. "Well, that's not quite what you meant but it's what I took to heart. Deep down, I've known what I wanted since I was a little girl, but I allowed pressure from Father, from you, to cloud my thinking."

"I never—"

She touched a gentle hand to his lips to still the rest of that protest. "Of course you did. I don't blame you for that. I blame myself for allowing you to have that kind of control over me. You were doing what you thought was best, what was required of you by all our traditions, by all our rules of conduct. Well, I've never been one for following rules."

That wrung a reluctant smile from him. Encouraged by the fact that he still listened, she continued.

"Yes, I wanted Father and you to be proud of me, but I didn't let that interfere with my decision to marry Reeve. He was what I wanted for myself, not for the good of the family name or anything else that you men dwell on. I wanted him for me, for my happiness. If things had been different and I had married Jonah to please the Sinclairs and the Glendowers, I don't know if I would ever have felt the contentment I feel right now. I did the right thing, for me. You see that, don't you?"

"Now I do. I was a little slow to be convinced."

She pursed her lips. "Just a little? Deacon, I love you, but you are so dense sometimes. How a man with your intelligence can be so singularly dim—" She broke off, sensing from his bristle of defensiveness that she was taking the wrong track. She regrouped behind a smile. "I love you, Deacon, and I want you to be happy. What is it that you want for yourself? Not for Father, but for yourself?"

"I don't—"

She cut off his stiff reply with an impatient wave. "Yes, you do. You wouldn't be so miserable if you didn't."

His brows puckered. Anger touched his tone. "What do you want from me, Patrice?"

"Honesty would be nice. Openness. We've had little of that between us over the years. You never know, I might even be able to help you."

He didn't laugh or say something sarcastic. That in itself proved how forlorn he was. Patrice's heart broke for him, but she couldn't do anything for him until he was ready to do for himself. To begin with, he had to admit what was in his heart.

"At one time, I could have helped myself to everything you have here—a lifetime with the woman I loved, a baby to carry on our family name, a happy home, all of it, Patrice."

"What happened?"

"Just what you said. I let the idea of duty and Father's dreams get in the way. And now someone else has everything I ever wanted. And I have my empty nobility."

She rubbed his coat sleeves, stunned by his unexpected candor. She returned it. "Are you sure you've lost it?"

He made an anguished noise. "She's married to another man, Patrice. They're living together under the roof I wanted to provide for her. I'd say that makes her pretty much out of my reach."

"Does she still love you?"

"What? What difference does that make now?"

"It's the only thing that really does matter, Deacon."

"I betrayed her, Patrice. It's my fault her father died in prison."

"A woman can forgive a lot of the man she loves. Is she in love with her husband?"

Again, the blank look. She held to her exasperation. "Deacon, she was alone, deserted by all she'd known and loved. Can you blame her for grabbing at the first chance of rescue? She might be grateful, but that's a poor substitute for true feelings."

"They share a child, 'Trice. That's a bond not easily broken."

"No, it's not."

She debated then on whether she should tell him what she knew. Would knowing that he was William's father clear the path toward his happiness or just compound his misery? She'd seen the wistful softening of his gaze when he looked down upon her slumbering son. Was it fair to deny him the privilege of feeling those tender emotions for a child of his own? Or would the knowledge of how much he'd missed already be too great a pain to forgive? Garnet had kept the truth from him. She'd had her reasons, and from what she knew of the situation, Patrice had to respect them. But she loved her brother and knew how much he'd be capable of if just allowed the chance to express himself. In his mind, Garnet was the only woman for him. Having experienced that certainty herself, she couldn't make light of it. But was now the right time for her to interfere?

"Does she love you, Deacon?"

He raked a restless hand through his hair and admitted, "She loves what we had together but now believes it was all a lie. I don't think she'd believe me if I told her the truth. And why put us both through the torment of what we'll never have?"

"Don't be so sure it's impossible," was all she'd say.

Because he was right. The bond between a woman and the father of her child contained a strength she wouldn't have understood before Jonah was born. Even if Garnet didn't trust her brother, that connection still pulled them together. And gratitude for the man who'd rescued her couldn't compare.

"Don't give up, Deacon. You may be closer to that happiness than you know."

"You have a beautiful wife."

Monty stopped chafing his hands against the miserable cold and cast a sidelong glance at Roscoe Skinner. "Yes, I do. I'm very proud of her."

"As smart as she is lovely, a talented hostess, a shrewd businesswoman."

"Yes, my Garnet is all of those things." His affability took on an impatient edge, waiting for the other shoe to drop.

"I probably shouldn't say anything . . . "

"What is it, Roscoe?"

"It's just that I've developed a respect for you and a fondness for the lady and I would hate to carry tales that would distress people—"

"What's on your mind, Skinner?"

"Your wife is young, so you can forgive her a certain . . . impulsiveness."

"Just say it!"

"I came upon her and Sinclair in a rather indelicate meeting. They didn't see me, so I place the matter entirely at your discretion. I only beg that you not judge your wife too harshly."

Monty was silent for a long moment, his mind churning over the possible meanings of "indelicate." None of them were good. Finally, he said, "Garnet is, as you say, very young. And she has an unfortunate weakness where Sinclair is concerned. He has managed to confuse her sound judgement before."

"They knew each other before? I'm sorry, it truly isn't any of my business—"

While Monty might pretend to be eager for a sympathetic ear, his reasons for disclosing so much of the truth was part of a far different plan. A plan that revolved around Skinner and his niece. Time to set the stage for that particular relationship while planting a firm wedge between Garnet and Sinclair. He knew Roscoe was attracted to his niece. What man could help that? Now, he needed to engage the man's protective instincts to nudge him subtly in the right romantic direction.

"They met during the war. Sinclair . . .

seduced her to gain information for the Con-
federates. She was vulnerable and alone and
believed the cad completely. Even after he had
her father arrested as a traitor and imprisoned.
The man was in poor health and didn't survive
his incarceration. As a friend of her mother's, I
was only too happy to step in and assume her
care."

"So it's no accident that you bought his plantation," Roscoe mused, looking suitably disgusted by Sinclair's manipulations.

"She told me it was to ruin him but I'm beginning to suspect it has as much to do with her
unhealthy attraction to him."

"Then your wife is not from Pride."

"No, she and her father had a modest farm in
the Cumberlands. So you see, she hasn't the
inbred skill to protect herself from a man of Sinclair's cunning."

Roscoe Skinner knew a moment of rapturous
delight. Oh, this was too good, too perfect. He'd
made two mistakes in his life and here they
were, both ready to be remedied in one place, in
one swift stroke of retribution. Fate had delivered them into his hands. It had always been his
plan to seek out Sinclair, but the woman, she
was an added extra.

"Mr. Skinner, you could do me a great service
if you would stay close to my wife, using your
presence to remind her of her place and purpose. I don't trust Sinclair. I know he's not above
breaking her heart all over again to gain back

what once was his. A man like that has no conscience, no allegiance, no loyalty."

"An apt description of a dangerous man." A
description that fit him just as snugly. "You are
wise to worry. I would consider it a privilege to
protect your wife's honor." A privilege and an
unexpected pleasure.

"In fact, might I go so far as to ask another
rather . . . unusual favor of you?"

"Of course."

"Should something happen to me, would you
be willing to see to my wife's care and protect
her from Sinclair? If you agree, I would certainly
make it worth your sacrifice."

And as he guided their carriage into Pride,
Roscoe Skinner listened with concealed glee and
adjusted his plans to include this bonus discovery. He would have his revenge against the one
man who'd bested and ultimately thwarted him
and he would claim all that mattered most to
Deacon Sinclair . . . his property, his life, and his
woman all with Montgomery Prior's blessing.

Chapter 19

~~⟶⟶⟶~~

Did she love him?

Deacon's attention drifted from the drummer trying to sell him a sample display of some new wonder tonic to the always distracting arrival of Garnet Prior. He had a brief smile of welcome for William before the boy's mother met his stare. Her impersonal look never failed to rile him, discounting the fact that his expression was almost identical. They could have been total strangers instead of lovers who were or were not in love with one another.

Did she care?

The way she doted on her escort's every word confused the issue. Deacon glowered at Roscoe Skinner, wondering why the man never failed to put his hackles up—other than the fact that he now stood in Deacon's place, both on his properties and at Garnet's side. He'd thought Garnet shared his uneasy opinion of the man but her behavior had contradicted it today. She held lightly to the man's arm and blushed at his flattery while joining in his laughter. Deacon's jaw ached.

"Can I set up a display for you?"

He turned back to the annoying salesman with a curt, "What?"

Ordinarily, the appearance of a drummer was an anticipated event. They arrived with the scent of the city still clinging to their coats like coal dust from the train. They knew all the latest news, all the baseball scores, the weather up north, the health of folks four counties over, and they shared that information generously with any who would listen. Only this morning, Deacon had no patience with the endless prattle. He eyed the bottle of tonic: an elixir of "exotic" herbs suspended mysteriously in a generous solution of alcohol behind tinted glass.

"What exactly does this potion do?"

The drummer beamed at him and launched into his pitch. "It cures headaches, fullness in the head after eating, dizziness, dots before the eyes, shooting bodily pains, and dyspepsia, and gives a cheerful warming glow to the whole body."

"Probably due to the fact that it's almost all alcohol," Deacon mumbled dryly. "Does it work?"

Now the drummer looked blank. "Excuse me?"

"Does it actually do anything other than produce a stupor that numbs the unfortunate sufferer into forgetting his ills?"

The sharpness of his tone brought Garnet to lean on the counter with a diplomatic, "Is there a problem here?"

"No problem, Mrs. Prior. Mr. Morganstern was just enlightening me on the restorative powers of his tonic. Perhaps you'd like to tell Mrs. Prior about your product. This is her store, so the buying decisions are hers. I'm just the counter help. Please excuse me."

Before Garnet could voice the displeasure sparking in her dark eyes, he slipped away from them for the preferable company of the town banker, Hamilton Dodge, accompanied by his stepson. Christien immediately bounded off to greet William.

"Business is booming."

Deacon accepted Dodge's observation with a cynical smile. "Skinner has them convinced they're all wealthy while he sucks off his high percent of interest."

Dodge grinned. "Most of them would say you just described me."

"At least you give them enough to live on. His rates are going to starve these people."

"And Mrs. Prior has nothing to say about that?"

"She says it's the price of doing business and that they are responsible for understanding their own finances."

Dodge made a noncommittal noise. "Considering most of them can't do more than make their mark, those are high expectations."

"Mrs. Prior may have a fine head for figures, but her standards are impossible to live up to."

Dodge gave him a look, but refrained from comment.

"Are you here to place an order for cigars, or to listen to my complaints?"

"I'm all set on cigars, and I'm not opposed to hearing your complaints, but I'm actually here to follow up on some rumors I've overheard. I figured, what better place to ferret out gossip than the source of most of it?" He nodded toward the glowing stove and the gaggle of gabbers holding court around it.

Deacon gestured to the office for a modicum of privacy, not wanting to fuel rumors while trying to uncover the truth of them. There was nothing unusual about the store manager and the town banker doing a little business over the record books behind closed doors.

"What's on your mind?"

"What do you know about these new improvement bonds?"

Deacon smiled. "Afraid of the competition?"

"If I was, I wouldn't be here talking to the prince of liens. I'm all for community improvements, depending on who's backing them. I hear it's Judge Banning looking to get himself appointed to county supervisor."

"And that worries you?"

"Like inviting a convicted bank robber to count my money at night."

"Good morning, Mr. Dodge. Is there something I can do for you?"

Dodge was all smiles as Garnet entered the office. " 'Morning, Mrs. Prior. Aside from bringing Christien over to visit your boy, I wanted to stop by and let you know that I've examined Mrs. Collier's financial statement as you requested. I think she'll be an excellent business risk for your rental space."

"I'm so relieved." That relief didn't translate well to her expression, which remained pinched and preoccupied. "I suppose there's no reason she shouldn't begin moving her things upstairs." Why did she look as though she wished she could find one?

"I'll let her know."

Her gaze darted to Deacon, then away. "I've told Mr. Morganstern he could set up a temporary display of his product and we'd keep track of how it sells for future ordering."

"Just what we need, more snake oil."

Her stare focused and sharpened. "It's our business to supply people with what they need."

"Or what we tell them they need." He picked up an order form and handed it to her. "Have him fill out that top part. There should be some room on the counter next to the Gray's and other miracle cures."

When she took the form and left without some quip or challenge, Deacon looked after her in concern, wondering what troubled her.

"Thanks for not saying anything in front of Mrs. Prior."

Deacon glanced at Dodge. "Why not?"

"Because her husband is behind this bond business. What do you know about him?"

"Not enough. I've got some feelers out through some rather unconventional channels. I'll let you know."

"Do that. Something's not as it seems about him and that hired man."

"Skinner?" Now Deacon's intuition quivered as well.

"I've seen him someplace. I just can't put my finger on it. But I will. Until then, don't turn your back on him."

"Don't worry," he murmured, eyes narrowing as Roscoe Skinner assisted Garnet with her wrap. His hands lingered upon her shoulders just a moment too long for Deacon's liking. Then, as if feeling his displeasure, Skinner met his glare.

And smiled. Like a crocodile.

"What are you doing?" William whispered in alarm, as a paper of fish hooks disappeared into Christien's pocket.

"Shush." Green eyes flashed about to see if anyone had observed the deft sleight of hand or his young friend's reaction. But as usual, no one paid any attention to them. He made no attempt to put the item back, and instead moved along the counter to the selection of Rodgers and Wolsten-holm knives safely encased under glass. "Boy, would my uncle like one of them frog stickers."

"What'd you take those fish hooks for? They're not yours. You have to buy them or it's stealing."

"Oh, it is not."

"Is too."

"Well, don't go making a big fuss about it. Here." He pressed the packet into William's hand. "There. You take 'em."

"I can't. It'd be stealing."

"Naw. It ain't stealing. Everything in this store belongs to your mama, so it belongs to you, too. If you wanted to give 'em to me, it'd be a gift, not stealing."

It sounded logical but still not quite accept-able. "I'll go ask my mama."

"You big baby," Christien hissed angrily. "Jus' forget about it. I was planning to let you go with me."

"Fishing?" His eyes rounded.

"As soon as it gets warmer. But you can forget about it if you go blabbing to your ma."

William looked from the forbidden hooks in his hand to Christien's empty palm. In a quandary over what best to do, he chose his mother's teaching over his new friend's bribes.

"I'm putting 'em back."

With a disgusted frown, Christien waited for him to return. "I suppose you're gonna tell on me."

That had never occurred to William. He shook his head and Christien was all smiles again.

"Wanna come play at my house? I gots tin soldiers made in France."

"Really?"

"Paris, France."

"I'll have to ask."

"You go do that, baby boy. I'll wait for you at the door." He walked that way, his hand trailing along the counter top with a nonchalance that disguised his palming of whatever lay in its path while William hurried to his mother.

"Mama, Christien wants me to come to his house."

She glanced outside at the overcast sky. "I don't know, darling. It looks like it could rain." Then her gaze fixed on the figure of Constance Collier, with her swinging stride and glorious hat.

"If it rains, we'll play inside. Say I can go. Pleeeese!"

Distractedly, she waved her hand. "Stay inside."

"Thanks, Mama."

And he raced off before she thought to ask him how he meant to get home, automatically assuming the Dodges would bring him either back to the store or out to the Manor.

"Good day, Mrs. Prior. Was that your little boy?"

"My son, William."

"A handsome child. Have you made a decision on the room?"

"You may move in anytime you're ready."

Her gaze shifted to the two men emerging from the office, lingering over the taller of them. "Perhaps Mr. Sinclair could spare a moment to help me with some of the heavier items."

She said it loudly enough for him to hear. Gallantry wouldn't allow him to decline.

"I'd be happy to, Mrs. Collier. Mr. Rosen comes in in just a few minutes and I'll be able to slip away."

Garnet smiled fiercely. "I'll leave you in Mr. Sinclair's hands, then."

"Yes," the widow purred, as if she could think of no place she'd rather be. She sauntered over to the counter behind which Deacon had turned. The tonic sharper was busy stacking his medicinal wares. "Mr. Sinclair, would you happen to have a supply of laudanum? I've had trouble sleeping off and on since my husband died and find it soothes my nerves."

Deacon looked surprised, then cautious. "You're aware that it can be dangerous if taken in excess, aren't you?"

She laughed and gave a negligent wave. "Good heavens, there's no danger of that. As I said, I just use it when I can't sleep." She waited patiently for him to bring a vial up from beneath the counter. Her hand closed quickly about it. "Thank you, Mr. Sinclair. You are a true life saver."

He watched her tuck the vial in her bag and wondered if he were doing her any favor at all.

* * *

"Mr. Skinner! Mr. Skinner!"

Roscoe turned to see the spindly telegraph operator waving him over. He recrossed the busy midday street and ambled up on the porch. "Mr. Hargrove, isn't it? What can I do for you?"

"I'm waiting on an important message and can't leave the office. I got a reply here for Mr. Sinclair that he said was urgent."

Roscoe eyed the folded missive as it fanned back and forth, charmed like a snake. What could Sinclair be expecting? "Would you like me to deliver it to him? I'm going that way." He smiled wide to disarm the other man.

"I'd sure appreciate it."

"No problem. Happy to do it." He extended his hand, still smiling. It lay in his palm, weighing with importance—importance to Deacon, which could mean importance to him. With a tip of his hat, he tucked the message into his coat and started back toward the mercantile. By the time he'd woven in and out of horse traffic, Gates Hargrove had disappeared. Roscoe stepped up onto the boardwalk, purposefully strolling past the store on his way to Sadie's. He sat down to a strong cup of coffee and biscuits swimming with gravy, then leisurely drew out the letter, savoring the suspense.

His idle curiosity stropped razor sharp when he saw the heading, recognizing the name and the governmental office.

Son of a bitch! How had the man figured him out so fast?

Rushed by trepidation, he scanned the brief contents, then frowned. Though there was no name affixed to the information, it definitely didn't concern him.

Or did it?

He reread the terse documentation. *Defrauding the government, served two years. Stock speculation, insufficient evidence to convict. Suspected of land fraud, selling false claims, misrepresenting banking institutions, insufficient evidence to bring charges. Wanted for questioning in Philadelphia and Wilmington in separate bond scams.*

Then the last tell-all line: *British expatriate.*

Montgomery Prior, you sly dog.

Handing the information to Deacon was, of course, out of the question—at least, until he could think of some way to use it to his best advantage. And he'd have to think fast before that fool from the telegraph office asked if the message had been received.

Tapping the explosive news against the table top, he sipped his coffee and schemed. And finally, he smiled as the perfect plot evolved: the means to garner him what he wanted—the land, the woman, the revenge. All it would take was a little blackmail . . . and perhaps a murder.

"Slide it in a little farther, more, more, yes, yes, that's right. Yes."

Spoken with Constance Collier's husky encouragement, even the directions for moving her furniture took on sexual overtones. Deacon eased his shoulder back from the big display case he'd been angling to catch the light from the top of the stairs. When he'd offered to help their new tenant set up shop, he'd had no idea she came equipped with back-breaking pieces of oak and enough purring innuendo to make a man go through the rest of his life at eager attention.

He glanced around, only to get an eyeful of her rounded backside as she bent to arrange some boxes. With that lightly bustled derrière waving in a tempting dance, he found himself mesmerized for a long moment. He took a rather tight breath.

"How's this, Mrs. Collier?"

She turned and that was worse. With hands on her knees, her torso twisted, her neckline dipping away from a surprisingly generous bosom, she had a sensual allure he was all too aware of.

"That's fine. And please, it's Constance. We're going to be friends, aren't we? And I'm all for relaxed formalities."

Her small smile filled in between those lines.

And why not?

She was attractive and obviously found him the same. She saw him as Deacon Sinclair, store clerk, not the Deacon Sinclair of Sinclair Manor sadly fallen upon hard times. She didn't know his history, his failings, his humiliation. Her interest was summed up in the slow sweep of her gaze from feet to face, with several meaningful pauses in between.

He'd been bemoaning his solitary status, and

here was an appealing answer. A widow looking for the comforts of a man in her life again. No dramatic emotional issues, just simple, satisfying sex.

And for a long moment, he considered the possibility.

He watched her rearrange her bags of feathers and frills. Her movements weren't graceful, but rather crisply efficient, and that he found appealing as well.

Why not? Did he want to spend the rest of his life alone, tortured by the evidence of what his future could no longer be?

Since seeing baby Jonah cradled in his sister's arms, he'd been more acutely aware than ever of what he was missing.

So what if he didn't have a big fancy house and thousands of fertile acres? Did that make him less of a person, less of a man? Did that strip away all his value? Apparently, Constance Collier didn't think so. Perhaps it was time he stopped viewing himself by what he possessed rather than by who he was.

Amazing. All it took was one lusty widow to alter his entire perspective on life.

Taking his smile as an invitation, Constance closed the distance between them. When her arms slipped over his shoulders, he had no objections to her kiss or to the feminine feel of her pressed up against him. His response to both was healthy and encouraging.

"What's wrong?" she whispered, as he pulled

away. "Am I moving too fast for you? My social graces are sadly out of practice."

Deacon stepped back. He was still smiling, still pleasantly flushed by the intimate contact. And a sudden clarity flooded his mind.

Constance released him, frowning slightly, confused by his reaction. "I'm sorry. Do you find me unattractive? You aren't married, are you?"

"No. No to both things. In fact, I owe you my thanks."

She was a quick and clever woman. "Why does that sound more like a good-bye than a hello?"

"My life is . . . complicated. You've just opened my eyes to some things I've been blind to, and for that I thank you."

Her smile was rueful. "But you're not interested."

"Tempted, but—"

"Not interested." She sighed, not at all offended by his unexplained rebuff. "Please tell me there are other eligible men in this town."

"Eligible—and, I'm sure, more than willing to go beyond temptation."

"Then I'll remain optimistic."

"Deacon?"

He was unaware of how the simple sound of Garnet's voice impacted both body and mind until Constance's face lit up with understanding.

"Ah, I see," she murmured. "Yes, complicated."

Garnet appeared on the open stairs, pausing as she took in the two of them together. Though her features betrayed nothing, it was a moment before she could speak naturally.

"Have you seen William? I thought perhaps he'd be with you."

She took his breath away. After all the years, all the changes, all the agonizing choices that pushed them apart, she was the only woman to work so sweetly upon his soul. He'd known it when he'd ridden away the first time and the certainty was stronger now. They were meant for each other. And now, instead of avoiding it with bitterness and anger, it was time to deal with those complications that kept them from finding happiness.

"Is he here?"

Her worried prompt shook him from his concentration. "No. He's probably still at the Dodges', playing with Christien. Do you want me to go check?"

She backed down a step, her shadowed gaze still drawing a connecting line between him and their new tenant. "I'll go. You stay and make Mrs. Collier feel welcomed."

He was so stupid.

Of course, she still loved him. It was evident in the pained smile she gave the two of them. And in the way she hesitated, just for an instant, before descending the stairs.

She loved him, and as his sister told him, all was not yet lost.

Filled with renewed purpose, he made his excuses to a too-intuitive Constance Collier and went below, hoping to catch up to Garnet. The time for brooding was done. Action was long overdue.

He saw a figure moving toward the front of the dimly lit store, but it was Herschel Rosen finishing up the sweeping. Garnet had already gone.

"A fine day's business," Herschel commented, leaning on the broom.

"Yes, it was. A good day." He looked about the well-stocked room, feeling a surprising sense of accomplishment. He shook his head, truly mystified. Who would have thought Deacon Sinclair would take pride in clerking behind a counter?

"I haven't told you how grateful I am for what you've done."

He glanced at the other man. "What have I done?"

"You got me this job. You gave me purpose again. And for dat, I thank you."

"I didn't—"

"Please, no modesty. It's a time for truth. I had my doubts at first. I did not think you could embrace this work, but you've proven me wrong. The customers trust you. They listen to your advice. Dat's not something a man can learn—how to gain the respect of others. I am happy to come here each day to work beside you, Deacon Sinclair. You are a good man.

There, I've said it. Words I needed to say dat you probably hear much too often."

A good man . . .

"No. It's something I haven't heard at all." What surprised him more than the sentiment was the way it brought a lump of emotion up to wedge in his throat, making his words sound thin and strained.

Herschel patted his arm and carried the broom back into the store room. He returned with his hat and coat. "I will see you in the morning, then. We have that shipment of horse collars coming in. And I want to show you how to read the merchandise marks so you can learn the bookkeeping."

That was an unexpected honor, being invited into Herschel's secret circle of mark-ups and profit margins. Garnet knew it, of course, but it was her store and she had that phenomenal head for figures.

And that phenomenal figure.

Restless energy growled through him. He held the door open, anxious to be on his way.

"Good night, Herschel. I'll see you in the morning."

And just then Constance bustled down the steps, heavy cloak concealing her charms just as her smile for Deacon disguised her disappointment.

"I must be going, too. Myrna will be waiting supper. Good night, gentlemen."

They both murmured polite responses, then

Deacon received Herschel's wink with a slight scowl. Yes, he needed a woman. No, that woman was not going to be Constance.

He was latching the heavy window shutters when the front bell rang again. Thinking his partner had forgotten something, he was slow to turn around. Then, when he did, he was momentarily taken aback.

It was Roscoe Skinner.

"If you're looking for Mrs. Prior, I believe she's over at the banker's home." Hostility rippled through his words.

"No, actually, I'm here to see you." Skinner smiled, a feral baring of his teeth. "I came to say good-bye."

A swift spike of satisfying good riddance was tempered by Deacon's mild reply. "You're leaving?"

"No. I'm not. You are."

Chapter 20

～～◯◯～～

William enjoyed playing at the Dodges'.
Mrs. Dodge, who was as beautiful as the
fairy queens in the books his mother read him,
was as nice as she was pretty. She didn't follow
them around, warning them to be careful, to
stay warm, not to run so hard or go so far, as his
own mother did. He knew his mother worried
that he might get too tired and have one of his
attacks. She fussed so much because she loved
him. But still . . . sometimes it was nice not to be
reminded or to see the fear pop up in her eyes
every time he got a little winded.

He knew she was thinking about Grandpa
William, who had died in prison, and that scared
him. He didn't want to think about dying, not
when he finally had the chance to play like a normal boy his age who had his first friend.

Christien said he was a friend, but sometimes
he didn't act like it. He was mad about what had
happened in the store, but he'd smiled and pretended he wasn't. After they'd had battles and

308

won wars with his fancy soldiers, had built corrals for his kitten out of blocks and picture books and grabbed for the most jacks, Christien had given him that funny smile and emptied out his coat pockets. They were full of all sorts of odd things from buttons and a hatpin to a small can of pomade and fruit jar rings.

"Where'd you get all this stuff?" he'd asked with wide-eyed innocence.

Then Christien's grin had widened as he'd revealed with an unholy pleasure, "From the store." And he'd waited, just daring William to do something about it.

William studied the handful of ill-gotten items in horror. "You have to take it back."

"Who's gonna make me?"

"Your mama will."

"If she knew. But who's gonna tell her?" His jewel-bright eyes narrowed in challenge, trapping William in an unwanted dilemma. When he said nothing, Christien sat back smugly. "I didn't think so."

At the sound of Mrs. Dodge's tapping footfalls, Christien gathered up his treasures and greeted her with an endearing smile.

"You boys ready for some hot chocolate?"

Christien bounded up. "You bet, Mama."

William remained seated on the rug, his brow furrowed, his gaze somber.

"Don't you want any, William?" Then, with a mother's intuition, she prompted, "Is something wrong, honey?"

"If somebody takes something that don't belong to them, like something from my mama's store, is that stealing?"

Christien froze up, his stare glittering with warning, and for the first time, with a vulnerable alarm.

Starla frowned. "Why, yes, honey, it is. Why are you asking?"

"Christien said it wasn't and I said it was. Just wanted to know for sure."

"Well, Christien knows better. Stealing is stealing, whether it's candy from the store or money from Mr. Dodge's bank. It's wrong and it's against the law."

"Would we get put in jail?"

She smiled indulgently. "No, honey, but your daddies would switch you until you wished they had. Now, come on down for that chocolate."

William trotted behind her with a sullen Christien bringing up the rear. After the mugs were emptied and the chocolate smiles wiped away, Starla shooed them outside so she could start dinner. It didn't take Christien long to get over his silence once they were alone.

"Think you're pretty smart, huh?"

"I told you it was wrong."

Galled by the other boy's self-righteous attitude and by the fact that he'd been made to be afraid, Christien shoved William hard into the porch rails. William grabbed on in surprise to keep from falling down. By then, Christien was up close, in his face.

"Think you're smart, huh?" he growled. "Think you're better'n me, do you?" His expression grew sharp and crafty as he smiled. "I got news for you. You're just a little bastard boy."

William blinked away massing tears. Bastard. He didn't know what that meant, but it sounded ugly the way his friend said it. "I am not!"

"Are too! Heard my mama and Miz Garrett talking about you."

Frightened by Christien's mocking sneer, he demanded, "What did they say?"

"They said that man you're living with ain't your daddy." He grinned as his words had the desired shock effect.

"He is so!"

"My daddy don't live with me, but at least I know who he is. Guess that makes me better'n you, don't it?"

Chest tightening up with a denying pain, William gave Christien a push, knocking him down on his behind with teeth-clacking force. He hadn't done it to be mean or get even but just to get away. He slipped off the porch at a run, heading not toward the safety of the store but out into the gloomy drizzle of twilight.

To try and run from the pain of truth.

"I'm not going anywhere except home for dinner." Deacon slipped on his overcoat, dismissing Roscoe with his indifference.

But that wasn't Roscoe's plan.

"You don't have a home to go to, Sinclair.

You're living under a borrowed roof with borrowed dreams and on borrowed time. That time's run out and I'm stepping into that dream. What was yours is going to be mine. All of it, Deacon. All of it."

Deacon stared at him for a long moment. Then, instead of the anticipated alarm and desired dread, he gave a short laugh and snapped, "Are you insane?"

Roscoe stiffened. This wasn't the response he wanted. "You don't think I'm serious."

"I try not to think of you at all and when I must, it's as an annoyance. Now, please excuse me."

Roscoe grabbed his arm as he started to pass, surprised by the hard muscle he found beneath the aristocratic trappings. And angered by the hard edge of superiority in Sinclair's expression when he looked from the offending hand on his sleeve to Roscoe's face, intimidating him into letting go.

"Still think you're a cut above everyone else, don't you, Sinclair? Even measuring out tobacco plugs and ladies' calicoes. You think these folks would still respect you if they had any idea who you really were and what you've done?"

Deacon wasn't mocking him now. His features were still, his eyes bared blade-cold. Encouraged, Roscoe went on.

"You think they'd want you handling their children's readers and their household monies if they knew how many men you'd killed or allowed to be killed just to save yourself? That you let Jonah Glendower step in front of a firing squad to give you enough time to get away? You could have given him the information to carry and accepted your own fate. A brave and honorable man would have, but not you. You wanted the glory of delivering the message yourself. Your vanity cost that innocent man his life. That innocent man was your own sister's fiancé and you hid behind him, letting him spill blood that should have been yours."

Again, Deacon wouldn't give him the satisfaction of appearing guilty. "So what if I did?" was his cool reply. "I made the decision I was trained to make, not the one I would have preferred to. Jonah couldn't have made his way back to Richmond with that information and we both knew it. He didn't have the experience in covert work. I had more to offer the Cause, so he stayed and let them capture and execute him. And I'll live with that for the rest of my life. But it was war, Skinner, and I did the job I was trained to do."

"And you were the best, weren't you? The best at deceiving those who trusted you, the best at inventing lies, the best at making those stone-cold choices that cost other men . . . and women . . . their lives and livelihoods."

"Yes," he answered with the flatness of truth, not pride. "I was."

His answer angered Roscoe further. "You may not have a problem with it, but that's not how Garnet Davis Prior sees it."

Deacon showed no outward reaction, but the

slight flicker of his eyes told Roscoe all he needed to know. He pressed on ruthlessly.

"Funny, how folks get to believing what they want to believe, just like they see what they want to see. She wanted a hero and there you were, a shiny substitute for her father. And her daddy, she put him up on a pedestal so high, God had to step aside to make room for him. But she wasn't seeing things the way they were, was she? You were just a spy, using her to get information. And her daddy was just a sickly old man who turned into a traitor because unlike you, he didn't value his country more than his family.

"She thinks he went to prison as a scapegoat for something you did. She believes he was a martyred hero who suffered and died for the Cause, not a weak man who sold out his side to save himself. She thinks you sent those false orders he was arrested for. But you didn't, did you? He did. He sent them for us, and a whole battalion was cut to pieces in a crossfire. How do you think she'd like hearing that truth? That instead of a hero, her daddy was responsible for those men's lives?"

Deacon moved so fast, Roscoe had no opportunity to defend against the hand that closed upon his windpipe, crushing, lifting him up onto his toes. Up close, his glare glittered with frightening intensity, the eyes of the man Roscoe had talked about—the man who could kill without conscience.

"But you're not going to tell her, are you?"

"Not unless you force me to," he wheezed. "Let me go. Now!" He went flat-footed, with jaw-snapping impact.

"What do you want, Skinner?"

Because he sounded more impatient and irritated than he did trepidatious, Roscoe took his time, massaging his throat before replying. "I want you to know that you're not the best anymore."

"All right, I'm not the best. I've admitted it. Now will you stop these dramatics and tell me what I've ever done to you?"

"Done to me? You don't even know, do you? You destroy men's futures so casually, you don't even pay attention to who they are."

Deacon looked closely and shook his head. "I don't know you. We've never met."

"Oh, but our paths have crossed many times over the past five years. I regret that I can't spend a bit longer filling you in on everything but you'll just have to go on in suspense. But go, you will."

"You've yet to give a solid reason as to why I'd want to."

"Her father's fate isn't the only secret I can tell Mrs. Prior. This came for you." He passed Deacon the telegram. "I don't know how you meant to use that information but I could make it very unpleasant for the lady."

Deacon scanned the news, his expression never altering.

"Imagine," Roscoe drawled, spelling out the

worst case scenario with relish. "The poor folks of this community who've survived the ravages of war finding out that they're being bilked by a professional con man. They'll be lucky to escape with the clothes on their back. If that gets you thinking you can step right back inside your fancy house, guess who's next in line to hang onto that mortgage? Monty was real set against you getting it should anything happen to him. So he put it in my name as guardian. And that would leave him, you, and the little lady all out in the cold."

"What. Do. You. Want?"

"I want you gone. I want you to disappear. I want you cut off from everything that's ever meant anything to you, and I want you to spend the rest of your days knowing that I'm responsible and that I'm enjoying those things."

"And if I go?"

"I'll be a happy man and content not to rock the Priors' tidy boat. As long as you stay gone. So, what's it going to be, Sinclair? Do you pack up your things and slip out of Pride tonight, or do you ruin her life all over again? Because she'll think it was you. After all, you were the one who sent the telegram. Who would have more to gain by soiling her good name . . . again?"

Deacon said nothing. His granite-hard jaw worked in silent frustration and fury.

And Roscoe Skinner smiled, finally gifted with the sweet sense of victory.

"I have business to attend to this evening. When I get back, you'll be gone. No word to anyone, no fond farewell letters—just gone. Understood?"

"Oh, yes. I understand you quite well."

"Then you know I'm very, very serious."

Again Deacon let his silence be his answer. Pleased with his sufficient show of domination, Roscoe was satisfied enough to gloat, "Have a nice life, Sinclair. I'll be enjoying yours."

When Skinner was gone, Deacon let his breath escape in a slow hiss. "In your dreams, you son of a bitch," he vowed to the darkened room.

Who Skinner was and why he claimed such a harsh vendetta no longer mattered. The important thing was to protect Garnet. He'd failed her before and he would not do so again. He cursed Prior for involving her in this new misery, then paused. Did Garnet know? Was she a part of his scheme to scam funds from the citizens of Pride? No. He didn't believe that. She would never hurt innocent people. She'd been justified to go after him, but even in taking her revenge, she'd been careful to see his mother didn't suffer for it. She didn't know what Prior was up to, but that left her no less vulnerable to the town's fury. He was the one who manipulated through lies, not her.

While standing in the empty store, he thought hard and fast on how to recover without losing all. Getting out of impossible situations was what he did best. Skinner was a fool, blinded by his own intentions. If he knew anything about Deacon at all, it was that he never accepted failure. And he never surrendered.

He'd confront Prior and get him to publicly confess his past to eliminate the damage Skinner's information could do. He'd shelter Garnet from any slur of awareness or participation. If Prior was in the midst of plotting, as Roscoe suggested, then it was the dapper Englishman who'd be absent from Pride this very evening. And he wouldn't be leaving with Garnet.

That was the other situation he'd clarify.

Did she love him?

He'd wasted enough time wondering.

Patrice had asked him what he wanted and he'd hedged in his answer. Now he knew. He wanted Garnet and her little boy. He wanted to make his world around them, whether it be in his family's grand home or in humble quarters in town, whether he was a plantation aristocrat or a simple store clerk. If she would have him. If she could forgive him.

If she loved him.

He couldn't make the past five years of pain go away, but he could see they didn't perpetuate into a lifetime of regret.

And it all began with one question, one he'd been terrified of asking, because once the answer was known, whether it be yes or no, his life would be forever changed.

But wasn't any change better than the lonely

limbo he'd been drifting through for most of his years?

With or without the woman he loved, tonight he would begin over as just Deacon Sinclair, separate from past glories, free of inherited expectations, ready to accept what the future would bring on his own terms. And the emancipation felt wonderful.

He took his first deep breath as a free man. It caught in his throat, then expelled in a shaky rattle as he recognized the figure pushing through the front door on a gust of rain and urgency.

"Garnet, I need to know—"

She tossed back the hood to her cloak and the sight of her expression ended his declaration. Strain and fright etched her face into dramatic angles and hollows. He reached out to catch her by the arms, alarmed by her trembling, by her suddenly dependence upon him.

"What's wrong?"

"I can't find William!"

Her tight-throated claim hit Deacon like an unfair punch, making him realize for the first time that he cared almost as much for the little boy as he did William's mother. Never mind who the child's father was, he was part Garnet, and therefore dear to him.

Seeing more than just potential danger to the boy in Garnet's hurried breathing, he took her pale face between his palms, cradling it, forcing her to focus on his calm expression.

"Slow down," he commanded with a quiet

authority. "Relax your breathing or you'll be no good to him at all. Breathe, slow and easy."

He held her gaze until the wildness began to abate. Her hands came up to cover his, clutching with a controlled desperation.

"Talk to me," he urged.

"I don't know where William is. He and Christien got into a fight and he ran off."

"He didn't come here. He didn't try to find you?"

She shook her head, tears brightening in her eyes.

"Where else might he have gone? Think, Garnet. Who else does he know in town?"

"No one."

"Would he have started back to the Manor on his own?"

Alarm leapt in her gaze. "But that's miles and miles."

"Would he have started back on foot if he was upset?"

She took a few quick breaths, thinking as her child might. "He could have. He doesn't have a very good sense of distance or of his own limitations." Her expression sobered. "He might have tried to walk back alone."

"When did he leave the Dodges'?"

"About an hour ago." Her voice faded and broke at the thought of her child alone, out in the cold and dark. She surrendered gratefully into Deacon's surrounding embrace, willing to transfer some of her burden onto his capable shoulders.

"If he hasn't stopped someplace, he could have made good headway by now. It's dark, so I'm sure he's stuck to the road. He won't be hard to catch up to. What were the boys fighting about?"

She shook her head again. "Starla couldn't get Christien to tell us. William is a sensitive child, but he's also a sensible one. He gets that from his father."

Deacon felt the faint pull of her smile beneath the curl of his fingertips along her cheek and jaw.

"It's not like him to do something so impulsive. So dangerous. Deacon, I'm afraid—"

His arms tightened. "Don't be. We'll find him. Where's your husband? And Skinner?"

"I don't know. I haven't seen either of them."

"Then we'll start searching ourselves. He won't have left the road. You're right, he may be upset, but he's not stupid. We'll find him."

Her tension eased with belief, and Deacon hoped that wishing it could make it so. But William was just a child, and children didn't always conform to logic. There was no use worrying Garnet until absolutely necessary. They would focus on the road between Pride and Sinclair Manor. Then, if worse came to worst, he would alert all their neighbors for a search of the woods. He wouldn't think about how hard it would be to find one little boy in the darkness. Not until he had to.

But he would find William. There was no way he'd allow another source of sorrow into Garnet's life. If it took all night. If he personally had to look under every bush, behind every tree. He owed her that much and more. Tonight, he would find her child, and for the rest of his life, he'd work on that "more."

Garnet rode in the buggy in what had become a chilling sleet. Deacon flanked her on horseback, hunched against the weather and holding a lantern high. A thin beam of light wavered from it, just enough to illuminate the sad condition of the road. They took turns calling for William. Garnet's voice grew increasingly hoarse. Deacon could hear the panic she tried to hide in its uneven tones, and he admired her for her bravery while fearing the worst. The night was brutal, the icy rain slashing through his heavy coat to burn right to the skin. What chance would one frail little boy have after suffering the elements for over an hour? Garnet had to be thinking the same thing.

He was staring out into the darkness, trying to see beyond the weak pool of lantern light, when Garnet gave a sudden cry. The buggy had stopped. He reined in beside it, chest tight with alarm.

"What is it?"

"I'm stuck. These damned roads." She sounded more angry than frightened, which was good.

Deacon swung down off his horse, immediately sinking to his boot tops. Wading through the mire, he circled the vehicle to assess the problem. The problem was the county's method of providing road drainage by heaping soft dirt up in the middle of the lane to encourage runoff. What it encouraged was a sticky hill and slushy ruts that snared the lightweight buggy like a gnat in honey.

"I'm going to push. When I holler, you whip up the horses."

"All right."

After finding firm purchase for his feet, Deacon leaned his shoulder into the rear of the buggy. Shouting "Go," he levered his weight against the conveyance, hearing the slap of reins and Garnet's demand of "Get up there!"

His feet slipped and he dug in deeper, pushing steadily until the buggy rocked forward, then broke the muddy suction to roll rapidly ahead. Off balance, Deacon plunged headlong into the muck. Cold ooze filled his mouth and nose, choking off his curse. By the time he skidded and scrambled to his feet, Garnet had the buggy free.

"Are you all right?"

"Fine," he spat out along with a mouthful of grit. He was wiping his face on his sleeve when he picked up on a faint sound, one sweet enough to offset his cold misery.

A child's voice.

"Mama!"

Chapter 21

It was with tremendous pleasure that Deacon lifted one shivering boy up to his weeping mother. William was wet and cold, but otherwise seemed no worse for wear, but Garnet needed further assurances as she clutched him to her.

"Are you all right, darling?"

"I'm sorry, Mama. It got dark so fast and it started raining and it was too far to go back and I was too tired to go on, so I found that big old tree over there to sit under and figured I'd wait for you to come get me."

Clever boy. She squeezed him until he squirmed. Smart boy, like his father.

"Let's get him home and into some dry clothes."

She nodded. Home, with Deacon and her son. She embraced the idea, too weary to deny herself the simple joy of it. With William tucked against her side, she drove the rest of the way without incident. She saw the lights of the Manor ahead, a beacon in her storm of worries and doubts, a safe haven for her family. And for the first time, she felt its welcome.

"I'll take him."

She passed William into Deacon's uplifted hands and the reins to one of the stableboys. With the sleepy boy enfolded in one arm, Deacon helped her down, then secured the other about her waist. She leaned into him, exhausted from the gamut of emotions, needing his strength just to get her to the door, where they were met by an alarmed Hannah.

"What happened?"

"Mama, see a hot bath is drawn for Mrs. Prior and get her settled in."

Garnet was quick to protest his order. "No, I have to see to my son."

"You see to yourself before you fall ill. I can take care of Will." His tone brooked no further argument. It was the voice of the master of the house. She might have resisted his command if not for the tender way he held her child tucked under his chin. Her objections melting away, she gave an assenting nod. Obediently she followed Hannah up the stairs, too tired to examine the complexities of her mood, too vulnerable to Hannah's motherly concern not to place herself completely in her care.

While the bath was being readied, Hannah undressed her as if she were a helpless child. She'd forgotten how wonderful it was to surrender herself to loving hands. There were times when she could scarcely recall her mother's face, and others when she seemed so close that Garnet could almost smell her perfume. Hannah combed out her hair, reminding her of when she wasn't alone, when she'd felt safe and secure with a mother's love. How she'd missed that feeling and needed it now to restore her flagging spirit. With eyes closed, she gave herself over to the pampering sensation.

"He'd make a wonderful father, you know."

Garnet kept her eyes shut, afraid the other woman would see tears in them as she whispered, "I know."

"Your son is so like him when he was a boy, so serious and yet so tender of heart."

Garnet swivelled on the stool, grasping at the opportunity. "What changed that? What made his heart so hard?"

Hannah smiled wistfully. "He might pretend it is, but I don't believe it."

"Then why won't he let anyone get close to him?"

"He's afraid to, my dear. He's afraid if he lets down the barriers even for a moment, he won't be able to put them up again."

"Would that be so bad?"

"No. But he thinks it would."

"Why? Please, I need to know. For William's sake. And my own."

"My husband was an exacting man. He expected perfection from himself and from all around him. Deacon was his son, made in his image, a reflection of who he was and what he might have become. And that image had to be perfect. I can tell you, it wasn't easy to bear those expectations, but Avery had a way of making you want to meet them. Both the children idolized him, but his demands took such a toll. Patrice reacted to the strain with rebellion, Deacon with rigid compliance. He struggled so hard not to be a disappointment. I watched my husband make my son into a man I didn't know and couldn't reach, and there was nothing I could do to stop it."

"He's lost, then." All her anguish resonated in that brief summation. But Hannah shook her head.

"No, not lost—misguided. Avery put him on a path of discipline and denial, but he's my son and Patrice's brother, too. He could be coaxed from that road by the promise of a reward greater than his father's approval."

"And what would that be?"

Hannah smiled. "I think you know, or you wouldn't be here."

The water arrived then, a parade of steaming buckets emptied into the huge tub in the sitting room, where a fire burned invitingly and the scent of chamomile beckoned. As Hannah went to check on William, Garnet sank beneath the suds, letting the heat soothe her body's tensions as Hannah's words had her mind's. Soon the chill of the night and the frightening episode seemed far removed. Then there was only relief and reflection. And images of Deacon Sinclair. The way he'd looked with William in his arms.

The passion in his voice when he'd said, "I came back for you." Dared she believe what her heart told her? And if he loved her, could that love withstand the truths she had to tell? Or with truth, would she lose him forever?

She wouldn't know unless she took the risk.

"You had your mother worried, Will."

William wiggled into his nightshirt, then met Deacon's gaze reluctantly. "I know."

"If you knew it would upset her, why did you do it?"

" 'Cause I got mad at her, I guess," he mumbled, sinking under the covers and wishing he could pull them over his head.

"Why were you mad at your mother? Did she scold you about something?"

He looked glumly at the man sitting on the edge of his bed, needing to tell someone the secret that writhed inside him like a pocketful of snakes. "No. She lied to me."

Deacon's brows soared. "Your mother? About what?"

He wouldn't believe him, William knew. Adults tended to stick together when one of their own was challenged. Christien had told him that. Christien had also told him a fact that had rocked his world. What if he was wrong? What if he was lying just to get even? Of all the adults he knew, he respected Deacon Sinclair the most. He would know who had told the lie.

"Will, what did you and Christien fight about?"

He liked it when Deacon called him "Will." It made him feel more grown-up, less like the sickly little boy his mama fussed over. What if Deacon thought less of him after finding out the truth? That horrible thought held him silent.

"I thought we were friends," Deacon said, with enough cajoling to break through William's resistence.

"Maybe you won't like me anymore if I tell you."

"Will, no one's without faults or mistakes. Friends forgive those things. I don't have enough friends to be willing to lose any of them."

"He called me a bastard."

"Oh. Well, that's not a very nice name. Sometimes grownups use bad words when they shouldn't—"

"He didn't call me a name. He said I didn't have a father." His chest jerked beneath the covers as he struggled to uphold Deacon's statement that men didn't cry.

Deacon frowned, angry lines appearing on his forehead. "That was a mean and untruthful thing for him to say. Why would he say that to you?"

" 'Cause he heard your sister, Mrs. Garrett, saying so to his mama."

Patrice?

Why would Patrice suggest that Montgomery Prior wasn't William's father? Unless she knew it to be true. And if Will wasn't Monty's child . . .

The breath left him in a sudden rush.

My God!

William was his child. His and Garnet's.

His.

"I told you you'd be mad," William mumbled, watching the changes in his expression and drawing unhappy conclusions.

Deacon forced himself to breathe and to smile—or at least make a reasonable facsimile of one. "I'm not mad at you, Will. I could never be mad at you."

He bent to gather the boy into an affirming embrace. He drew in the scent of rain and fresh soap and warm child along with an intoxicating truth: this was his son. Why hadn't he seen it? His sister had; his mother had. Now he knew the reason behind her poignant expressions. This was her grandson. The future of the Sinclair name.

Why hadn't Garnet told him?

The sudden chill of that question set him back from the boy like a swift dose of the sleet outside.

Why had Garnet given him another man's name?

"There's my adventurous little dear."

Hannah stepped into the room and Deacon's heart took a tender turn when he watched William's features light up at her approach. There was a bond between them already. And he knew, seeing it, that he would never be satisfied playing the friend when he could have the reward of acting as father.

Hannah slipped her hand over Deacon's shoulder for a gentle press. The gesture was an automatic claim of her affection, one he'd rarely had time to acknowledge in the past. On this night of secrets and surprises, it was a stabilizing anchor he clung to in gratitude. She glanced at him with a mother's intuitiveness, seeing his distress and confusion, knowing its cause without having to hear of it. Her quiet smile comforted him just as her soft words encouraged.

"I'll finish tucking William in. You should go speak to Mrs. Prior. I think there are issues you need to discuss."

An incredible understatement.

"Where's Monty?"

"He went into town to meet with Mr. Skinner. I believe they were planning to play cards until the early morning hours."

She was telling him he had a clear window of opportunity to be alone with Garnet.

"Well, dear," she cooed to William. "Shall we finish that story I was reading you?"

Her slight push to Deacon's shoulder urged him to go make his own happy ending. As she assumed his spot on the edge of the bed, he bent to touch a kiss to her brow, followed by the impulsive claim, "I love you, Mama."

The words came with surprising ease and the reward of having her gaze lift to his in teary surprise and pleasure far surpassed the risk of saying them.

Now that he'd had some practice, it was time to speak them to the one woman who mattered most.

* * *

Deacon paused outside of the room that had been his and should have been theirs. He struggled to focus his thoughts amid the uncommon swirl of his emotions. There was so much that needed to be addressed, so much to be said. He needed to prioritize them but for once his methodical logic failed him. Control fled when he depended upon razor-sharp faculties to defend against Skinner's threats. Objectivity faded when he considered how best to handle the situation concerning his son. A mass of conflicting feelings as frightening as they were foreign, he was at a loss with himself how to proceed.

With a small step, he decided.

She answered his tap on the door with a panicked abruptness.

"William?"

"Is fine," he assured just as quickly. "My mother is reading him a bedtime story."

The fortifying edge left her on a heartfelt sigh. What remained was a weary vulnerability that played havoc upon Deacon's already frayed sensibilities. Instinct told him to take a step back, to free his mind from the sensory assault of her nearness. She'd just gotten out of the bath. He could smell the oils upon warm skin that lay bare beneath the wrap of her robe. Her long black hair had been piled on top of her head during her soak and now tendrils of it escaped, clinging damply along her neck and the sides of her face.

He couldn't resist one strand curving along her cheek, reaching out to tuck it back behind her ear. And once his fingertips grazed her soft skin, he couldn't pull them away. They lingered at the juncture of stubborn jaw and sleek throat, riding her jerky swallow, testing the sudden hurry of her pulse. She put her hand over his, meaning to draw it away, then similarly stilled by the heat of contact. Her fingers stroked over the backs of his, exciting sensations both restless and dangerous.

"Thank you, Deacon," she said at last, her voice barely a whisper. "I don't know what I would have done if you hadn't been at the store."

A small smile escaped him. "You probably would have done just fine. You're a strong, resilient woman, Garnet. It's one of your most captivating qualities."

And the unexpected praise captivated her. Her uplifted gaze searched his for the reason behind his words. "I didn't feel particularly strong or capable. I needed you to be there."

"I'm glad I was. And I deeply regret the times when I haven't been."

He watched the confusion of doubt and desire cross her features. Then, surprisingly, she smiled in some amusement and lifted her other hand. He stilled his initial recoil to accept her touch, tensing as it brushed over his cheekbone and down to his chin.

"Mud," she explained, humor warming her tone in a way that relaxed him wonderfully.

"It's all over me, I'm afraid." He'd taken off his soiled outerwear down to his slightly damp shirt sleeves, but the front of his trousers were caked with remnants of the road.

"I've never minded a little honest dirt."

She leaned into him, her hand sliding behind his head, her cheek resting over his heart. And after the briefest pause, his hands skimmed over the nap of her robe, spreading wide at the small of her back and spanning the hollow between her shoulder blades to pull her closer still. A perfect fit, two into one. It seemed only natural for her to tip her head back, for his mouth to find hers with an unerring fervor. Sweetness remembered, paradise recalled.

Deacon waited for some objection to surface, for his moral conscience to interrupt what was flaring so quick and hot between them. But it wasn't a whisper he heard; it was a roar.

Our son. The mother of my child.

And he realized the truth of what he'd told his sister in envious ignorance: that bond between parent and child was one of emotional steel, strong, unbreakable, inseparable. He could never let them go, not ever. Skinner's threats, Monty's existence, conscious thought itself fell away as he parted her lips to plunge to her soul in one claiming thrust.

He'd gone half crazy surviving off the brief memories they'd made between them all those years ago. The stolen kiss, the secret yearnings, that one mad moment on the balcony had stoked them to a wildfire intensity that burned out of his control. He'd longed for this intimate reunion, had imagined it down to the most minute detail, but impatience rattled those good intentions and urgency ruled.

He tore from her kiss, breathing in harsh snatches that fueled rather than tamed the passion. His mind was a hot blur, his body a fierce pulse of need. With one swift motion, he swung her up in his arms. With a few purposeful strides, he deposited her atop his bed. The sight of her there upon his coverlet, her lush mouth kiss-bruised, the disarray of her robe exposing soft shoulders and one sleek thigh, snapped the only thread of restraint holding him together. Even a second of delay meant torture.

Then she tugged at the belt to her robe. Parting the fabric, she opened for him like one of his mother's precious roses, passions unfurling from delicate petal to tender center. When her arms lifted in invitation, he was quick to cover her with his weight, with his kisses, with the reacquainting scrub of his palms over exquisite surfaces. Her hands dipped to his trouser band with no trace of hesitation, opening it, slipping inside along the taut furring of his abdomen, lower to capture the hard beat of him in her hands. Encasing him, stroking him, squeezing until a sound or a word groaned from him and he snatched her clever hands away, holding them tight in his own shaking grip.

It was no little girl's gaze that met his, filled with wonder and reverence. It was a woman's stare, all smoky and hot with knowing expectation. His emotions shuddered.

"I've wanted you here in this bed since the first time I saw you," he told her in rough urgency.

"I don't want to be alone in it again," was her equally gruff reply.

Their hands met at his hips to shove down his pants. Hers rubbed along his thighs, moving up to cup the hard curve of his buttocks. Kneading taut muscle, tugging him against her in a rhythmic beat, encouraging him with that explicit motion to finish what he'd started on that upper porch. To fulfill what simmered deep inside her by bringing it to a boil. She lifted her knees, parting them. She was all bubbly heat already, which he discovered as his hand slipped down between them, sifting through inky curls, slipping through damp folds to test the temperature of her desires. Finding them volcanic.

She moved restlessly beneath him, hips lifting as her hands pulled down, creating an exquisite friction where his hardness channeled along her feminine grove. His body grew rigid with strain. Her spine arched, a soft, needy moan wavering from her as her naked breasts flattened against his damp shirtfront. The sound intensified as his hand swallowed up one plentiful globe, molding it, shaping its nipple into a turgid peak, then feeding it between the pinch of his thumb and forefinger into his mouth. Sensation shook her at the first fierce, startling suction, then became a stabbing pleasure as the pulsing echoed the bump and grind of their hips and the slow, steady dip of his fingers inside her ready heat.

"Deacon," she pleaded, as her breaths quickened into ragged little gasps. She was shaking apart inside, muscles tensing, nerves dancing, skin quivering as if provoked by a thousand tiny shocks. Showing no mercy, he continued the erotic attack at each sensitized point until tremors massed low in her belly and raced along her thighs. The balls of her feet punched down into the mattress as she said his name again.

His tongue mashed her nipple against the cut of his teeth and she came in glorious abandon.

Even before she began to spiral down from that high plane of pleasure, he buried himself within her, catching those tight, milking spasms at their pinnacle and pushing them further, faster, to reach the heart of her with every thrust. With no chance to recover, she found herself lifted to another soul-shattering climax. It quaked through her limbs, rattling down her spine, exploding at the core as he burst inside her in scalding pulsations.

For a long minute he didn't move, couldn't move. Reaction twitched through him in nerveless shudders. He waited.

He'd expected the guilt to come afterward. He knew it would be there, just knew it. Another sin heaped upon the many others to punish him. But all he felt was sinfully good; relaxed, relieved, and reborn.

Garnet was his. William was his. No one else had a claim to either.

Now was the time to tell her, the time to come clean with all he'd discovered. But the moment he lifted his ridiculously heavy head off her shoulder, he was met by the sight of her satisfied smile. Everything inside him went to mush. God, she was beautiful. And brave. Think of all she'd endured when she'd thought he'd abandoned her.

He did abandon her. There was no escaping that ugly truth.

Beautiful, brave, and resourceful. Alone and afraid, she'd found the means to take care of herself and the child to come. He would never fault her for that, not ever. Montgomery Prior would have his eternal gratitude for taking her in and raising their child. But that's all he would have. Woman and child were now out of his reach.

And he had to make sure they were safe.

Seeing the frown lines gather above the distancing chill of his gaze, Garnet experienced a shiver of dread. She brushed her fingertips along his jaw, sampling the tension there.

"Deacon, don't."

Surprise softened his expression. "Don't what?"

"Don't pull away from me."

The remote glaze melted from his eyes, leaving all the warmth and devotion she'd dreamed of. And a glint of wry humor. He nudged his hips into hers. She felt him stir inside her, a slow awakening that soon pulsed with renewed life.

"I hadn't planned to, angel. At least, not for a while."

It wasn't what she'd meant, but it would more than do. She moved her legs lazily so that the soles of her feet stroked his calves and thighs. Her fingers made idle circles about the muscle groupings on his arms. Just touching him with such casual intimacy excited powerful emotions. Possession was foremost among them. In her heart and mind, he would never belong to another. He would be hers. If only reality could be so obliging.

Noting the sudden glimmer in her eyes, it killed him to think it might be regret. Deacon bent to take her lips in a long, reassuring kiss, not letting up until he'd coaxed her tongue into play with his. He'd be damned if he'd let her feel guilty about something that was meant to be. Him and her and their son. Meant to be.

First, to convince her. Then to take action.

He lifted up onto his elbows, his expression growing serious even as his body grew more impatient with the idea of delay.

"We need to talk," he began. It didn't help that she'd begun to raise and lower her hips in tiny, devastating pulses.

"We need each other," she contradicted, a reasonable request, considering how he'd doubled in size inside her. Her thumbs grazed the jut of his cheekbones, her fingers spreading wide to capture his head, directing him back down to greet her sweet, wet kisses.

The gentle rock of motion escalated into a sea-swept tempest. Tidal passions roared, surging madly, wildly, to break finally upon a peaceful shore . . . where they lay entwined for a timeless moment, lulled by each other's breathing.

Until the sound of Boone galloping down the hall roused them. And the slam of the front door brought them up and apart.

Garnet shoved against his chest as footsteps pounded up the stairs. "Quick." She gestured to the sitting room. "Dress in there."

He snatched up his clothing as Garnet arranged her robe. Just before he ducked into the other room, he paused to catch her anxious gaze. A brief flare of sentiment calmed her. Her faint smile sent him on his way.

Deacon wrestled on his muddied trousers in the dimness of the dressing room. He didn't have time to wonder what kind of evidence he was leaving on the hardwood floor. As he stuffed in his shirttails, he cast a look around him, stunned by what he saw.

He saw a man's bedroom, with signs of it being fully occupied.

If Montgomery Prior was sleeping in this room, did that mean he wasn't sleeping with his wife?

Then chaos took hold.

Garnet answered the pounding at her chamber door. An anxious house servant burst out, "Mrs. Prior, it's your husband. He's been shot!"

Chapter 22

Clots of mud disappeared as recently disheveled covers were thrown back to receive an insensible Montgomery Prior. Deacon stood in the background as Garnet and Hannah listened anxiously to Doc Anderson's prognosis. It wasn't good. Monty had taken a bullet to the chest, a dangerous wound for even a young, fit man, lessening the odds for an older, sedentary gentleman who'd lost a great deal of blood. The situation was grave, each second critical. If Monty held on for the next twenty-four hours, his chances to survive doubled. If no fever set in, the percentage kept increasing. What the doctor stressed was the immediate constant care he'd need. Both women volunteered to see someone was always at his side.

Helpless to do much more than stay out of the way while the ladies set up a hospital room with quick efficiency, Deacon lingered by the door-way, distressed by his own dark thoughts.

How much better everything would be if the Englishman died.

He hated the idea, and himself for thinking it, but a rational part of his brain recognized the truth of it. If Monty quietly slipped away, Garnet would be free to marry. She'd never need know about her departed husband's past and he could correct any overtures Monty had made so far to bilk the people of Pride. Skinner would lose his leverage, but if Roscoe was right, Deacon would lose his chance of ever getting his home back.

He watched Garnet bending over the gray-haired gentleman to carefully blot his forehead. Moved by the tender sympathy in her exquisite face, he realized that having the Manor and his inheritance was a far distant goal. Having Garnet and the child they'd made between them was everything.

Monty's survival or demise wouldn't change that fact.

Then Garnet's gaze lifted, meeting his for a brief, telling moment. In the dark pool of worry, he could see deeper eddies of distress. Because she'd been unfaithful in the same bed her wounded husband now occupied? Because she couldn't trust that the moment of passion between them would develop to something more? He saw the splintering doubt in that fleeting communion, an unanswered pain of past betrayal and fresh uncertainties. He deserved that from her even after the beautiful love they'd made. She needed more from him now. More than physical pleasures. She needed words. She needed to hear the truth to wash away the tinge of his dishonorable actions. He wanted to reassure her that his motives were solid, that his love would overcome the stain of infidelity. But they were not alone and she looked too quickly away.

What if her guilt placed an insurmountable wall between them? Deacon began to frown.

"Tough old bird, isn't he? Who would have thought."

Deacon's glance stabbed to where a pale Roscoe Skinner leaned on the door jamb at his side. While he might plot the old fellow's death, he didn't like the idea of Skinner taking pleasure from it.

"Who shot him?"

At Deacon's terse questions, the women turned toward them.

"Mr. Skinner, should you be up and around?" Hannah cried worriedly.

"Thank you for your concern, ma'am, but the doctor said I was in no danger. Blade just grazed my ribs. Nothing vital got perforated."

"What happened on the road, Mr. Skinner?"

Roscoe grew somber at Garnet's directness. "Your husband was carrying a stack of investor's money. The attack was unexpected. It happened so fast, I couldn't have prevented it."

"Who pulled the trigger?"

"Tyler Fairfax."

That news stunned even Deacon, who wouldn't

have believed the scheming drunkard could
have fallen any farther in his esteem. But cold
blooded murder? For financial reasons? It could
have happened that way. Could have, but he
suspected it didn't.

"Now that I know Mr. Prior is holding his
own, I aim to go after Fairfax myself."

Skinner's hard claim alerted Deacon. Roscoe
was going hunting, and it wasn't to bring Tyler
back alive. If Monty died and Tyler didn't survive
to tell his side of the tale, Skinner's word would
be all they had to go on. And that didn't sit well
with Deacon. Skinner's word wasn't something
he'd take at face value—not knowing as he did
that Skinner had more than one face.

"Where do you plan to look?"

"He's wounded. At his home, at his sister's,
then I'll start checking with his friends. Don't
worry, Mrs. Prior. I'll find him. And he'll pay for
what he did to your husband." And as he turned
out into the hall, he gripped Deacon's arm, turning him out for a private word. "And you'll pay,
too. Don't think you're getting off easy, Sinclair.
I'll take care of you when I get back. You might
want to make yourself scarce before I do, or
things will get ugly, real ugly."

Deacon smelled Garnet's unique scent as she
moved to stand beside him as Roscoe wobbled
down the hall. He was almost afraid to look at
her, afraid he'd see regret, remorse, or even
anger over what had happened between them

while her husband was being attacked. He couldn't bear the thought of her guilt.

But Garnet wasn't thinking in a carnal direction.

"Do you believe him?"

He started at her low, calm question. "Skinner? No. Not until someone backs up his story."

"What if Monty never wakes up?" Anguish colored her voice, making him wince at his earlier thoughts. She obviously loved Monty, regardless of the nature of their marriage.

"That's why I have to find Tyler before Skinner does."

He started again as her fingers brushed across the back of his hand to slip into his palm. His closed up for a heartening squeeze.

"Find him, Deacon," she urged. "I don't want any doubts to remain. Not about anything."

He nodded, giving her hand another press. "And then we need to talk."

"Yes," was all the encouragement she'd give him, before sliding her hand free and returning to her husband's bedside.

Deacon saddled his horse and spurred it in the opposite direction that Skinner had gone. He had the advantage, that of knowing a thing or two about Tyler Fairfax and who he would first think to go to if he were in any real peril.

If she hadn't been up with Jonah's feeding, Patrice would never had heard the knock.

At least, she thought it was a knock.

She'd tucked the sated baby back into his bassinet, then gone downstairs to put the infant's soiled linens to soak. She stopped in the kitchen to pour a glass of water for herself and was carrying it across the front foyer when the noise brought her up short. Someone or something was on the porch making that weak thump against the solid panel.

Made cautious by harsh experience, she padded on bare feet into Byron Glendower's former study. Trembling hands a contrast to her cool demeanor, she drew a loaded pistol from the big desk and returned to the hall. If it was nothing, she wouldn't disturb her husband and child in vain. If it was something, she wouldn't be caught unprepared.

The freezing rain had finally stopped leaving a heavy mist rising from the ground in a cold, thick curtain. The stables were silent, no sign of disturbance there. She stepped out onto the porch warily. That's when she saw a single horse cropping on their corner bushes. Its reins were trailing on the wet grass. Its empty saddle was dark and slick with an all too recognizable stain.

" 'Trice . . . "

The sound came from behind her, making her heart leap and the gun in her hand jerk up in self-defense as she whirled back toward the house. The glass in her other hand shattered on the stone porch floor as it fell from nerveless fingers.

"Oh, my God! Reeve, come quick!"

Even as she shouted for her husband, Patrice was kneeling down before the figure slumped next to the door, searching out the source of the terrible blood flow.

"Patrice? What is it?" Reeve barreled through the door dressed only in long underwear washed to a faded pink. He carried a rifle, expecting anything, ready for everything. Except the sight of his onetime friend bleeding all over his doorstep. "Tyler." He looked to his ashen-faced wife. "How bad?"

"Bad," she answered, tears in her eyes.

"Let's get him inside and I'll go for the doctor."

Tyler gripped his arm, dragging himself back from the brink of unconsciousness. "No," he whispered hoarsely. "Deacon. Bring Deacon. No one else."

Reeve carried him murmuring insensibly into the front parlor, draping his muddied, bloodied form across a newly upholstered sofa.

"Any idea what this is about?" Patrice asked, as she tucked a pillow behind his lolling head.

"With Tyler, it could be anything. A falling out with his cutthroat friends, his bastard of a father, who knows? I know I don't like leaving you here with him like this, not knowing what kind of trouble he's bringing behind him."

"Reeve, we have to help him."

He met her solemn stare for a long moment, then nodded. "Of course we do."

Theirs had been a lengthy friendship marred by the changing times. But fond memories couldn't be dismissed as unimportant, so they would do what they could, regardless of the danger that might be even now following on his heels.

Reeve gestured to the pistol she'd placed on the table at the end of the sofa. "Keep that within reach. I'll be back as quick as I can. Hopefully your brother can shed some light on this, though I can't see him and Tyler involved in anything together."

"Be careful."

He nodded, kissed her hard and was gone.

" 'Trice?"

"I'm here, Tyler." She took up his hand, pressing it comfortingly between her own.

"Don't let me die."

"I won't. I promise. After all, you saved me once. Now I can return the favor."

A faint rueful smile etched his taut features. "Then we'll be even and owing each other nothing. Then you can finally get rid of me."

"Don't be silly. You know Reeve and I will always love you, just as we do Starla. You just make it hard for us sometimes."

"I know, darlin', I know." But his eyes closed and his smile sweetened with relief. "Maybe I can make some of it up to you tonight."

Reeve was leading his stallion Zeus from the barn, tacked and ready for a fast trip to Sinclair Manor, when he heard a single rider approach in a hurry. He eased his rifle from its scabbard in case their predawn visitor had more than a courtesy call on his mind. Then he stuffed the barrel back in its sheath when he recognized the lean, upright posture of his wife's brother.

"Tyler?" Deacon called as he swung down, not questioning where Reeve was headed before daylight.

"Inside."

"Alive?"

"When I left."

"Anyone else know he's here?"

"Nope. He was sending me over to get you. You mind telling me what's going on?"

"I'm hoping Tyler can answer that."

He greeted Deacon with a faint smile.

Deacon cut right to it. "Was it Skinner?"

"That son of a bitch," Tyler mumbled in agreement. Haltingly, he filled them in on Roscoe's treachery, ending with, "I should have known not to turn my back on him."

"And he should have kept a better eye on you, as well. You nearly carved out his spleen."

Again, the faint smile. "Meant to. Prior?"

"Hanging on."

Tyler's eyes slid shut, his energy lapsing. His breaths came shallow and fast. "Patrice says I'm not dying. What do you say, Rev? Figure you'd put it plain."

"I'm not a doctor," he replied, not meeting his sister's plaintive gaze. "But it looks pretty bad."

"Guess I'd better talk fast, then." He drew a

slow, bracing breath and began. "Skinner's my fault. I brought him here. Prior wanted someone to oversee the properties and keep an eye on you, and I remembered Roscoe from the war years. Figured I could plant him at the Manor and keep tabs on what was going on."

"How did you know him?"

Tyler smiled. "We boys with bad reputations tend to find one another. He was tradin' secrets for the highest price. He did a few things for me now and again and I told him a thing or two. That's all I'll say about that. But I remembered him having a particular dislike for you, Rev."

"Why? I don't know him."

"You were in the same brotherhood."

"What are you talking about?"

"Your code name was 'the Reverend,' his was 'Hermes.'"

Things fell into place for Deacon. Hermes. He'd never met the man, but he knew the name of the infamous counterspy he'd helped expose. Before the court martial could convene, Hermes had escaped and disappeared. And now he had resurfaced to take his revenge upon the man who'd turned him in as a traitor.

"There's more," Tyler whispered, his voice failing, his breath growing weaker. "Roscoe, he was responsible for Jonah."

Deacon, Patrice, and Reeve exchanged quick looks. It was Reeve who answered.

"We know who was responsible for Jonah dying. The two of us are right here."

Tyler shook his head. "No. Roscoe set a trap for Deacon and Jonah sprang it. He meant for it to be you, Rev. Then, before they executed you, he was going to slip in and offer to get the information you were carrying through to Richmond. He would have been a hero and you would have been dead. That was his plan."

"But he hadn't counted on a real hero stepping in," Reeve interjected softly, choking up at the thought of his half-brother's sacrifice.

Deacon stayed focused on the current problem. "So you brought him here to finish what he started." There was no time to delve into the complexities of emotion ricocheting between heart and mind. He'd said it was duty where Jonah was concerned, but Roscoe's suspicions were closer to the truth than Deacon had been willing to accept. He had wanted to be the hero. He had wanted the glory for himself. And he'd never stopped suffering for the results, not ever. Jonah had died bravely, his sister's fiancé. And he'd let it happen. Knowing it was part of a plot conceived by Roscoe Skinner lessened some of that blame—some, but not all. Never all. In some ways, it made him even more culpable. Skinner had sought his death, not that of an innocent martyr to the Cause. It was no longer an impersonal matter of war. It was a very personal attack.

Now he knew who. He just needed to know why.

"If I'd wanted you dead," Tyler was saying,

"you'd a been buried long ago. I just wanted him to make some mischief so nobody would see what I was up to."

"Getting the judge appointed county supervisor so you could pretty much run Pride as you saw fit."

Tyler grinned at Deacon. "Always was too damned smart. Knew you'd pick up on it 'less you was distracted. Figured Roscoe would keep you busy. Should a figured he'd come to see me as a liability sooner or later."

"He's saying you tried to kill Prior and stole the money."

Tyler's gaze sharpened in alarm. "He's lying." He looked to Patrice. "You don't believe that, do you?"

"Then you'd better plan on staying alive to prove it." Deacon looked to Reeve. "Keep him here and keep things quiet."

Reeve nodded. "Where are you going?"

"I'm going to set a trap for a traitor."

Chapter 23

After a quick stop in town at the break of day to speak to Dodge and Noble Banning— Dodge because of his Yankee background and his contacts with those still maintaining a loose martial law and Noble to obtain his legal counsel— Deacon returned to the Manor, numbed with weariness but alive with anticipation. It took him several determined minutes to finalize his case against Roscoe. The law was already after him, and now he would see the man hanged. His threats lost their power. That accomplished, Deacon had only one remaining purpose.

Prior was still unconscious but breathing stronger and resting easier. His mother was sitting at the Englishman's bedside, and again he experienced a twinge of concern. She seemed awfully committed to a married man. An irony, considering he was planning to steal the man's wife.

After exchanging brief words and learning that Garnet had retired to get some much needed rest, Deacon headed wearily for his own small room in back. His mind spun with the question of what to do about Garnet.

It didn't appear that Prior would die, despite the seriousness of his wound. If that was the case, would Garnet be willing to risk the scandal of divorce to begin a life with him? Would Prior let her and the boy go without a fight? He dismissed the thought of using blackmail as leverage. That would force him into the same mold as Skinner. That's not who he was anymore.

Would Garnet believe him if he told her his motive was love?

That was the big question. He had nothing to give her except a history of lies. Would she always wonder if he'd only wanted her as a means to get back his properties? Or to claim his son? He'd have to work long and hard to convince her otherwise. But first, some sleep; then he'd seek her out for a little long-overdue truth-telling.

He pushed open the door, sliding out of his coat as he stepped inside. Then froze.

For there asleep on his bed was Garnet Prior, her hair spread across his pillow, encasing it in ebony silk.

The gentleman he'd always prided himself on being would have discreetly backed out and left her to her rest. He closed the door quietly behind him, not caring what that made him. She woke at the sound, regarding him through quiet eyes that showed no alarm or displeasure.

"You said we needed to talk," she murmured in

a sleep-roughened voice that tightened every fiber of his being. "I thought I'd wait for you here."

"It's rather hard to concentrate on what I wanted to say with you lying over there like that."

Her smile was gently coaxing as she patted the mattress beside her. "Then come over here and do your talking."

A temptation man wasn't meant to resist.

Draping his coat over the back of a chair, he crossed to the bed, pausing at the side of it while Garnet unwound like a supple cat from the covers to sit up, the movement all unplanned sensuality. Before his resolve totally crumbled, he told her, "What I have to discuss is serious, Garnet."

"Then you'd better kiss me first."

A logical request. He wouldn't be able to concentrate until the roar of his blood was cooled. But how to quiet a fire by pouring on kerosene?

His hand slipped under her chin so long fingers cradled her upturned face. The gaze that met hers was intense and steady. She waited, dreading the distancing veil sure to drop over that quiet gray stare, covering the lambent passion, the naked need displayed there for her to see. She waited, knowing he would draw back into himself, becoming the cool, unapproachable stranger who might share the heat of his mouth but never the warmth in his heart. She waited for those impersonal changes to barricade the man she'd touched so briefly behind a wall of rigid defensiveness where he would remain just out of reach. She waited, emotions pooling around a deeper regret.

But as he bent toward her, there was no shuttering of his expression. His eyes remained open as windows to a troubled soul right up until the magical instant when their lips swept against each other's, sealing that intent gaze behind the lowering of his lids.

Their mouths moved together, seeking the most satisfying fit where tongues could meet in an intimate dance that imitated other pleasures they'd shared. To Garnet, it was a generous and expressive offering, not a bold claim of what she couldn't help but give. Along with the slow, hungering pursuit of her response was a richer heartfelt yearning, one that couldn't be and never had been pretended. She knew with a certainty that her quest for the real Deacon Sinclair was answered in his searingly honest kiss, in the revering caress of his fingertips along her cheek and jaw. It was an honesty that made her tremble, for now that he'd revealed his heart, she must similarly bare her conscience.

And that prospect terrified her.

Even as her arms encircled his waist and her body molded itself along the hard length of his, she slipped from the safe, consuming passion of his kiss to the neutrality of her head upon his shoulder. Chiding herself for being a coward, she asked him to take the first healing step.

"What did you mean when you said you came back for me?"

"I was on an assignment, Garnet," he began with a flat-toned candor that made her fear what he would say as much as she desired to know the full truth. "I was sent to find a way to break your code, and I was prepared to do anything it took to succeed. Not just because the Confederacy needed it, but because my personal vanity wouldn't allow me to fail. Skinner pegged that right about me."

"Skinner? What does he have to do with any of this?"

"Nothing directly, but he and I were both involved in espionage on the deepest, most dangerous levels. I can't count the number of times I put on a Union uniform or pretended to be captured so the enemy could coax information from me through bribery or force—*false* information, of course. I worked alone and I trusted no one. And I was damned good at what I did."

She shuddered slightly, imagining it. With his detachment, with his ability to focus completely upon a single goal, she could well conceive what a deadly weapon he became for the Confederacy.

"So what was your mission?"

"We had some vague intelligence that your father was the code master and I was sent to infiltrate your farm and family. I didn't know Davis had a daughter. You were a surprise."

"I'm sorry." She meant it to be a wry comment, but somehow her heart got tangled up in the words and they came out in a broken whisper.

"I'm not." She closed her eyes as his lips brushed against her hair. "You did what family, conscience, and the whole Union army failed to do. You distracted me from my duty. You made me question what I was doing and why. In the face of your courage and conviction, I felt like the lowest cowardly criminal. I fell in love with you, Garnet. That wasn't supposed to happen."

She heard an entirely new tone in his voice, one of humility and regret. She'd thought that was all she wanted from him—that acceptance of responsibility, that quiet apology. But it wasn't enough.

"Then why did you betray me?" All the pain in her heart spilled out in that one question.

"I wasn't going to. When I rode out, I'd decided not to say a word."

She leaned away from him, needing to read that truth in his soul-baring gaze. "Then why?"

"My father's dead, Garnet. But I didn't know about it when I met you. It was just part of the lie to earn your sympathy, to prey upon your own devotion to your father."

She grimaced at that brutal telling. "Go on."

"I didn't find out until after I turned in my first report, the one in which I said I'd learned nothing at your farm. At that point, I'd begun to make plans of my own, plans that didn't involve the survival of the Confederacy or the propagation of my father's dreams. They involved me and the woman I wanted to spend the rest of my life with."

"But your father wouldn't have accepted me any more than he did your Jassy. I had no proper lineage, no benefit to bring in marriage."

"I didn't care. For the first time in my life, I didn't give a damn what he thought. Until I found out he was dead."

He broke eye contact. Garnet tucked her palm beneath his chin, redirecting it so he couldn't hide the conflict going on in his heart and mind.

"And you were devastated," she finished for him. "Not to have admitted all that you knew would have been a betrayal of him and what he meant to you. I understand." Those same feelings were a constant torment to her.

"What he was to me was an unloving and unforgiving figure who dominated my life, who made me ashamed to feel or think for myself. He had no respect for who I was or who I might have become. All he wanted was to see himself reborn in his son. It was the thought of his disappointment that made me amend that report. Even after he was dead, I was afraid to displease him. I'm sorry, Garnet. I never meant for anything to happen to you or your father. I didn't know they would burn your farm. I didn't know your father would die in prison. I wasn't supposed to care."

"But you did."

He covered her hand with his and pressed the side of his face into it. Still he didn't look away. "I went back for you. I was going to take you to my family to protect you, to keep you safe until I could come home. But you were gone when I got there. And you found someone else to protect you."

There was no blame, no accusation in that last statement. Now was the time to tell him the truth.

"Deacon—"

"How much do you know about your husband?"

His sudden somber question interrupted her confession. "What do you mean?"

"How well do you know him? What do you know about his past?"

"Not much," she admitted with a perplexed frown. "He's a good man. He took me in without question, without . . . judgment. He's caring and kind. He's—"

"A thief, Garnet."

"What?"

"He has a criminal record in Britain and in New England, and he's here in Pride to con my neighbors into investing in a nonexistent improvement program so he can make off with their money."

Her eyes welled up in confusion and denial. "I don't believe it."

"I wired a contact of mine in the government. He sent back a list of convictions and suspected involvements. Skinner intercepted the message and he was blackmailing me with it."

That cut through her anguished mind. "Blackmailing you? Why? Why would he think hurting Monty would bother you?"

"Because he knew I couldn't bear the thought of bringing ruin to your life twice. Tyler Fairfax didn't shoot your husband, Skinner did. To get back at me, to get my properties, and to have you."

"Me?" That squeaked out in dismay.

"Because I turned him in as a counterspy and ruined his reputation, and now he plans to destroy my life by taking everything I value."

She swallowed jerkily. "And you value me?"

"You and our son."

Our son . . .

Before she could assimilate and answer that shock, she received another in the form of a sneering voice.

"What a touching declaration. And you're a fool if you believe a word of it."

Roscoe Skinner stood at the partially opened door. He was wet, disheveled, and breathing in harsh gasps. And his eyes were stone cold.

"You see, Mrs. Prior, men like us never tell the truth about anything, do we, Reverend?"

Deacon set himself in front of Garnet, cursing his lack of a weapon. He had only his wits for a defense. He'd survived on them for years, but never had the stakes been so high.

"Like us? We're nothing alike, Skinner . . . or should I say, Hermes."

Roscoe blinked, then loosed a jeering smile. "You found Fairfax."

"Before you could kill him. And he was in a talkative mood. Give it up, Skinner. You've no place to go with this. You've no leverage, no secrets, no place to hide."

His gaze narrowed as he tried to probe the truth from Deacon's slitted glare. "You're wrong. When I tell the lady—"

"He's already told me," Garnet interrupted.

"And I'd rather deal with the truth than live under the manipulation of your lies."

Roscoe's gaze darted between them as his mind spun furiously to find another angle for his revenge. Deacon cut him off at the knees.

"Once again I'll expose you for who and what you are. I can weather the scandal. I'm among friends. But you, you're an outsider, a bad influence. And when Prior adds his testimony to Fairfax's, you'll be in prison, although I'd rather you be put before a firing squad. Wasn't that your plan for me? You've lost, Skinner. Admit it."

Outflanked and outmaneuvered, Roscoe smiled grimly. "I'll concede for the moment, but all isn't lost. Not yet. I may not be able to strip you of all your treasures, but I won't be leaving empty-handed." His expression stilled with deadly intention. "Tell me what you did with the money."

It was Deacon's turn to smile smugly. "What's wrong? Wasn't it where you hid it? You should have kept it with you. You should have known I'd be one step ahead of you."

"You're wrong, Sinclair." And he pushed the door the rest of the way open so they would have a clear understanding of what he meant.

William stood beside him, the muzzle of Skinner's pistol wedged under his chin.

"Now, where is my money?"

Chapter 24

"No!"

     Deacon snatched Garnet back as she started to lunge off the bed. He shared her horror and alarm, but now was a time for cooler heads and careful actions.

"Let the boy go, Skinner. He has no part in this."

Roscoe's smile was a fierce grimace. "I don't think so. He's my only chance of getting out of here alive, and we both know it."

"Let him go!" Garnet cried, straining against Deacon's encircling grip. "Take me instead, just let the boy go."

"Tempting, but he'll be far less trouble. You see, Mrs. Prior, I've dealt with your family before. I was the one who convinced your father to work with us. It took some persuading, but in the end, he was happy to comply."

"You liar! He would never have helped you!"

Roscoe shook his head sadly. "You enlighten her, Sinclair."

"You go to hell."

"I was the one who paid a visit to that quaint little farm. I wanted to meet the woman capable of charming Reverend Sinclair from his duty. I planned to sample you for myself. Imagine my disappointment when you slipped through my fingers."

"I don't have to imagine it," Garnet spat. "I could see it burning for miles, you bastard."

Roscoe chuckled. "Charming."

"Let the boy go," Deacon stated again. "It's me you want, not some innocent child."

"Is anyone truly innocent? Take this boy, for instance, already stained by the sins of his mother and father. You are his father, aren't you?"

Deacon's voice cut like steel. "You harm him and I'll see that it takes you a long, long time to die."

Roscoe's laugh became a grating cough. He clutched the boy tighter, the muzzle shifting to his temple. William stood still and silent, though his whitened lips quivered. His eyes were fixed on Deacon with a pride-shattering confidence, as if he hadn't the slightest doubt that rescue would be forthcoming. Deacon wished he shared that faith as he restrained Garnet from doing the same crazy things he was considering within the panic of his mind.

"I want the money, Sinclair."

"Then you'll let the boy go."

"No. I'll let the boy live. He comes with me."

Garnet sagged on weakened knees, her wail of protest slashing Deacon's heart. He shook his head. "The boy stays here with his mother. You take the money and disappear. You're a professional. They'll never find you."

Roscoe gave another raspy laugh. "They won't, but you would, wouldn't you? You're just too damned good at what we do. I'd spend the rest of my life waiting for you to pop up and calmly slit my throat. No, thank you. It ends between us right here. We both know that."

Garnet took his meaning like a staggering blow. She could lose both of them in the next few moments, both the man she loved and the child she adored. It couldn't happen that way. She wouldn't let it. She straightened, making herself a shield in front of Deacon.

"Take the money. I'll make sure he doesn't follow you."

Skinner looked from her determined features to the penetrating chill of Deacon's glare. "Sorry, ma'am. You're one hell of a woman, but you'd never be able to hold him back. He's too much like me."

"You're wrong. He's nothing like you. He's put the past behind him. Once you're gone, you'll be just another unpleasant memory. He may be the driving force in your life, but you're nothing in his."

Deacon saw by the sudden cold glitter in Roscoe's eyes that those were the wrong words to say to him. He read of the man's irrational jealousy, of his consuming desire to be first, to be better. And that would never happen as long as he believed Deacon had bested him.

"He won't be doing me any favors by letting me live, Garnet, and he knows it. He knows that I'll spend the rest of my life wondering why I didn't catch on to him sooner, knowing that my slowness and stupidity almost cost your husband his life. Who do you think this town is really going to blame? They'll blame me for bringing the likes of him here, then not protecting them against him. He knows if I go after him, I'll lose you, and if I stay here, the fact that he got away with the money will eat at me like a disease. Either way, he wins and I lose."

Roscoe smiled, liking the twisted logic behind his claim and the idea that Deacon would suffer long after he was gone. Liking it very much.

Deacon sighed heavily, his shoulders taking a defeated slump. "I'll get you your damn money, Skinner, then you get the hell out of my life. Enjoy the fact that I'll spend the rest of my days behind a dry goods counter while the woman I love lives under my roof with another man and you're living high off my mistakes."

"Get it."

Deacon relaxed his hold on Garnet reluctantly, needing to know she'd do nothing rash. "Trust me," he whispered against her hair, and he was rewarded by the briefest of nods. It was enough.

Not sure what he was up to, Garnet remained

still, her heart pounding in her throat, her desperate gaze locked to the sight of her son with a gun to his head. But she trusted Deacon, just as William did. His words might suggest resignation, but his muscles were coiled tight and ready to strike. Perhaps Skinner, in his vanity, had forgotten that the Confederacy had bred no deadlier warrior than Deacon Sinclair.

She didn't move as Deacon stepped away from her. She heard him rummaging behind her, retrieving the cash from its hiding place. Then he was beside her, a reassuring hand touching her between her shoulder blades. And between his palm and her back, she could feel the definite imprint of a pistol.

"Here." He tossed the bundle of greenbacks to the floor at Roscoe's feet, then adopted a sullen glower. Hampered by his wound, Skinner tried to bend down but couldn't.

"Pick up the money, boy."

As William knelt down, Roscoe grabbed onto his shirt collar for control, but his attention was on Deacon. And his smile was cold and shrewd.

"As much as I like the idea of you wallowing in misery for the rest of your life, I'm afraid I can't quite believe it. All in all, I think I'll be better off knowing that you're dead."

He leveled the gun on Deacon, giving William a sharp jerk to bring him to his feet. The boy cried out and that was all it took for one hundred plus pounds of fur and fury to launch itself on the gunman.

As Boone's jaws clamped around the arm restraining William, Roscoe released him to shake off the big animal. William scrambled forward, and before Deacon could catch her, Garnet lunged toward the boy, putting herself in the path of Deacon's aim. Boone became a bristled barrier in front of the child. And with a survivor's instincts, Skinner seized Garnet, exchanging one hostage for another.

But this time, Deacon had a pistol leveled at his forehead.

Struggling to control a squirming woman who did everything she could to plant her elbow into his injured side, Roscoe finally had enough of it and stilled her with the rap of his gun butt against her brow.

"Mama!"

Deacon's gaze went flinty and ice cold.

Roscoe dragged Garnet's limp form up in front of him, hiding behind her as he edged back toward the door. Deacon took a step to follow and Roscoe's pistol touched to her temple.

"Don't try it, Sinclair." He cocked the pistol, backing out into the hall. "You're not that good."

"Yes, I am."

With that steely claim, Deacon fired. His entire life stopped in a heartbeat as Garnet was pulled over backward to land on top of Roscoe as the roar of a gun's discharge echoed down the hall. On the periphery, he heard screams and shouts of alarm, not even registering them as coming from the servants, from William and his own mother. His whole being channeled down to one narrow, desperate focus: on the woman lying motionless on the floor.

God, let me be as good as I needed to be.

Roscoe Skinner was dead, a neat hole in the center of his forehead, no longer a threat to anyone. But had he had time to pull the trigger in a last gesture of hatred and defiance?

He took a stiff step closer.

Her eyes were closed, her features gently composed as if she were sleeping. The blood in her hair and pooling brightly on the floorboards beneath her head said otherwise.

He went weak. Darkness and despair dropped him to his knees, where he was vaguely aware of Boone brushing past him. As he wondered numbly how he was going to survive, the dog began whining and licked at Garnet's face. After a moment, her hand lifted frailly to push the slobbery-tongued animal away. And Deacon's breath returned in a mind-blinding rush.

She was alive.

Wedging her elbows beneath her, Garnet angled up, one hand touching the nasty split Skinner's gun butt had made at her temple. She gazed blankly at Deacon, then blinked.

"Deacon, are you all right?"

He grinned wide. "Well, you wanted me on my knees, and here I am."

She returned his smile, bewildered and disoriented until she saw William. Her arms flew open and the boy was quick to fill them.

And never had Deacon witnessed a sweeter sight.

Roscoe Skinner's body was removed and the nearest authority sent for. Monty stirred from his stupor and was able to confirm all that Tyler had said about the attack on the road. Doc Anderson, fresh from pronouncing that Tyler would indeed survive, checked on the Englishman to his satisfaction, then took two small stitches in Garnet's brow, assuring her the scar wouldn't show beneath her hair. Deacon gave his statement, then retired to the parlor to pour a deep glass of bourbon. He was startled by the sudden press of Boone's nose into his palm. Gently he rumpled the dog's ear.

"Nice work, old friend."

The dog sat contentedly at his side, tongue lolling out in a happy doggy grin. Deacon returned it somewhat wryly. That was one less problem on his mind. The dog approved of him.

He'd just taken the first sip from his glass when he became aware of a small, frowning visage at the door.

"Will, is everything all right?"

"Are you my father?"

The boy's bluntness took him aback for a moment. "What does your mother say?"

"I haven't asked her. I was hoping you'd tell me."

Such a somber soul. How could he have looked upon the slender boy with his direct eyes and proper manner and not have seen himself? He smiled slightly, still uncertain of how to proceed.

"Would you like it if I was?"

His sober expression never altered. "I'd like that more than anything."

"So would I. Let me talk to your mother and we'll see, all right?"

He nodded and ventured a faint smile. Then another serious thought struck him. "What should I call you?"

"How about Deacon for now." And "Daddy" later. A giddiness even the entire bottle of bourbon couldn't produce swirled about in his mind and warmed deep in his belly. *Daddy, not Father.*

"I'm going out to play with Boone. Think that'd be all right . . . Deacon?"

"I'm sure it would, as long as you stay close—and dress warm."

"I will," came the promise that settled satisfyingly in his soul.

God above, he wanted that boy to be his own. Not just in fact, but in name as well.

From out in the hall, he heard cautioning words: "Stay close and dress warm."

"I will, Mama."

He was smiling as Garnet stepped in.

"What?" she asked in bemusement.

"That's an amazing boy. So resilient. So like his mother."

"And his father," she added softly, her telling gaze saying everything without words.

The sensation of fullness about his heart just kept getting bigger. He had to turn away or risk shedding some very unmanly tears.

Garnet wasn't sure what to make of the sudden presentation of his back. Was he displeased? Angry because she'd said nothing? She couldn't guess and she couldn't read anything in the squaring of his posture. She ventured on like a blind man groping along an unfamiliar road.

"That much was true about what Skinner said. What about the rest of it? About my father?"

He looked at her then, his gaze steady, unwavering, totally sincere. "That wasn't true. Your father never betrayed anything—not his country, and certainly not you. He was a true hero with unbreachable integrity, nothing like Skinner . . . or me."

Those were the words she wanted—needed—to hear. But were they the truth? Or was Deacon Sinclair acting the part of her hero by keeping her father's memory unsullied? He would never tell and she knew she could never ask again. She would believe because he wanted her to, and all the pain of the past was laid to rest.

That left their current complications.

"You said you love me. Another truth, or a means of manipulating Roscoe?"

"That's always been true. Right from the first. I just didn't know how to express it until it was too late."

"Is it?" she asked softly. "Too late?"

"I asked you to trust me earlier today and you did. Was that just for then or for always?"

She couldn't answer right away. There was no simple reply. Trust implied more than just belief. It signified that truth be told. And there was one more deception she hadn't revealed.

"Yes," she said at last. "I trust you with all the things that matter to me the most. With my love and my child."

"And your future?"

Again she was silent, afraid to assume too much.

"You've let me make love to you and you've provided me with the fruit of that union. I wasn't there when you needed me most, but I'm here for you now, and I want to be part of your life and Will's."

She stared at him through eyes large and luminous.

"Garnet, I want you to be my wife. I know that means giving up all this. I can't provide you with a grand house and fancy things. The woman I met didn't need them. What about the woman you are now? It'll mean divorce and taking the whispers and shunning that goes with it. We might even have to move away from here to make a go of it."

"You'd leave Pride?"

"I have no pride when it comes to you. Nothing matters except us being together. I've got nothing against Prior. In fact, I'm damned grateful to him for stepping in when I should have been taking care of you. But I'm here now, and he's just going to have to let you go. I'll talk to him and make him see it's the right thing to do. No blackmail, no threats, just man to man. You love me, that's our boy, and we need to be together. I'll talk to Noble Banning. He can tell us what needs to be done, what papers need to be filed—"

"Deacon."

"I don't plan to go through another day thinking of you wearing another man's name and my son calling him 'Daddy.' "

"Deacon, Monty and I aren't married."

"He'll just have to—what? What did you say?"

"Monty isn't my husband, he's my uncle."

He froze like a poleaxed steer, unblinking, not even breathing while she faced him down boldly, dreading his reaction to come.

Then he chuckled, the sound escalating to a great shout of laughter. Practically in tears after the awful anxiety she'd suffered in anticipation of his temper, her own flared hotly.

"What's so funny?"

He took a breath to get his mood under control, but his eyes still danced with a wicked appreciation. "I should have known you'd have a head for more than just figures. You would have made a formidable spy, Garnet Davis."

"I should explain—"

He took her in his arms, drawing her tight against him. His mirth had quieted into a tender admiration. "You don't have to explain. Not just now."

He took her lips in a sweetly savage kiss, ravishing them thoroughly until her knees were boneless and she lay limp upon his chest. As her eyes flickered open to the sight of his adoring gaze, they were suddenly awash with silly tears of gladness.

"Marry me."

She blinked, scattering the dampness. Her breath faltered briefly and her answer escaped on a sigh. "Yes."

His mouth collected the salty traces from her cheeks in a leisurely sweep, then returned to her to exact a lingering possession. He leaned back at last to regard her soberly.

"Now, how do we get rid of the husband you supposedly have already?"

Montgomery Prior was propped up in bed being spoon-fed his soup by a tenderly solicitous Hannah Sinclair. Still pale and slightly haggard from his recent ordeal, Prior managed a smile for both of them, then regarded Deacon rather shamefacedly.

"I believe we have some things to discuss, don't we?"

But they weren't the things Monty expected.

"Garnet has agreed to be my wife, and we'd like your blessing."

Hannah sighed happily and murmured, "It's about time." Deacon looked to her in surprise.

"Mama, you knew and didn't tell me?"

"About William, from the beginning, about the marriage, I'm afraid I have to admit to some rather shameful eavesdropping. It took me a while to convince him that you'd be the best thing for her. I didn't tell you because you had too many other things to figure out first." She smiled. "And I see you have." Her glance chided. "Really, darling, you didn't think I'd be throwing myself at a married man, did you?"

He flushed. That was exactly what he'd thought and he should have known better. He turned his attention back to Monty who was no longer smiling.

"I realize that you felt you had to protect her, from scandal . . . and from me."

"And from myself," Garnet added softly as her hand tucked inside Deacon's for an intimate linking. "But not any more."

"It's not going to be easy and I don't pretend it will be," Deacon continued. "We'll have to leave here and start over someplace new. We won't have much but I promise you, I will provide for Garnet and William. You won't ever have to worry about that."

Monty's lips twitched in a secret smile. "Why would you have to leave? All of this is Garnet's, after all."

Garnet stared at him, confused. "What do you mean? I came to you with nothing. You provided the funds—"

"No, my darling, *you* provided them. With the

trust left you by your grandparents. They might not have approved of the rash step your mother took in running off with your father, but it was always their intention of seeing you well cared for. As the last of your family, it was left in my hands. And I never touched a penny of it for myself. It's yours upon your marriage—your legitimate marriage."

"But you didn't tell me. Why?"

"If you'd known the house and the money were yours, what would you have done? You would have thrown it all at him in a foolish passion before discovering what you needed to know. Then you would have had doubts for the rest of your life." His gaze filled with tender wisdom. "Now, you'll have none, and neither will I."

"But I don't want to live with her under this roof pretending a lie. I want her and the boy to bear my name. That means more than all of this." Deacon's gesture encompassed the room that he'd dreamed for five long years would embrace him and his bride. But his dreams had changed, and the setting no longer mattered.

Monty sighed. "I can see just one solution. I'm going to have to die." He waved off the shocked protests. "Now, now, I have no plans to really expire. We only have to make the people of Pride believe I have. I've been homesick for my native England. It's time I returned. Once I'm on my way, you can announce my passing, and after a brief but heartfelt mourning, you can wed again. The property will naturally transfer to Garnet's new husband."

The logic was so simple, it was brilliant.

"But you can't travel alone," Garnet protested. As much as she disliked the idea, she said, "I'll go with you, of course. William can stay here with Deacon and Hannah." After all, she'd waited five years, what was a few more months? Her heart filled with an empty ache anticipating the pain of separation.

"I'll go."

They all turned to stare at a calm and determined Hannah Sinclair.

"I've always wanted to see England."

"Mama—"

"Oh, darling, don't look so shocked. I've lived my life for my father, then my husband, then my children. I should like to live the rest of it for myself, if you don't mind." Her hand rested meaningfully upon Monty's shoulder and his hand covered it in an affectionate press. "We won't be able to come back here, of course, but you can visit us."

"Mama, there are things you should know," Deacon began grimly.

Hannah smiled. "Dear, I know them already. Monty has confessed his sordid past to me and has promised no more shenanigans. We'll live comfortably at his family's estate and I'll make sure he's not tempted to stray." She watched her son's face for signs of what he was feeling, unable to discern his thoughts from the blank expression he wore. "Deacon, I'm asking for your blessing, now."

"I will miss you, Mama."

She rose and came to embrace him, cherishing his unrestrained response.

Monty cleared his throat. "There's the matter of the money. I'm afraid I just couldn't help myself when the opportunity presented itself. Such dishonest men, so ripe for the taking."

And for a moment, Deacon considered just letting Monty go with the cash. Then he thought of a better revenge.

With one arm about his mother and the other about his soon-to-be bride, Deacon had an answer. "I'm thinking of running for county supervisor. We could use some decent roads around here, and it would please me immensely to strip some of the influence from certain citizens of Pride by establishing a fair and legitimate bond for improvements. After working at the mercantile, I've listened to every possible grievance, and I think my neighbors will trust me to find some solutions."

"You mean your *friends*," Garnet corrected gently.

"Yes. My friends."

Leaving Hannah and Monty to plot the Englishman's "death," Garnet backed Deacon up against the wall in the hallway. After first checking for any possible witnesses, she stretched up to kiss him soundly.

"I'll be glad when we don't have to be so discreet."

"I told you I'd wait forever for something that I want."

Her gaze probed his warmly. "Welcome home, Deacon Sinclair. All that you see is yours again."

His hands delved into her dark hair, tipping her face up to his. "I see everything I need right here. Shall I get down on my knees again, or do you believe me now?"

"My heart never doubted; it was my mind that took some convincing." Her fingertips traced over his lapels. "What do we do now?"

"I want to find our son and tell him that soon he can call me 'Daddy.' "

Garnet's eyes shimmered with pleasure. "Kiss me first."

That was one command he happily obeyed.